Set in the Sea

Q. T. Porta

Grosvenor House
Publishing Limited

This book is published by
Grosvenor House Publishing Ltd
Link House
140 The Broadway, Tolworth, Surrey, KT6 7HT.
www.grosvenorhousepublishing.co.uk

A CIP record for this book
is available from the British Library

ISBN 978-1-80381-497-1
eBook ISBN 978-1-80381-559-6

Acknowledgements

It has taken a long time to complete a story set by the seaside with turbulent tides and shadows following silhouettes striding forward in the sunlight.

In retrospect, my family have given support, surprises, and strife, however it would have been impossible to finish the novel without their empathy and encouragement.

The temptation is to only thank each person who has offered kindness, but recognition is to be given to those who cast dark shadows because they redirected my life towards new opportunities. They had a part to play. Therefore, they appear in the metaphorical closing credits, but will not be in the sequel.

The guidance and help from Grosvenor House Publishing Ltd is much appreciated and needed. From a fledging storyteller to a published author and fulfilling a lifelong ambition.

And last but by no means least, I give a wave of appreciation, to each reader who takes their time to purchase the book. Your support is more than I can express in words which may not be the best marketing pitch, but I hope you get the drift. ☺

In trust the story will raise your spirits and will create a space to set aside the distractions albeit for a moment.

Q. T. Porta
2023

CHAPTER 1

A cacophony of noise alerted those entering the station of the chaotic scenes playing out in front of them on the concourse of Victoria rail station.

"Due to signalling problems throughout the afternoon, there are delays to all services leaving Victoria. Rail tickets will be accepted on buses and underground stations. We apologise for any inconvenience caused. Please keep checking the departure boards. Further updates will follow."

The public announcement was met with a unified groan and grumbling. The crowd of passengers gathered and swayed as if one flock eager to migrate from the hustle and bustle of central London.

"Told ya, should've left earlier," Pam said, "I'll miss Corrie!"

Martha shook her head in disbelief. "I despair, honestly, really! We've just been to Buckingham Palace on the day and time The Queen became Britain's longest reigning monarch and you're moaning about not seeing Coronation Street!"

"I know, was really great," replied Pam, "but could've left earlier?"

"I give up!" Martha snapped. "But before I scream, and it won't make a slightest bit of difference in this din, I'm going to the Ladies. Hold my bags and please do not lose my tea towels!" Martha battled through the throng, leaving her lifelong friend besieged by weary commuters. The tantalising fragrance from The Pasty Shop, small retail unit, motivated Pam to squash past her temporary close acquaintances; dragging the treasured cargo wrapped carefully in tissue papers, inside Buckingham Palace gift bags, behind her back. Pam scrambled around the bottom of her black faux leather handbag to find loose change to pay for one traditional pasty and large English breakfast tea. Precariously balancing the hot drink in the same hand holding the precious luggage she heard Martha's words filled with frustration. "Where she gone now!?" As Pam turned to try to catch the attention of Martha, the corrugated cardboard recyclable coffee cup fell on the floor.

"Oh, for goodness sake, look where you're going!" The sharp retort was delivered by an angry young man, dressed in a light grey double breasted 2-piece suit with thick white pin stripes heading off into different angles as the flared trousers rested haphazardly on the black heeled boots. The outfit was emblazoned with a canary yellow shirt with white collar and cuffs. The grey candy stripe extra-long polyester tie was competing against the silk plain aquamarine pocket square for attention.

"Sorry! Was an accident." Pam's attempt at an apology fell on deaf ears as the rail rage increased in volume. "Stupid cow! Could've burnt me and ruined my suit!"

"Ruin that clown suit? Gotta be kiddin'! Couldn't get any worse if you tried?" Martha's interjection raised a ripple of laughter from the audience.

"Keep your nose out of it! What's it got to do with you?" The disgruntled man directed his instruction at Martha, not realising the consequence.

"It's got everything to do with me. You don't insult my best mate and get away with it. Who do you think you are? Was an accident, she said sorry, so just get over it!" Martha's face filled with a deep hue of red and continued, "you ain't perfect. Have a look in the mirror! Second thoughts, don't bother, it'll crack!"

Martha picked up the empty cup and Pam put serviettes on the floor in hope they would absorb most of the liquid.

"Can't leave you for a minute!" said Martha as they walked off arm in arm.

Amidst the notifications of 'delayed' and 'cancelled' on the departure boards, a sign of hope; the next train to Wishym Bay was due to leave at 19:00 from Platform 3.

"Need to go to the loo!" The angst on Pam's face predetermined the sense of urgency.

"Watch where you're going, yeah?" Martha replied with a smile, "I'll meet you at top of platform. If train comes in, I'll save you a seat."

The train trundled out of Victoria station filled to the brim with exasperated passengers relieved to be free of the confines of the impromptu departure lounge with excessive air conditioning and minimalist style and lack of seats.

"Phew! What a day." Martha exclaimed as she looked at Pam who was pinned against the window by the fellow passenger busily inserting the key into the tarnished metal lock on the side of his vintage tan leather briefcase.

Pam grimaced, "Yeah! A hot cup of tea could come in quite handy now!"

Martha chuckled and reached into her gift bag. "Hope Maeve will like this; it's got lots of information about the history." She sounded pensive as she held up the book entitled: The Royal Line of Succession, however, felt comforted by the purchase of the official souvenir guide of Buckingham Palace, as an accompaniment.

"Maeve will love it!" Pam's affirmation veered towards consideration. "How she gettin' on in school?"

"Not good." The weight of an anxious mother pulled Martha's gaze down.

"Only few days into Year 3, she'll be great." An offer of reassurance from Pam did not lift the burden but prompted Martha to lift her head. "How's Maddy getting' on?" Pam asked.

"Oh, she's alright. Got in with a group of friends before summer holiday and they seem to be stickin' together this term. No doubt there'll all be over for her birthday party." Martha frowned in anticipation of the rowdy celebration.

"She's 16 not 6," Pam's reaction was shared with a louder volume than intended, "wot, you think they'll want to play pass the parcel and musical chairs! She'll be out clubbing."

"Just like you," Martha quipped, "dread the thought. Anyhow, are there any nightclubs in Wishym Bay?"

"There's a Bingo Club," Pam replied sarcastically, "she'll love that!"

At Bromley South station the pressure cooker of passengers eased as many stepped off the train to the delight of those still on board.

"At last! I can breathe." Pam sighed with relief and placed her handbag on the adjacent empty seat. "Did you see his briefcase – thought they went out with the Ark?"

"Retro look is fashionable," Martha replied, "had enough space for your pasty, so ain't all that bad."

"Pasty is all squashed now! Have you got any cereal bars left?" asked Pam.

"No, we scoffed all of them on the train this morning. How can you still be hungry after sandwiches and cake in garden café?"

"They were tasty but could've done with a couple more," said Pam, "talking of tasty, did you see that Army Officer? He'd make you want to stand to attention!"

"Think everyone saw him after all the fuss you made. Like a kid in a sweet shop."

"Be great to work there!" Pam picked up her mobile, "let's have a look at the website."

"Look for what?" Martha asked with trepidation.

"Ah, found it, vacancies. Retail shop assistant, sounds ideal especially when working with Army Officers!" The zeal for a spontaneous act did not surprise Martha but still gave her cause for concern.

"Oh Pam! You only moved to Wishym Bay last Friday. Now you want to go back working in central London. Give me strength!"

"You're an old worry guts," Pam protested, "will be really exciting meeting all those handsome men and maybe see The Queen."

"How can I break this to you; the Army Officer, as handsome as he is, does not work in a shop, and sadly, don't think Her Majesty will be poppin' in to buy a new tea towel!"

"You're no fun anymore!" Pam protruded her lower lip in an exaggerated childish sulky pout before asking, "talking of no fun, is Brian enjoying his new job?"

"Oh, stop it!" Martha retorted. "Brian's okay. Job in Canterbury ain't bad. Bit different from The City, to put it mildly, but he'll get used to it."

"More people his own age, be better for him. Can't keep up with all those youngsters."

"Talk for yourself," Martha laughed, "you ain't no spring chicken."

"Only two months older than you. Like fine wines we get better with age."

Martha looked up towards to her mind calculator and said, "Brian's sixty this year – how does that happen?"

"You'll be gettin' your old age pensioner passes." Pam teased her best friend, and over enthusiastically threw a torn wrapper, stuck to the last three polo mints: resulting in it hitting a fellow passenger sitting across the aisle.

"Do you mind!" exclaimed the white-haired lady wearing a navy wool crepe two-piece skirt suit complimented by a classic bow tie white silk blouse. The antique bronze diamante butterfly brooch worn on her left shoulder matched the design of the hair clip, clutching the bun of fine hair tightly to the base of her neck. "I am trying to read my book! We could all do with a bit of peace and quiet after the mayhem in Victoria. I will be writing a letter of complaint to Network Rail; animals are treated with more respect!"

Martha and Pam were unsure how to react to the rant without prompting a further outburst.

"Sorry." Pam said sheepishly, resembling a naughty child scolded by a parent.

Martha diverted her eyes to Pam's mobile and mouthed "switch it off!" The notification sound: *Robot*, echoed through the air as frequently as the requests from Martha to change the setting to the do not disturb option.

"Like being on the school bus," Pam whispered.

"What school bus?" asked Martha, careful to reduce the volume of her voice. "Me and Betty went on normal red bus. Alright for you – just walked home, via Whitgift Centre most days. I had to go straight home for tea, not hang around with boys in shopping arcade."

Pam teased, "Little Miss Perfect; bet it was like *The Waltons*, all sitting down together, saying grace."

"Ha! Ha! Very funny. Dad used to be late in most nights. So, sat with Mum, Bobby, and Alfie. They scoffed their food before going out with the boys."

"And the girls!" Pam joked about Martha's older brothers.

"Yeah, remember loads of girls after Bobby. Mum said he had gift of the gab."

"And pulling!" Pam shrilled with laughter at her own joke about Bobby's reputation of having numerous girlfriends. Two-timing was a worthless hobby for him unlike his younger brother, Alfie, who was more interested in playing darts in the local pub.

The subsequent glare from the prim fellow passenger prompted Martha to give Pam the crumpled copy of a free newspaper, The Metro, which was squashed in the back of a nearby seat. An attempt to keep her quiet and avoid another argument.

Martha had a flashback of her childhood home in South Croydon. A standard terraced 3-bedroom house purchased with a loan from Martha's maternal grandmother. Her mother,

Daisy, married Jack Burtin in 1957 aged 18, against the wishes of her family. The nickname 'Jack the lad' was an apt description however Daisy tolerated her husband's addiction to 'booze, birds and betting' the label his work mates, on the building site, used to describe his behavioural traits. The minimum salary from her job as a shop assistant in BHS (British Home Stores) in central Croydon, did not cover all the costs of running a home therefore could not afford to leave Jack nor face her mother sniping, "I told you so!" The additional income, after Jack trained to be a scaffolder, was sufficient to support the family. Daisy took on the duties of a traditional full-time housewife. A role she cherished and tackled each challenge with vigour.

The rumbling on the tracks as the train picked up pace induced Pam to nod off with her mouth open but not snoring nor dribbling, much to Martha's relief. The daylight dimmed and the lights in the houses shone like beacons on the landscape. *'What a year'* Martha thought as she reflected on the previous nine months that had seen her domestic life tipped upside down. The steady job her husband, Brian, had in The City of London was snatched from him at the bequest of management consultants, hired to streamline the business. The corporate mantra was 'Restructure to Reinvigorate' when translated meant a reduction in operational costs. The goal, not advertised on the company intranet, was to vigorously encourage, manipulate, those who could be easily steered to take the voluntary redundancy package. The alternative, being managed out, was not an attractive proposition. The true underlying aim, not captured in official version of the minutes, was conveyed in passive aggressive clues interspaced during the annual review appraisals in December 2014. Hidden between the lines was the message; only dynamic personalities will endure the changes i.e., youthful characters could easily be moulded to fit in with the ruthless ambitions of the global corporate machine and energised shareholders, to increase profits and the overall remuneration package of the board of Directors. To bolster the bonuses of middle management to sustain morale and increase the magnitude of envy held by junior members of staff, masquerading as ambition. Leaving the firm of Auditors, VAC (Valuation Adroit Consultants), was a paradigm shift - impacting his self-esteem and relationship with his family. The fall out was immense. The move to Wishym Bay was instigated by Martha. '*A fresh start by the seaside,*' she thought, '*would surely help motivate her husband and three daughters to see things in a different light.*' Although the transition was in its infancy the waves of resentment were increasing in height and frequency and continued to erode the foundations built on sand. Martha remained hopeful in her evaluation, '*It'll be fine, especially now Pam's near me. Once we get the house redecorated – they'll love it.*'

Martha and the white-haired lady exchanged a smile as they watched Pam leaning over and falling into a deep sleep. As the train pulled into Wishym Bay, Martha tugged Pam's jacket and said, "Come on sleepy drawers, time to go home!"

***

CHAPTER 2

"Maddy, call me!" the distressed strain on Martha's voice cracked and tears filled her eyes as she slammed her mobile down on top of the 1950's kitchen cabinet with red drawer and door fronts, and satin nickel effect bow handles. Signs of wear and tear on top of the cupboard were remarkably minor, after decades of bearing the weight of a hive of activity in the heart of the home. The minimal heel of Martha's black leather ballet pump caught the edge of a torn piece of the cream vinyl flooring. She stumbled forward and hit her wrist on the side of the stainless-steel sink.

'*Stupid girl! Where can she be?*' Martha thought as she rubbed her joint to ease the pain.

Martha resorted to the usual tactic of keeping busy when her mind was consumed by worry.

The mugs and plates were given an intense clean; a daily domestic chore reintroduced whilst the wait for the repair to the second-hand dish washer entered the third week. The need for a larger dish rack on the draining board, to the right of Martha, was moving up the wish list. The pint glass temporarily housed the cleaned cutlery; it tipped over towards the gap between the sink and neighbouring red cupboard, resulting in a teaspoon falling into the rift.

"Seriously!" she thought as her fingers probed into the cobwebs. The exploration successfully unearthed the teaspoon and a white plastic fork, stained with tomato sauce, wrapped in a paper-thin napkin – suspiciously like the one Maddy used with her take away fish and chips. Remnants of the boiled egg, Maeve had for breakfast, clung onto the spoon handle. She was not keen on eating before going to school, driven by her distress. However, when Martha used her favourite old-fashioned, pink, and red, elephant egg cup, a present from Granny Daisy, it rekindled her appetite. Maeve cut long thin slices from a mixed selection of sliced bread: *Warburtons Milk Roll* and *Hovis Tasty Wholemeal* medium loaf. The result of her culinary decorative skills was six proud *'soldiers'* on parade, spaced evenly and meticulously turned out, on the pale pink side plate.

Brian's breakfast, a mug of black instant coffee, was a hurried affair: not creative nor considerate for his family. *'Must remember to add coffee machine to the kitchen essential list,'* Martha made a mental note and allowed herself one light moment of distraction as she thought, *'Pam will moan George Clooney is not here to pour a cup of Nespresso for her.'*

Project 49*WB* was scheduled to be completed in different phases subject to the required funding and the agreement of the Steering Committee i.e., all members of the family. The meetings took place during mealtimes which, sadly, were few and far between. Martha was the designated Project Manager, secretary, and co-ordinator. Brian reconciled the accounts but had not yet come to terms with the move and enormity of the task ahead of them – renovating a five-bedroom house. Martha's pitch of a home with a sea view was dampened when the realisation hit them; the supposed splendid scenery was blocked by a garage and overgrown trees set firmly in the land on the other side of the road. Martha relished the idea of an en-suite bathroom not only for her but also for Philomina and Maddy. Philomina commandeered the loft extension, referred to as a studio flat, due to the need to concentrate on her PhD, and privacy when inviting friends to stay which had not happened since moving to Wishym Bay. Maddy was ecstatic to have her own den, so that she could stay in her room for days with only a few breaks to top up her food supplies. She tried her best to persuade her mum to let her have a microwave in her room, but the request was met with a firm no from both parents. The compromise was a kettle, small fridge, and store cupboard, for snacks and cutlery, with the caveat all utensils would be cleaned daily. Maeve selected the bedroom with a sea view, albeit restricted, and vintage lily rose floral wallpaper which she earnestly requested not to be removed during phase 2 of the project plan i.e., decoration of the bedrooms.

Martha looked in puzzlement at the different tones of the indistinguishable flowers on the wallpaper above the cupboard with red doors. They seemed to be a mixture of large daisies, dandelions, and outlandish orange clovers. The kitchen was divided into a mixture of 1960s designs and flat pack, medium-density fibreboard, units from MFI - the original Ontario maple colour fading into a neutral beige. Martha liked the cabinet pantry. The glass door cupboard at the top of the unit and the drawers appeared weary but the enamelled drop-down work surface reminded Martha of visits to her maternal grandmother, Florence, in South Croydon. The Cadbury's chocolate fingers, stored in the mid-section, were a special treat for Martha. Her brothers were given *Jamboree Bags* to keep them occupied before they joined in with the ad-hoc football games in the street.

Phase 1 of Project 49WB included the kitchen, sparse adjourning breakfast, and utility rooms but the top priority was a new boiler closely followed by a security alarm to cover the entire house and outdoor space.

Martha grabbed the mobile with soapy hands as soon as the ring tone hit the first note -

"MADDY – where are you?"

"What's wrong M?" Pam asked whilst wiping sleep from her eyes and moving her legs slowly from the warmth and comfort of the double polyester duvet without a cover.

"Oh, it's you! Didn't notice name in rush." Martha sounded dejected.

"That's a nice wake up call for your BFF," replied Pam, "what's Maddy done now?"

"Wish I knew. Have to find her first!"

"Probably still in land of nod - sleepin' off her birthday night" Pam yawned and earnestly searched for the appropriate reassuring words.

"Well, she ain't sleepin' it off upstairs! Managed to bluff off Brian before he left for work and didn't tell Maeve – she'll get in a right state worrying about it."

"If she turns up here with her tail between her legs, I'll text you." Pam said as she pulled open the two pieces of faded material across the ill fitted curtain poll. The purchase of new curtains and other furniture in addition to all the DIY jobs raced through her mind, particularly the search for the elusive money tree.

"Thanks mate. Who'd want to be a parent with all this hassle?" Martha ranted, "how can she be so selfish? Takes two minutes to call. Ain't difficult!"

"Battery might've run out," Pam extended an excuse followed by advice, "have a cuppa an' breathe, but knowin' you, house will be cleaned from top to bottom before the rebel returns." Martha tried to restrain her anger. "Just phoned school to give excuse she's sick. Don't think they'll accept hangover as an illness. I'll probably get fined! Anyway, must get back to tidying kitchen. What you doin'?"

"Gettin' toast and jam." Pam shared her slow start with a sense of guilt, so elongated the description of her activities, "still got boxes and suitcases to empty. I'll have a go at them after cuppa an'…." Martha interrupted sharply, "You were goin' say, cuppa 'n' ciggie, weren't you? If I catch you with cigarettes, I'll scream! You promised – not in your new home."

"Just habit, sayin' that." Pam moved the ashtray near the opened kitchen window. The dangerous decision to delay fixing a smoke alarm was facilitating the continued use of the contraband.

The first tap of the letter box did not attract attention, so a louder double tap jolted Pam from her slumber, back under the duvet watching the TV programme, *Lorraine*.

"Wait a minute!" called out Pam as she rushed to take the ashtray into the garden and shove it in the rusty BBQ – a remnant from the previous owner. Pam hoped the tin structure would help hide the smell. "Comin' now!" Pam skipped over the stones on the concrete garden path in her bare feet resulting in a pebble sticking to her heel. There was not time to find her fluffy pink mule slippers. A spritz of Impulse body spray entitled *Tease* intermingled with the smell of nicotine but did not mask the distinct odour.

"You look worse than I feel!" Pam greeted Maddy on her doorstep.

"Can I hide 'ere for a while?" Maddy pleaded. "Can't take Mum's nagging."

"Of course, but one condition; I'm texting your Mum now – yeah?"

The dishevelled teenager shuffled into the small hallway of Pam's one bedroom bungalow, squeezing past the unpacked boxes. "Need to use your loo."

'She's here. Let her stay for while?' The response sent to Pam's text was instantaneous.

'Cheers! She ok?'

'Yeah. Tired. All ok – wiv Aunty Pam.' ☺

The loud coughing from the bathroom filled Pam with dread and sparked memories of the numerous times she cleaned up after her mother.

"If you gonna throw up, don't do it in bath! Plug hole still blocked."

There was no reply and no pause in the groans. Pam opened the door to find Maddy's head leaning over the toilet. "I'll get you a glass of water and fresh clothes."

Maddy tied back her hair and splashed cold water over her face. The reflection in the bathroom mirror showed a grey complexion and dark circles under her eyes. She rubbed toothpaste on her finger, and she gave a quick swirl around her teeth in an attempt to remove the vile taste in her mouth. The mismatch of light blue track suit bottoms, long baggy pink tee shirt and black spotty socks was not a desirable fashion statement but a vast improvement on the stained clothes that lay in a heap on the bathroom floor.

"Where can I put these?" Maddy asked in a feeble hoarse whisper.

"Leave 'em there. Gotta find launderette soon. Washing machine goin' be delivered next week."

"Okay if I sit in garden?" Maddy did not want to be ill over the belongings spread throughout the bungalow.

"Yeah, I'll get the camping chairs – sure they're here somewhere."

The uneven paved area in the back garden made the chairs rock sideways however the drinks holder just about managed to hold the glass of water for Maddy.

"Dry toast usually does the trick?" Pam looked at Maddy to gauge the reaction.

"Not now." Maddy grimaced. "Thought you given' up smoking?"

"Trying," Pam replied with embarrassment and shrugged her shoulders.

"Need a stronger air freshener." Maddy looked up at Pam and they connected by sharing a gentle laugh. "You be alright?" asked Pam, "Gotta have a quick wash an' get dressed. If you need loo just shout!"

Pam found Maddy leaning over the side of the chair, sleeping off an all-night birthday celebration. Maddy willingly accepted the offer to lay down on Pam's bed.

"Hankies, bottle of water and shopping bag – strong one – you know, bag for life, just in case you can't make it to bathroom." Pam pointed to the rustic, pine-effect, slim bedside cabinet as she sat on side of the bed and turned off the small flat screen tv perched on the white chest of drawers.

"What's his name?" Pam asked.

"What do you mean?" Maddy replied defensively. "Don't waste your smelly breath lying. It's Aunty Pam you're speakin' to not your dad."

"Mick." Maddy surrendered; gave up the information reluctantly and turned her head towards the wall.

"Tell him to leave love bites on another part of your body, tricky to hide when they're on your neck."

Maddy's natural blusher broke through the pale complexion. "How old is he?" asked Pam.

"Thirty-two" Maddy looked shamefaced.

"Married?"

"Nearly!" Maddy replied.

"Well, that's a new one," Pam smiled, "guess he's engaged?"

"Yeah. Gettin' married next month."

"Ah, one of those," said Pam.

"Whaddya mean?" Maddy looked perplexed and her thumping headache prevented her from making sense of cryptic clues.

"One last fling!" Pam derided the arrangement. "Mind you, that type don't stop flinging. Bit of paper don't stop 'em."

"Said, he might call off wedding," Maddy looked at Pam for justification but unfortunately Pam tuned into the reality channel. "Don't think he's tellin' truth somehow. His ego must be off the scale - conquest of a teenager. But he can't show off on Facebook."

"I can!" Maddy's rebellious streak filtered through her aching body.

"Maddy! You're not stupid," Pam enthused, "just think about damage it'll do you. Doubt if he'll be bothered." Maddy frowned but she did not have the energy to get into an argument or storm out as was the usual reaction if challenged.

Pam could see Maddy's eyelids closing slowly but felt obliged to ask, "You're being careful?"

"It's okay, we stay at his mate's house in Studd Hill. He lives near Reculver."

"That's not what I mean, and you know it!" Pam retorted.

"Oh that! Yeah, get all sorts of things at school now! Boots have good choice!" Maddy giggled hoping she may shock Pam. Her attempt was fruitless.

"Sure your dad would love to know what you're spendin' allowance on! Hope Mick buys some?"

Pam pulled the duvet over Maddy as she slipped into a deep sleep. '*Silly girl*' she thought, '*same old story, don't change. Why are we so stupid?*'

Pam returned to the garden to retrieve the cigarettes from the enclosed BBQ and sat in the camping chair, nervously expecting it to collapse. The seagulls hovered overhead and the noise from the neighbouring car repair shop drifted into the hazy rays from the sun. Weeds popped up amongst each minute gap in the concrete paving slabs. It was nice to have a private, albeit noisy, outside area. For the first two years of her life, she lived with her grandmother, Doris, and made the most of a compact back yard. Pam's mother, Gillian Docker, had to move them into a council flat in West Croydon, after enduring and witnessing abusive behaviour from her stepfather and Doris' second husband: Bill Denton.

After decades of battling with alcohol and smoking Gillian conceded defeat in 1992, aged 49. Following a traumatic birth and medical malpractice, she was not able to have any more children. Resentment and anger were periodically directed towards Pam. The excessive amounts of Gin erased the memories and emotional pain temporarily. Gradually the quantity and strength of alcohol increased as she became immune to the toxic cocktails. Pam learned to make excuses for her mother and clear up after self-destructive benders. Cocooned in her bedroom, she kept busy by filling in colouring books using a mixture of crayons, pencils, and paint. The materials acquired from the stock room in the store, Woolworths, where Gillian worked as a shop assistant. Other hobbies included cutting out paper dolls and a variety of outfits and dreaming of all the things she would buy from mail order catalogues when she meets 'Mr. Right.' All these activities helped drown out the noise from the mismatched male visitors. Despite numerous requests, Gillian did not disclose the name of Pam's father.

***

CHAPTER 3

Low lying cloud formation rested on the sea momentarily before dispersing into fine strips of lace; threading through the crisp blue sky as the autumnal wind picked up and raced over the pier. Maeve wanted to look at the various memorial plaques on the pier railings before starting her Poppy collection duty, at the supermarket Morrisons. The rollercoaster and fair ground rides were securely locked eagerly awaiting to ignite the adrenaline rush for daring passengers. It was half term for most of the schools in the locality therefore it promised to be a fun filled weekend. The visitors relished their temporary freedom from the monotony of the proverbial hamster wheel of daily chores and commitments.

Maeve cleaned the debris left by the seagulls with travel size wet wipes taken from her pink, vintage floral print, backpack bought from the local Cancer Research UK charity shop. The two outer small pockets, secured with the same style of square silver-coloured buckles, as attached to the lid, were put to good use. Packed to the brim with white and black reels of cotton, sewing needles clinging to a minute Union Flag fridge magnet, spare buttons, safety pins, hair clips, pencil, biros (blue and black), pocket tissues, plasters, silver pencil sharpener, eraser, and smallest size pad of yellow sticky notes.

"There are so many different names," Maeve observed. "Do all their family and friends come to visit?"

"I think they do," replied Martha. "Although, it may be too far, for some, to travel."

"But they will always miss them, won't they?" Maeve asked earnestly.

Martha paused to construct a suitable reply for her youngest sensitive daughter. "Yes, they will. Love does not pass away. It moves to a different place in our heart. Stored carefully to help comfort us when we feel sad."

"Will it help if I clean the signs?" Maeve tugged at her mother's coat to try to get her to turn around. Martha quickly wiped away the tears streaming down her cheeks; making the excuse she had dust in her eye. The incoming tide of grief was bottled up, for now. However, the despair would bubble up again, forcing the lid to come off.

***

The clash of supermarket trolleys, the hurly-burly and chitter chatter caused Maeve to wince. Martha quickly tuned into her daughter's unease and tried to reassure her by saying, "Look Maeve, there's the table. Let's make sure we are shipshape. We need to report for duty."

"Well now, who do we have here?" Padraig Cloherty, a veteran, representing The Royal British Legion, reached his hand out towards Maeve. She retreated behind her mother's coat and closed her eyes.

"Oh, I'm sorry." said Martha as her natural blusher shone through the powder foundation, haphazardly applied whilst checking her middle daughter, Maddy, was safely asleep in her bedroom.

"No worries at all," Padraig smiled, "let's get our new volunteers ready for action!"

Martha readjusted the red ribbon supporting the box of poppies, held out in front of her and Maeve held the collection tin tightly. Padraig directed them to their allocated position just by the entrance of the supermarket. Customers were enthralled by the brooch Maeve hand crafted: worn on the left side of her navy-blue woollen coat with black buttons except for the top one which had been replaced with a red anchor button, as a tribute to the charity.

Maeve moved slowly towards the 4 wheeled mobility scooter. "There you go my dear," said the occupant wearing a bright orange hooded quilted jacket. "You can have two pounds, as you're doing such a grand job." Maeve wore a gentle smile and replied in a whisper, "Mummy has the poppies. Oh, I forgot to say, thank you."

"Your mammy is blessed to have such a beautiful daughter." The enthusiastic daily shopper pushed her wiry white hair behind her ears, revealing gold coated emerald claddagh dangle earrings.

"Oh dear!" exclaimed Martha. "I am falling behind in my duties. Would you like me to pin the poppy on your jacket?"

"Yes, that'll be grand. Your daughter shines as bright as a moon beam. A true Galway girl."

"You are kind. My name is Martha, and this is Maeve."

"Now then, that's a good old Irish name, I've not heard for a good while. Well, I'm Bridget."

"Lovely to meet you," said Martha. "Thank you for your generous donation."

A sense of relief intermingled with the pride Martha felt for her daughter. Volunteering was one option to encourage Maeve to socialise. She loved living by the seaside but the move to a new school resulted in excessive bullying and days off due to mental stress. At the age of seven, Maeve started Year 3 at St. Bernadette's Catholic primary school, in Sea Street, with trepidation. The teachers and children in her old school accepted the idiosyncrasies however these were now used as weapons against her which hit hard. She was reeling from the spiteful comments.

"Is the tin too heavy?" asked Martha. Maeve nodded as she put her weighty collection of donations on the floor. "Okay darling, let's go back to the table."

"My, my, young lady, we could do with your help again," Padraig greeted Maeve in a loud cheery voice.

"We really enjoyed it, didn't we Maeve?" Martha searched for a response but her daughter sort refuge in her double breasted, long black wool, flared coat.

"Oh, I know just how you feel." The empathy and sincerity of the comment emboldened Maeve to look up towards the elegance of a demure elderly lady, petite in height, but with an inner strength that shone through the façade. "I am signing off duty now."

Martha nodded. "I'm waving the white flag. My feet will not forgive me if I stay much longer."

"I know the feeling. I'll just check if Mr. Bentley needs anything or water for Bobby, then I am heading home for a nice cup of tea."

They looked with admiration at the shiny black coat of the Labrador, Bobby, a faithful and long serving guide dog. "They both put me to shame," said Martha.

"My dear old dog could not cope with a tour of duty," replied their kind-hearted fellow volunteer.

Maeve exclaimed excitedly, "I love dogs!" Martha was taken back by the enthusiastic outburst of joy. She could not remember the last time Maeve was so exuberant and spoke loudly enough to be heard clearly.

"Now, now. We mustn't stop… uhmm, sorry I did not catch your name."

"Angela. Am afraid my name badge fell off. Do you have a dog, my dear?"

Maeve clammed up and stood behind her mother. "Please excuse Maeve, it's a bit noisy and she's overtired. Staying up too late reading books. No dog for us, we have a cat called Tabitha. She is queen of the castle. Sorry, we don't want to delay you anymore."

"Oh yes," Angela laughed, "cats can be prima-donnas. My old dog is too soft; would not hurt a fly. I need to go now but hopefully see you for another shift." As she waved goodbye Maeve stood in the shadow of her mother and proffered no reply.

"Come on sweetheart, time to go home. You have been brilliant. Maybe we can come back another day to see Bobby and bring him some treats."

"But, mummy, he's not allowed to eat on duty!"

Martha leant down and hugged her daughter.

***

CHAPTER 4

Heavy rain bounced off the pavement and a bitter wind sharpened the chill biting through the different layers of clothing. The widening gap in the side of Pam's pastel blue trainers with light grey stripes: remnants from a closing down sale of an independent sports shop in West Croydon, soaked her zesty lemon trainer socks. Shivering with cold she walked through the muddy puddles towards the card shop. *'Look at Christmas cards,' she thought, 'help me dry out.'* The crowded store indicated that many others had the same idea.

"Put those back Johnny!" yelled an exasperated grandmother. "Told you before, look but don't touch! Stay there, while I stop your sister pulling the balloon stand over!" Johnny giggled and grabbed a handful of envelopes and threw them on the floor.

"Okay, okay, young man," a shop assistant called out, "no more please." Sympathy for the staff was reflected on the faces of the customers.

Pam perused the scrambled cards, to elongate the break inside the warm shelter, despite the dripping umbrellas prodding into her legs. A box of charity cards was selected. She did not share the excitement as displayed in cosy Christmas films.

The queue spiralled around the shop. Whilst waiting she looked at the section dedicated to boyfriends, fiancés, and husbands. A slither of envy crossed her mind, but it was overtaken by a sense of relief.

'At least don't have to waste money on that this year,' she pondered and continued to daydream, *'never know, could meet man who's fit and rich before Christmas.'* Her thoughts were interrupted by two questions announced loudly, "Who's next? Do you wanna a bag?" The cashier, weary from standing, and smiling falsely even at the most awkward customers, took the box to scan the bar code.

The crowd gathered by the doorway continued to grow and blocked the exit to relentless wet weather. Whilst Pam squeezed the new purchase into her black faux leather tote bag, she saw a poster in the window advertising vacancies for seasonal staff. Her immediate instinct was to run; risking the slippery pavements, but the worry about household bills, accumulating interest on credit card statements and need to furnish the bungalow took over, and she stopped in her tracks.

'Can't be all that bad?' she pondered. *'Money would come in handy.'* Pam was acutely aware Martha could not keep paying the minimum monthly payments on her credit card. The cost of Project 49*WB* was already over budget and the strain on her best friend was evident.

Pam pushed against the crowd to get back to the counter.

"Forgotten something?"

"No… Ah yes, do you sell stamps?" asked Pam, as tuts of disapproval echoed throughout the queue.

"Yeah. Six first or twelve second class? We don't have Christmas stamps at moment." The cashier displayed expert multi-tasking skills as she totalled up another bill whilst talking to Pam.

"Both please." Pam called out above the discontented muttering. "Is there an application form for job vacancy?"

"Yes, somewhere. Haven't got time to look; just bring your CV into manager tomorrow. Should be okay."

"Cheers! That's a great help. Good luck." Pam swiftly departed from the shop before the protest escalated into a riot.

***

"You're a bit early, just need to bring cat upstairs, won't be a minute!"

"No need to hide Tabitha, she's my friend!" Pam shouted through the front door of Martha's home which remained securely closed.

"Didn't expect you," replied Martha all in a fluster.

"Who were you expecting? Ain't got a fancy man have ya?"

"Oh, stop it. Waitin' for plumber. New boiler ain't working properly!"

"Can I come in now," asked Pam, "I'm drenched!"

"Yeah, but leave those sopping wet trainers on the doorstep. No one's goin' take 'em."

Pam took off her socks and blue, funnel neck, long sleeved zipped fleece jacket. Both items of clothing gave off a damp smell, so she dropped them, unceremoniously, on the hallway floor.

"Wanna cuppa?" Martha called out from the kitchen.

"Got anything stronger?"

"No!" came the sharp retort.

"Okay, spoilsport. Coffee would be great, with biscuits would be even better."

"Thought you were goin' shoe shopping?" asked Martha.

"Was on my way when it pelted down so dived in card shop. Got box of cards 'n' new job!"

"Really!" Martha laughed mockingly. "You went for interview dressed like that?"

"Had chat with lady; she told me to bring in my CV tomorrow."

"What CV?"

"Ah! That's where you come in. Need your help M?" Pam's expression regressed to childlike features.

"It'll cost ya!"

"IOU, okay? Give you cards for now 'n' take you for a drink on pay day." As Pam picked up her bag the magnetic closure clip burst open. "Drat!" she blurted out and tugged the box from the mishmash of objects, scratching the inner lining. "There're soaking!"

"Unlike cigarette packet at bottom of your bag!" The disappointment in Martha's voice was palpable.

"Am trying. It's hard, what with worrying about bungalow and everything else." Pam's excuses did not hold any sway with Martha; exhausted from being torn in different directions.

"Try harder!" the rebuke pierced the outer layers of the fabrication.

Pam took Martha's laptop to Philomina's studio flat on the top floor, to use the large printer. She was under strict orders to stay upstairs until the plumber left the house.

***

Pam tripped and scuffed the back of her black, stiletto heel, pointed, court shoes, against the kerb. Cursing under breath, she took a detour into the nearby café. *'Got about ten minutes'* she thought. The search for a black biro, in her neatly packed bag, minus the cigarette packet, was unsuccessful.

"What can I get you?"

"Uhmm … hot chocolate to take away, no cream, and a black biro for a few minutes, please."

The request was met with a puzzled look. Pam's garbled explanation caused more confusion.

"Only have blue pen, that okay?"

"Brilliant, thanks so much." Pam sat in a chair and sighed with relief. Although not a perfect match the blue ink hid the white scratch marks.

Pam left the half empty ripple, recyclable, paper cup by the side of a litter bin and took a deep breath. Once more, she adjusted the navy midi pencil skirt, borrowed from Martha. An elasticated waist was comfortable but had stretched too wide for Pam's flimsy figure. As she walked into Clipper Cards on the High Street a familiar voice called out, "Hello again, less busy today."

"Sure is," replied Pam. "Is the manager in? I can leave my CV with you if that's okay?" The nervous pitch of the questions unsettled the member of staff, so she tried to put Pam at ease.

"Yeah, she's just on a call. By the way, my name's Summer."

"Good to meet you, I'm Pam."

"Think I've seen you a few times? Daphine won't be long, she's really friendly as long as you do what you're told. Her nickname's Daffy but don't tell her I said that."

Pam chuckled with her prospective work colleague, but at a lower volume compared to the shrills of laughter she usually shared with Martha and Betty.

"Hello!" said Daphine, as she held the stockroom door open with her left foot. "Come in, I don't bite! Well not yet."

"Thank you." Pam tried to avoid the empty boxes, packs of cards and ribbon torn to shreds, scattered on the floor.

Daphine shouted, "everything all right Summer? Give us a buzz if you need help with balloons."

"Right, take a seat." said Daphine. "I'll just move those bits on the desk."

'There's no more space' Pam thought but smiled before sitting on the wobbly brown plastic chair.

"Okay, let's have a look at your CV. All seems good. Admin work but that'll come in handy. At this time of year, we hire for attitude as much as aptitude."

"I had temp job in Woolworths. My mum got it for me when I was a teenager."

"Now that's a blast from the past." Daphine's face lit up. "Loved pick'n'mix! I wanted to get Saturday job in our local store, in Liverpool, but dad insisted I concentrate on exams."

Pam nodded but felt embarrassed and sad because her mum took little interest in what she did inside school.

"You okay with all the hustle and bustle? It's hectic in lead up to Christmas. Heard you had a trial run yesterday.

"Yes, was busy. Summer done a brilliant job doing everything at same time."

Daphine evaluated Pam's reaction to the prospect of a crowded store and need to multitask. "She's great; need four of five with her skills and then we'd be laughing. Bet she told you my nickname was Daffy?"

Pam blushed and asked, "Can I phone a friend?"

Daphine and Pam laughed in harmony which was a positive signal.

"Tell you what," said Daphine, "I'll give you a chance and we'll see how it goes. Sound good?"

"Yes." Pam's voice crackled with nerves.

"If you bring in your passport and references before Friday, I'll give you a shift Saturday afternoon. You'll get a sweatshirt but other than that it's black trousers and flat shoes. You won't last an hour in those!"

***

"Hiya! What you up to?" asked Martha.

"Ouch!" Pam groaned. "Ow! Up to? I can't move."

"It's only your first day! What you been doin?"

Pam put a pillow behind her back, stretched her legs out on the bed and tapped the speaker option on the mobile. "What ain't I been doin! Talk about throwin' me in deep end!"

"Get a grip, it's a card shop, not the fire brigade!"

"Thanks for support M. You try blowing up balloons, folding sheets of wrapping paper and serving customers especially when there's only one card machine amongst three of us. Kept falling over wire and slipping on carrier bags!"

"Next time, pick them up! Anyhow, good place to meet the locals?"

Pam cried out in pain. "Don't even get me started on those brats runnin' around, messing up the cards and pulling things off the counter. And you won't believe it; sticking bubble gum on the calendars!"

"Children are naughty now an' then," Martha pointed out the obvious using a teacher's tone of voice, "Some of us don't act much betta, do we?"

"Yeah, but M, there's being naughty and there's being a vandal!"

"Honestly, you're such a drama queen!"

"Whatever! You're so lucky, Maeve's not like that."

There was a slight tremble in Martha's voice as she asked: "Do you wanna go for a drink? My treat to celebrate your new job."

"Sorry M, I can't even go to get a drink of water. Everything alight?"

"Yeah, okay." Martha replied in a whisper, "what's happening in Maeve's school is getting to me. Don't know what else to do!"

Pam felt guilty for moaning and tried to console her best friend. "They must do something. Headmaster can't keep defending bullies. Someone's gotta stand up to 'em! Where's she now?"

"In her room; bought her headphones so she can listen to audio books – keeps her occupied and calms her down."

"Bless her!" Pam thought, '*it's horrible to watch a sensitive spirited soul beaten down by cruelty and negativity for no reason.*' "What's Brian say about it? More importantly what's he doin' about it?"

"He's too busy. Doesn't want to interfere." Martha sounded dejected.

"You don't say!" Pam replied mockingly. "He has a meltdown if someone dares touch one of Philomina's books. Come over tomorrow, we can have a chat over a glass or two?"

"If only!" Martha groaned. "Have to make sure Maddy finishes her homework, and must talk to Brian about house, seem to be going nowhere fast! Then there's housework!"

"I'll pop in Monday, okay?" Pam asked. "Offered to help with delivery at shop on Tuesday."

"You're such a teacher's pet." Martha teased her lifeline.

***

"Hello, good morning," said Pam. "Daphine asked me to help with the delivery today."

"Oh, hello. I'm Indira. You're Pam?"

"Yes, I only started Saturday. You'll have to bear with me, still not sure where everything is."

"No problem. I've been here for over ten years, just work part time now, but know all the tricks of the trade. Daphine's been called to the store in Canterbury. She's doing a favour for the area manager in hope we can get more temps for Christmas."

"What time will the delivery arrive?" Pam asked.

"Depends on which way the wind is blowing," Indira said with a smirk. "Should be around midday. Two of the temps – Blake and Ben should be in about 10. We'll let them do all the heavy lifting."

"How long they worked here?"

"Only started a couple of weeks ago. They haven't worked in a shop before, in fact don't think they've had a proper job. There're keen, but just need to keep an eye on them, and make sure their mobiles stay in the lockers."

"I'll try my best." Pam said hesitantly.

"Indira!! 'So, Good Morning, Good Morning. Sun beams will soon smile through'."

The enthusiastic, youthful, wannabe singers belted out, in unison, lines of the famous song from the film, Singing in the Rain.

"My! My! You two are chirpy today!" said Indira. "Pam, can you look after the till while I get these two signed in. Press buzzer if you need help."

"Yeah sure," Pam looked up from tidying the cards and an emotional electric shock surged all over her body. '*Wowser!*' she thought, as her eyes absorbed the striking looks of Blake Dannreuther, a 24-year-old student, striding purposefully towards the stockroom. His shoulder length black wavy hair framed the chiselled cheek bones. Fantastic facial features were complimented by a toned physique, encased in skin-tight black jeans, earthy brown tee-shirt, and black fleece. Her stare was transfixed towards the door at the back of the shop.

"Anyone serving? I'm in a rush!" the disgruntled customer shouted.

"Sorry, yes, sorry, how can I help?" Pam stuttered and blushed; her mind distracted and her senses ignited by the vision who had just entered her world.

***

"Right, you lot, it's goin' be a busy day," Daphine raised her voice to get her team's attention.

"Busy making tea?" Ben's cheeky comment and smile eased the tension momentarily.

Overtired and irritated by increasing amounts of paperwork, Daphine lashed out, "You'll be busy goin' out the door, in a minute. Next phase of Christmas cards must be put out today. No excuses! Summer is on till one. Ben; help her and finish balloon orders.

Pam 'n' Blake; sort out those shelves in corner, need space. Then put new stock of boxed cards in order and tidy floor."

Pam, totally distracted, slipped on a giant plastic Santa sack, which had escaped from the clear cellophane wrapping, balancing precariously on the top shelf. "Oh no! Sorry." Pam's face burnt red with embarrassment.

"Mind yourself!" Daphine barked. "Don't wanna fill out the accident book. Got enough on my plate!" "Oh yeah, the area manager is coming in this afternoon. Make sure everything is tidy and you two," Daphine pointed to Ben and Blake, "mobiles stay in the lockers!"

A cocktail of chemicals made Pam giddy with excitement. "Okay, not sure where to start?"

"Let's start at the very beginning." Blake's smile melted Pam's pulsating heart.

"Sounds a good plan," said Pam. "You're far too young to remember that song."

"No, not at all, love musicals, and it's one of my mum's favourites."

Pam's effort to kneel on the floor caused her to stumble and Blake reached out to steady her arm which made her tingle.

"Am afraid my joints are not that flexible in my old age." Pam's effort at a joke was in vain however Blake smiled politely. *'Wish he could just stop smiling for a moment'* she thought *'can't think straight.'*

"I'll clear bottom shelf," said Blake, "and bow to your long-standing experience."

"Comedian as well as musical. You'll go far!" Pam simpered, looking pleased with herself.

After an hour of trying her utmost to focus on the allocated task, Pam noticed strands of Blake's copious wavy hair reeling around a hook protruding from the shelf.

"Hold on! Wait a minute!" Pam shrieked. The plea caused Blake to lift his head quickly and hit it against the edge of the metal rack.

"Ouch! Is that as painful as it looks?" asked Pam.

"Just a bit!" Blake's eyes watered with the sharp pain.

"Well, it is Friday 13th. Meant to be unlucky." Pam became increasingly concerned at the glazed look on Blake's face and said, "stay still and I'll get the hook out of your hair. Not a good look for your street cred."

Pam's fingers trembled with the sparks of tension. "If you keep movin' I can't reach it!"

"I'm not moving," Blake retorted. "Your hand's shaking!"

"Can't reach from this angle. Let me try from other side." Pam overbalanced and hit the floor with a terrific thud."

"That's definitely more painful than it looks!" said Blake. "We need danger money workin' here."

Pam groaned, "please help me up, think I've twisted my ankle."

Their hysterical laughter permeated through the stockroom door.

"Are you two doing any work!?" Daphine's initial sarcastic enquiry quickly turned into an order. "Blake. Front baskets need tidying! Then take over from Summer so she can go on lunch break!"

Daphine turned to Pam and said, "Sit down for a minute." She held out the brown chair with strands of ribbon wrapped around the uneven legs.

"Thanks. That's much better, getting' too old...." Daphine interrupted before Pam could finish.

"Maturity is what we need, in every way. We could get away with a bit of flirting, in our day. No one complained, and if they did it was mostly ignored."

"Absolutely, they called it a bit of a laugh, but weren't fun for a teenager. We daren't say a word." Pam's reflection of her past quenched the flames of hilarity.

"But we're in 2015, different world," Daphine said sternly. "First, I don't want to lose my job an' it ain't gonna do you any favours; not something we can put in your reference is it?

Pam floundered, not knowing how to respond, "sorry, uhm, didn't mean to cause trouble. There's nothing in it!"

"I weren't born yesterday!" Daphine snapped before giving out unbridled advice. "Nip it in the bud. It's only gonna end in tears. An older woman is a 'tick box' thing for young men. And there's no fool like an old fool!"

Daphine's words stung but Pam smiled, through gritted teeth.

***

CHAPTER 5

A rousing rendition of the national anthem encircled the memorial park and the last line of 'God Save The Queen' lingered in the air as the attendees of the Remembrance Sunday service glanced at the sky, yearning to re-connect with those no longer by their side.

The vicar's attempt to thank the event management committee and volunteers was lost in the turbulent sea breeze which drowned out the intermittent power supply to the microphone.

Bobby, the sturdy black loyal Labrador; proudly paraded his well-groomed coat and red poppy tag, polished to perfection. Beside him, Mr Bentley stood to attention with fellow veterans.

After the service finished, Maeve turned, saw Angela standing apart from the gathering and tentatively waved. Angela waited by the ornate iron gates, hoping for the chance to say hello to Martha and Maeve.

"Is your dog here?" asked Maeve.

"Oh no, dear. At one time, I would have been concerned about her barking but now it would be the snoring. She does sleep a lot."

"It is nice to see you again," said Martha. "What a lovely service. Admire then for battling against the wind. Couldn't hear all the words but good there's a big crowd."

"Yes, I am afraid we cannot win the battle against the elements."

Martha rubbed her hands together, "mustn't keep you standing out in the cold. We'll let you get back for your Sunday lunch."

"Not at all," said Angela. "It is a pleasure talking to you. Now Maeve, would you like to come to see Ginger? She would love to have a visitor."

Maeve tugged at her mother's coat and looked up with wishful eyes.

"Are you sure? We'll only stop a few minutes." Martha gazed at her daughter with an authoritative expression; managing expectations was a key factor in dealing with the sensitivity.

Maeve smiled and skipped along the pavement to the astonishment of her mother. The respite from her woes was a delight to witness.

The house on the corner with large turret caught Martha's attention. She thought it looked like a ship in dock ready to be launched out on the next adventurous voyage at sea. Maeve, intrigued by the height and size of the property, stumbled but was saved from falling by the secure grip of her mother.

Angela tapped on the front door and called out in a soft tone, "It is okay. I am here!"

Martha and Maeve, enthralled by the setting and reassuring words, smiled in unison.

"Best if she hears my voice before opening the door. She can get quite anxious at times."

In the hallway sat Ginger, a black cocker spaniel with a gleaming coat and wavy curly hair on her long ears. She gave a low-key bark as if to say, "Hello!"

"Good girl," said Angela. "Look! Maeve has come to see you." Ginger wagged her tail and stretched out her two front legs.

Martha held her daughter's hand for comfort and paid Ginger a compliment, "she is a star, look at her lovely coat."

Angela smiled. "You are probably wondering why her name is Ginger. Well, that is a story for another day."

"Can I stroke her?" asked Maeve. "Not now," replied Martha. "We have woken her up, don't want to cause too much trouble."

Angela looked at Maeve with empathy. "She will like that. Just walk slowly towards me and we can start the introductions." Maeve gently stroked the top of Ginger's head, and she did not move, but her tail swept energetically across the antique parquet flooring, set out in an Athene design.

"She likes you," said Angela. "I like her," Maeve replied tenderly.

"Would you like a drink?"

"That is kind of you," replied Martha, "but must get back to a grumpy teenager and equally grumpy husband. Need to start on the roast, otherwise there will be protests on the beach!" Maeve tugged at her mother's coat, and she instinctively recognised the urgency of the signal. "Could we use your toilet? I'm sorry, it must be the cold weather."

"Of course, upstairs, straight ahead. I am afraid the little room down here is out of action. I will get your drinks, what would you like?"

"Oh, thank you," Martha called over the banister. "I'll have a tea, and a Ribena for Maeve, please."

"Regrettably, I do not have Ribena but there is orange squash?"

"That'll be great, thank you." Martha replied and hurriedly searched for the bathroom.

They entered a period drama similar to exhibitions in the Imperial War Museum. Layers of dust heroically hanging onto a vast array or ornaments and artefacts. The classic floral print of the carpet, in admiral blue, laid on a cream backdrop. Frayed at the edges but snippets of the pure wool quality shone through the wear and tear.

"I'll come in with you, sweetheart. We have to be careful not to break anything."

The green and white striped hand towel, hanging on the mahogany towel rail stand, was pitied with holes and need of a visit to the launderette. Martha found a pack of travel tissues in her pocket and used them to dry her daughter's hands. There did not appear to be any radiators and the cool temperature generated a shiver. Curtains in the three smaller bedrooms were closed and dark shadows skated across the landing. Thick net curtains, with hand sewen-hems, covered the window in the main bedroom. The discolouration obscured the view through the large window.

Ginger wagged her tail as soon as she saw Maeve, carefully navigating down the Inca blue loose stair runner. "Your drinks are in the dining room," said Angela, "and have found some biscuits." Maeve sat at the table, nibbling the chocolate fingers, and tried to catch the crumbs whilst Angela and Martha exchanged small talk about Wishym Bay.

"Okay young lady," said Martha. "We best be going and leave Angela in peace."

As they were putting on their coats, Maeve knelt on the floor and gave Ginger a farewell pat on the head. A ray of sunlight hit the crystal glass pyramid prism paperweight, in the sitting room, and split into a rainbow of colours that projected onto the wall. *'So pretty.'* Maeve thought as she peeped inside the room with the large bay window. The blue and white nautical décor was the backdrop for ceiling high oak bookshelves, filled to the brim, and stunning silver ornaments. Taking pride of place on the windowsill was a hand-crafted replica of HMS Fairfax, fixed to a solid wood base. The centre piece of the setting was a Chesterfield high back wing chair, in velluto blue fabric, with yew feet in Queen Anne style. A Tweedmill silver grey, 100% pure new wool knee rug, in a herringbone design with double navy stripe, laid across the armrest. An empty cup, a copy of the Sunday paper, a cigar and ashtray, were placed neatly on the small square mahogany table, positioned by the right side of the chair. A pair of hard sole, black corduroy, well worn, slippers stood still under the table. The cream, hand knitted, chunky cardigan with dark blue buttons nestled in the seat.

"Can I look at the boat, please?" Maeve asked eagerly.

"I am afraid not, my dear. We do not go in there."

Martha felt a mixture of embarrassment and astonishment as to the keen interest and clear communication by Maeve but was confused by Angela's reference to 'we' but realised they had outstayed their welcome.

"Come on sweetheart, let's go back and finish reading your book. Before you ask, we are not getting a dog! Remember what daddy told you?"

Maeve nodded obediently but her eyes filled with melancholy.

***

After the front door closed, the emptiness of solitude encapsulated the home she once shared with her beloved husband, Victor. After 37 years active service in The Royal Navy, he moved to a desk job in the Ministry of Defence in Whitehall: part of the team working for the Deputy Chief of the Defence Staff (Personnel). He managed the work on behalf of DCDS in his role as Director Service Personnel Policy (SCS2 grade).

***

Gladys Griffiths waited for her sweetheart to return from World War II and at the age of 22 married Edgar Richmond in December 1945. Edgar served in The Royal Navy from the age of 19. Along with family and friends, who had acted as matchmakers, they learned to cope with rationing and all the other devastating consequences of a world war.

Various tours of duty led them to move home often however their children, Victor and Weston were both born in Plymouth. The discipline in the formative years of their childhood strengthened their characters and ambition to join The Royal Navy; to make their parents proud.

Edgar was astounded when gifted a house by a great aunt he vaguely remembered meeting, in his childhood, during visits to Whitchurch Canonicorum in Dorset. He spent many happy days in the summer exploring the stunning scenery with his cousins. The visit to St Candida & Holy Cross Church fascinated the curiosity of a child, but the creativity of their play-acting skills in the grounds did not amuse the nanny.

A scintilla of guilt rested on Edgar's shoulders after he moved into the house in Wishym Bay with his wife, in 1970, after the pace of his career slowed down. Both sons served in The Royal Navy which filled them with delight and unmitigated pride, especially when Victor was appointed as a Commander of a frigate during the Falklands Conflict in 1982. It was hoped that Weston would be part of the taskforce, but unfortunately ill health deprived them of that vision. The jealousy felt by the younger brother reared its ugly head on numerous occasions after 1982.

Gladys envisaged the large house in Wishym Bay would play host to family gatherings including grandchildren. Weston was pressured into marriage when his girlfriend shared the news of her pregnancy, without his prior knowledge of the announcement, at a family Sunday lunch. The cracks in the marriage appeared, instantaneously, after exchanging vows in a registry office. Tours of duty plastered over the uneven surface, and the birth of his son on 18th November 1968 provided a distraction.

***

Victor and Angela's wedding took place on Saturday 19th June 1976 in the Roman Catholic Church, Our Lady of the Assumption, in Wishym Bay. The June bride glowed with happiness and guests endured the intensity of the blazing sunshine as the photos were taken in the grounds. The high temperature caused no end of problems for Gladys who assumed control of the proceedings throughout the special day. Victor and Angela, happy in their own skins and confident in their commitment, watched Gladys run from one drama to another and become increasingly flustered. *'Mother resembles an overheated engine.'* Victor thought as he smiled at his beautiful bride. Edgar tolerated the heat after years of experience and engaged with the guests with aplomb. Angela's parents, Ernest and Ruth Oyston, took a back seat and embraced the joyful celebration. Victor formally asked Ernest for permission to marry his daughter which eased the initial apprehension. Angela listened to her parents' concerns about stepping out with a Naval Officer. The adage *'A girl in every port'* was referenced. On a more serious note, the extended periods of absence would be a strain when trying to bring up children, so they asked her to deliberate over all the consequences. The much-anticipated grandchildren did not arrive. It brought sadness to Victor and Angela but triggered a mixture of emotions in the family. Gladys regularly mentioned Weston's son, although there was little contact, and the ingenuity of the new line of products in the store - Mothercare, and she reached a crescendo by asking when to start knitting baby clothes. She stored a vibrant mixture of super soft wool on a shelf in her wardrobe.

***

Ernest and Ruth Oyston were steadfast and unyielding in their support for their only child. No glitz nor glamour but grit and determination to build a stable family home for Angela. Their desire for grandchildren was not put on public display and they reflected on the tragic loss of their first two children due to still birth. Ruth was shattered both physically and psychologically. The prognosis of not being able to have children broke their hearts but not their indomitable spirits. Ernest invested more energy into his vocation as a teacher. Ruth was a dutiful housewife, keeping their four-bedroom bungalow, in Whitstable, spotless. She dedicated her spare time supporting elderly relatives, the local Catholic church, and became an invaluable member of the community. The thickening of her waist in December 1946 was blamed on accepting the invitation to be a judge, tasting the various homemade mince pies, in readiness for the events during the period of Advent leading up to Christmas. Ernest told her to delegate some of her duties when she felt nauseous in the preceding months.

Angela was referred to as an Easter blessing after her safe delivery on Sunday 6th April 1947. Although premature she clung onto life with great fortitude and miraculously battled through the health challenges with the bravery of a lioness. At her baptism, the congregation marvelled how a delicate frame persevered.

Ernest and Ruth remained in Whitstable until the years caught up with them and decline in health weakened their resolve. Ruth's request to move into a care home in 1982 was heart wrenching. Angela tried to comfort her father and remained hopeful it was a temporary realignment of their domesticity. Her father needed respite from being a carer for his cherished wife, who was suffering from a deterioration of her gynaecological conditions. Ernest set out a plan to refurbish their bungalow in readiness for Ruth's return home, albeit a brief stay, until she regained her strength. The enthusiasm waned as the grip of loneliness took hold, and separation from his wife after fifty-three years of unwavering commitment, drained his reservoir of optimism. In 1984 at the age of seventy-nine he sold his home and with a heavy heart waved goodbye to a bedrock of his life for over five decades. Household duties weighed him down, even though the community and Angela helped as much as practical. The thought of living on his own for the rest of his life filled him with despair therefore he followed the advice from the local GP and moved to sheltered accommodation in Oakington-on-Sea, close to his darling wife. Ernest remained an insightful academic and put his talents to good use by setting up a book club, and organised quiz nights which the residents relished. Angela telephoned almost every day to keep her father up to date with details of her Service Families Accommodation and Victor's tour of duty. Ernest shared the news with Ruth who was slowly losing touch with reality but had enlightened moments of recognition and recalled moments from their honeymoon in Broadstairs which generated laughter; echoing the true happiness they shared.

Ernest could not fight off the brutal forces of pneumonia which took hold in the autumn of 1989. Angela was shocked how rapidly her father deteriorated and earnestly explained to her mother why *'darling Daddy'* would not be decorating the Christmas tree. The loss was devastating for them. The support from the community and Church in Whitstable navigated them through the darkest days. Victor would visit his mother-in-law during his all too short periods of R&R. The residents of the care home loved hearing tales of life in The Royal Navy, and they often sung *'All The Nice Girls Love a Sailor;'* much to Victor's embarrassment but the musical notes raised the volume of positive thoughts and lifted the dark clouds, albeit temporarily.

Victor usually extended their trips to the Kent coast to ensure his family obligation was fulfilled in Wishym Bay. Gladys cooked a banquet that would feed the neighbours and their families. The spare bedrooms in the house offered a welcome resting place for the night but they both dreaded facing the full English breakfast in the morning.

"I can't eat it – I'll burst!" Angela whispered.

"At first light, we'll go for a long walk by the seafront," said Victor, "and say we stopped for breakfast on the pier."

"Don't worry, I'll make sure you're mentioned in dispatches." Angela gently nudged her husband and they both laughed quietly, so as not to disclose their secret mission.

Edgar and Gladys thoroughly enjoyed living by the coast. They busied themselves in local council meetings, charitable organisations, and Gladys became a member of the Parish Pastoral Council. Veterans who served with Edgar were invited for weekends of reminiscing, golf, and fishing. Gladys was the epitome of the excellent host, and the preparations were tackled with military precision. One of the spare rooms was decorated as a nursery but unfortunately, they rarely spent time with their grandson and his mother rejected numerous requests to stay. The fault line in Weston's marriage was irreparable but refused to admit defeat to his parents and proffered a variety of excuses to avoid travelling to Wishym Bay.

The events in 1991 ripped through the lives of the Richmond family.

Following a joyful Choral Evensong in Canterbury Cathedral, Edgar politely declined their friends' invitation to go for a meal and stay overnight in their spacious detached home with a vast garden, in Bridge Village. He wanted to get a good night's sleep before attending a meeting at Wishym Bay Sea Cadets in preparation for a talk about service in The Royal Navy and discuss the final arrangements to join the team of Trustees on a voluntary basis.

"Please forgive us," said Gladys. "We will arrange another date, soon. I will call you tomorrow and we can compare diaries."

After a police investigation and post-mortem there was no conclusive proof of the cause of death on Wednesday 19th June 1991. The roads were dry, a cool breeze accompanied a cloudless sky and there were no obstructions, and hardly any other drivers on the road. As a matter of course, Edgar was breathalysed and not a trace of alcohol was in the result. After offering to help the Police with their enquiries, out of respect for the emergency services, Edgar blocked out the incident and did not talk of it again with his sons. Survivor's guilt set in, and the mere mention of Gladys' name set him off in a rage. He refused to attend grief counselling and to see his friends. The blockade built between him, and his friends eventually led to a self-prophesied isolation in which the anger, pity and shame roared out loudly, drowning out the maelstrom of bereavement. Alcohol was used as self-medication. Victor and Angela realised he could not be left alone therefore moved to Wishym Bay in 1991. Angela became a full-time carer; splitting her time between Edgar and her mother who was frailer. She was thankful the locations of residence were in close proximity.

Weston could not handle the grief after his mother passed away and had numerous questions that his father refused to answer. He moved to Gibraltar, leaving Victor and Angela to pick up the pieces. The topic of inheritance and the value of the family home was dropped into conversation before he emigrated, as a shot across the bow.

Edgar's internalised anger burst out, intermittently, and was fired at Victor. He empathised with his daughter-in-law however his words cut like a knife. The grief manifested itself into a wide range of physical ailments. Endless trips to hospital and medical appointments had to be organised. Home helps were hired to give Angela respite, but they would not tolerate the verbal abuse.

The passing of Angela's mother on Saturday 28th December 1991 was partially eclipsed by the pressure of being a full-time carer. The arrangements had to be discussed out of earshot of Edgar who refused to go to the funeral. The humble burial was attended by a small gathering, shivering in the snow, followed by an afternoon tea in the church hall. Edgar would not tolerate the guests in his home and insisted Angela had to keep busy. He snarled repeatedly, in a gruff voice, "We've just got to get on with it!"

Victor's attempts at reasoning with his father resulted in an amnesty temporarily. The vicious cycle came to a halt in 1996 when Edgar surrendered and welcomed the exit after five years of torment. A close friend of Edgar, who was an accountant, effectively managed the inheritance tax liability. Victor and Angela were relieved not to have face a hefty bill but had to face Weston, who turned up claiming half the property.

Victor did not want to sell the family home and did not want to endure an excruciating court case therefore raised the finances to pay a settlement to his brother. The lawyers prepared the necessary documentation, and the accountant arranged the payment to Weston with the caveat that he had no further claim on the property.

"It's alright brother," said Weston. "You're an old man, so when you go it'll be all mine. Next of kin an' all that!" The dismissal of Angela was cruel but no different from previous occasions.

Weston needed the money to fund his divorce and lavish lifestyle in Gibraltar. The expense of keeping a younger girlfriend and a new child was escalating each day and the enormous strain left his mind pounding.

***

Angela's world crumbled on 11th November 2005 when her devoted husband died of a heart attack at the age of fifty-nine. Victor was mapping out plans for his retirement and how he would make up for all the years away from his wife. Alas, the map was folded neatly and stored in their home.

Weston returned for the funeral and claimed a share of the property although Victor had re-written his will to ensure all his assets were left in the safe hands of his wife. The lawyers managed to stave off Weston's attempt to grab the investment his brother had worked for since the age of eighteen. Angela sensed his greed would motivate another raid even if it meant she would lose her home. The considerable cost of life in Ocean Village, Gibraltar, was spiralling out of control. The last of his savings was spent on a lavish wedding to his stunning bride who bolstered his ego, but he knew her loyalty was fickle, and only stretched as far as the amount in his bank account.

***

The vibrations of loneliness deepened in each room of her home on the Esplanade in Wishym Bay. Her dearest husband named the house, Anchor Tale. The ceremony included breaking a bottle of champagne on the front door but did not commence until Victor delivered a warning to the neighbours along with an invitation to drinks in the front garden. It was a jolly afternoon.

Major repairs to the colossal house, for a single occupancy, could no longer be passed over. Procrastination was not a trait in Angela's character, but the prospect of change sent a chill down her spine, and she was filled with dread as her home was steeped in memories. Although financially sound, she was acutely aware the cost of the renovation was daunting.

Angela returned to the large sitting room. The view from the curved window had not changed but the movement of characters inside the dwelling had changed considerably since 1970 when the Richmond family first acquired the property.

On the horizon a storm was brewing however a thin silver sword of light broke through the dark clouds in the direction of the resplendent twin towers of the medieval church at Reculver.

***

CHAPTER 6

A loud continuous beeping from the smoke alarm in the hall mingled with the black haze from the toaster that had seen over ten years of service. Martha opened the back door and tried to disperse the cloud of mist with a souvenir tea towel from Buckingham Palace.

"Can someone please turn off that noise!" Brian called out as he stood by the door of his office.

"We need a step ladder!" Martha responded angrily.

"We need a new house." Maddy smirked as she carried a bowl of coco pops to her bedroom.

"That's really helpful." Martha replied. "And what time did you come in this morning?"

"Dunno, watch is broken."

"Well, the only thing you'll be watching tonight is Maeve, because your dad and me are going out for a meal."

"You gotta be jokin'! What about Aunty Pam? She ain't goin' for a meal – she don't eat anything unless it's Weetabix, toast, or chocolate."

"Pam has a job," said Martha, "unlike you! She's working late so can't get here on time."

"Wot, with her toy boy?"

Martha was used to Maddy's sarcastic comments, but this piece of information was a revelation. She was wise enough not to let slip her ignorance. "Don't be silly, the temps at Clipper Cards are all students."

"She seemed to be studyin' something really close with him the other night, when I walked past shop!"

"You're imagining things," said Martha. "Back to real life, we are going for a meal with Betty and Ted. I'll check time with dad but if you've got any plans for tonight, cancel them!"

Martha pushed the black handled, stainless steel serrated steak knife towards the wire mesh inside the four-slice toaster, to try to dislodge the chunk of burnt crust torn from a thick white slice.

"For goodness' sake, pull the plug out!" exclaimed Brian. "You'll electrocute yourself!"

Martha jumped as the order echoed throughout the sparse kitchen furnishing. "You don't have to shout."

"It's just common sense," Brian snapped. "Don't tell me, we need a new toaster as well as everything else?"

"If we could sit down together and discuss the plans, we could work out exactly what we have to buy."

"Do not have time today," said Brian. "Promised Randeep, I'd finish business development plans and make a start on notes for next Tax Lecture, before Monday."

"What time did you book the table for?" asked Martha.

Brian's quizzical expression left Martha disheartened. "You've forgotten?"

"Thought we're going for Sunday lunch," Brian replied. "Anyway, they can't stay tonight."

"It's Betty's birthday – supposed to be a surprise!" Martha gasped. "Oh, don't worry, Betty took your numerous unsubtle hints and has booked a room in the B&B."

"Thank goodness for that. We can't invite anyone here."

"We can't live like hermits," said Martha. "The boiler is fixed now. Ain't all that bad?"

"Just look around you, it's embarrassing! Oh, but don't worry, Pam will always be on our doorstep, invited or not. She wouldn't miss out on free drink, food and not forgetting another interest free loan which she conveniently forgets to repay."

"Please give yourself a rest and come off that old merry-go-round for a few minutes." Martha's exasperated expression prompted Brian to pause from the repetitive onslaughts about Pam.

"We'll have to take Betty out for a drink," said Martha. "What time do you think you'll be finished?"

"Hopefully by eight," Brian delivered his reply from behind the locked office door.

***

Daphine locked the front door of Clipper Cards and yawned, "I'm done for! Goin' straight home to bed,"

"My feet are killing me!" Summer moaned.

"Ah, that's a shame," said Ben. "Was goin' take you to the disco tonight."

"You wish!" Summer replied.

"Not in mood to listen to you prattle on," Daphine snapped. "Ben, come to the bank with me. I'll see you lot on Monday. Indira is in tomorrow. You in Blake?"

"No, not this Sunday, club organised training in preparation for half-marathon." Blake replied.

"Yeah, remember, booked in calendar. Still think you're mad but whatever floats your boat. Right! I'm off. Cheers guys, beat sales targets today. Just got keep goin' to Christmas."

Pam stood on the loose hem of her black trousers and stumbled backwards.

"Steady on," said Blake.

"Oh, sorry; thanks," replied Pam blushing and giggling simultaneously.

"Didn't know Salsa class had already started?"

"Never mind Salsa, could murder a Spritzer!" said Pam.

"What's that?" Blake made the enquiry with a smile that contoured Pam's reckless make-up.

"It's white wine and… oh, never mind it's alcohol and it's got my name on it."

"Can add my name if there's space?" Blake stared at Pam with desire glinting from his rich brown eyes and alluring long eye lashes.

The awkward silence hung in the air for what seemed an eternity. Pam almost asked him to repeat the question but raised her head and resorted to her well-worn coping mechanism – humour.

"As long as you add your name to the bill, we've got a date." Pam winced at her ill-fated choice of words, but Blake enthused over the clumsiness of her flirtation.

"Whose idea was it to order the cocktails?" asked Pam as she staggered sideways.

"Two for the price of one," Blake replied. "You know how Daffy keeps going on about special offers."

"Sell them, not drink them!" Pam murmured.

"It was Happy Hour; rude not to?" Blake held out his hand to steady Pam. "Think we've moved on to the Cha-Cha-Cha."

"Comedian, musical and a dancer? Wow, that's what you call talent." Pam bit her lip and thought '*stop being so stupid and obvious.*'

Blake was amused by her adolescent approach and the role reversal boosted his confidence.

"Not really a dancer," said Blake. "But can do a wicked waltz with heel turns and everything. No, not really. Strictly Come Dancing is a favourite in our house."

"Bet it's your mum's favourite?"

"How did you guess?" Blake tantalised her with his smile each time he turned on the charm offensive. "Don't take this the wrong way, but you're not exactly walking in a straight line. Can I help hold you up until you're at the top of your street?"

"What a gentleman," Pam replied. "By garage, top of Pier Street. What's it called? Oh, yeah – Reg Silver. Thanks."

Pam misjudged the position of the latch and tripped into the gate. "Really should've had lunch."

"You alright?"

"Yeah, be fine," Pam replied. "Toast will do the trick."

"Bit dry for me," Blake laughed, "I'm getting chips on way home with lots of sauce. Had a nice time. Cheers. Next time, I'll pay for cocktails?"

"Great! I'll hold you to that," said Pam whilst fidgeting with her keys.

"Okay, you get in and practise those dance moves."

"Fab-u-lust!" Pam squeezed her eyes tightly and thought '*NO! – I didn't say that! NO!*'

"Take care." Blake waved as he turned to walk home.

His faltering steps came to a halt and rubbed his fingers through his magnificent mane of wavy black hair, an attraction for men and women. A myriad of impulses criss-crossed his mind. He thought '*I couldn't?*' Blake recalled a late-night conversation with his mate after a few ciders. Gio, an excellent student, met Blake whilst they were both in the gateway year of the five-year MB BS Medicine course at the University of East Anglia. His level of academic intelligence almost matched his enthusiasm for mature women. "They're more sensitive, and grateful," Gio would say, "good fun for a fling and, teach you a thing or two! Probably, not tech savvy, so, no dodgy photos posted online; especially by the married ones."

Gio did not keep in touch after Blake dropped out of university, but that insight into dating stuck.

He stood still and thought, '*worth a try, she's nice, and funny, what have I gotta lose?*'

Hesitantly he looked back but turned on his heels towards home.

The cry of despair caught his attention.

"BLAKE! You still there?" Pam squealed as she stood frozen in her doorway, confronted by a spider as large as her hand. "Blake! Please help. I need you!"

***

Plumes of sea spray hit the side of the pier and Betty found the sound to be refreshing and dramatic scene to be exhilarating. A brisk morning walk helped Betty to ponder the different locations for a bungalow suitable for their retirement. Ted, her husband of almost twenty-eight years, was relaxing in the B&B reading the sports pages in the Sunday newspapers.

Edward (Ted) Cooke, a Civil Servant since the age of eighteen, faced the last few months working in the Ministry of Defence with the same degree of calmness that his colleagues referred to throughout his career. Ted was her strength and stay, and Betty blossomed because the roots of their relationship were firmly placed in good soil. When she met Edward, he offered comfort after many years caring for elderly parents who both passed away at the beginning of 1987. Initially he was someone new to care for until their two children, Ramsey and Sindy arrived in 1988 and 1990, respectively. Both strong, highly academic, and self-possessed. Philomina, Martha's daughter, was born only four days before Sindy, but they were poles apart with regards temperament.

Ted had made enquiries about moving to Chiddingfold in Surrey. Village life was appealing, especially the Cricket Club, but he understood Betty would be happier, near Martha and Pam, if he checked out first. Some described Ted as grey but Betty knew the full range of the true colour palette.

Betty walked along the Esplanade. The properties facing the sea were appealing however it was prudent to keep a respectful distance from Martha and Pam. Although friends from school, she was not interwoven in the strong bond between the two fiery characters with sharp edges. Betty was more middle age in mind and outward appearance, but still enjoyed a giggle with the girls. Short bursts of reliving their youth and frivolity were harmless fun. Throughout her school years she was teased for her ginger curly hair. Martha and Pam tried to shield her from the most vicious comments. During one fracas in the playground, Pam pulled out a handful of hair from a classmate and shouted, "Any colour hair is better than no hair. If you pick on my friend again, I'LL PULL ALL YOUR HAIR OUT!" Needless to say, the incident resulted in a visit to the Headmistress 'office and a lengthy spell of detention.

In her maturity, Betty celebrated her flame filled hair, glasses, and widening waist. Ted loved her unreservedly. He did not compare or criticise her appearance nor character. Betty was acutely aware of the blessing and how many others did not experience genuine commitment.

Betty bought a bag of Cadbury Dairy Milk giant buttons from Tesco Express on the way back to the B&B as a peace offering for Pam. The labelling included the words *Big Share Bag* however Betty knew the concept of sharing chocolate was alien to Pam. The last-minute invitation to birthday drinks at the wine bar was met with a rebuff from Pam in a text message, '*Not asked at start means not wanted.*'

Betty thought '*I'll leave on doorstep if she's not awake, probably won't fit through letterbox.*'

Betty noticed the handsome young man with hair loosely tied in a man bun, closing the gate to Pam's bungalow. *'Bit old for a paperboy?'* Betty thought, *'don't be silly, Pam doesn't buy newspapers. Probably got wrong address?'*

***

"You awake yet?" Martha shouted as she opened Pam's front door with her set of keys. "We come bearing gifts, well, choccy buttons Betty left on your door step this morning."

"Yummy," Pam replied from the bedroom.

"I'll put kettle on," said Betty.

"Blimey, you must have worked the night shift," Martha quipped. "Look at the state of you!"

"Oh, ha ha, very funny. These are my best PJs."

"You had anything to eat?" asked Martha.

Pam yawned excessively and faltered a reply "Uhm? Not yet, get Weetabix, in a minute."

"Not sure what you're goin to have with it?" Betty asked. "There's no milk. I'll go and get some and bread; mould growing on what's left in cupboard. Anything else you need?"

"No thanks." Pam replied.

"C'mon lazybones!" Martha pulled Pam by the arm, "gotta get out of the bedroom at some point today."

Martha sat on camping chair and Pam sat on the floor, in the lounge, with her back resting against the wall.

"Where's settee on your list?" asked Martha as she shuffled to get comfortable.

"Ain't got a clue," Pam replied, "still paying for washing machine. How's Project 49*WB*?"

"Don't ask! Brian's too busy and all he wanted to talk about at lunch was cricket."

"Did Betty and Ted have a good time?" asked Pam.

"Yeah. Ted loves a Sunday roast. Didn't you fancy it?"

"Wot and 'ave Brian goin' on an' on about what I'm eating. *"Ooh Pam, why don't you have meat? Why don't you have parsnips?"* Pam mimicked her arch-nemesis. "Who on earth eats parsnips?"

"Get the door!" Martha called out. "Just popping to the loo."

"Only had full fat milk," said Betty, "but that's your favourite bread – Hovis soft white thick?"

"Brilliant. Thanks." Pam replied. "Got strawberry jam in fridge. Yum!"

"When did you get *2 in 1* air freshener?" asked Martha.

"Ain't got air freshener?" replied Pam.

Martha walked into the lounge with a pair of navy-blue fox pattern socks hanging from the hook of a wire coat hanger. "Is this a new fragrance?" she asked.

Pam's face reddened in a mixture of anger and humiliation.

"Where's this one come from?" asked Martha.

"Thought I saw a young man leaving your home this morning," said Betty. "Think it's time for coffee and chat."

"How young?" asked Martha.

"You two spying on me now? Why not put CCTV outside front door!" Pam snapped.

"Don't change subject!" said Martha. "How young?"

"Twenty-four," Pam replied sheepishly.

"Sorry, must be something wrong with my hearing. TWENTY-FOUR?" Martha exclaimed.

"Where did you meet him?" asked Betty. "One of those dating websites?"

Pam pulled at the top of her pink heart print fleece dressing gown and replied, "at work."

"One of the students?" Martha gasped.

"Yes," replied Pam. "Blake is one of the temps, he's lovely."

"And handsome from what I saw of him," said Betty blushing. "Nice hair bun!"

"So, he had time to do his hair but not pick up his socks? In a rush – mummy getting' his breakfast?" Martha teased her lifelong friend but was deeply concerned. How many more of these brief encounters could she withstand without having a nervous breakdown. Pam was tough on top but tender underneath.

"Don't be silly," Pam replied as she tugged at her pyjama top. "He had to go training with the running club."

Martha hugged Pam and said, "You better have a shower an' get tide marks off your neck. Oh! Wait a minute. There're bites! He's a quick learner." Martha and Betty chuckled.

Refreshed, after a long shower; Pam, dressed in pink leggings, navy-blue baggy sweatshirt, pink heart trainer socks, and fluffy pink mule slippers, knelt on a blanket spread out on the floor.

Betty brought out a tray holding mugs of coffee, toast with strawberry jam and chocolate fingers, she found in the fridge: in readiness for the in-depth investigation.

"So, how did you get him here?" asked Martha. "Don't tell me, he was just passing, and popped in for a cup of cocoa?"

"He came to my rescue!" Pam replied.

"Rescue from what?" asked Martha. "Did a seagull land on your roof?"

Pam shrieked, "It was a spider!"

"Wot?" Martha laughed. "You called out Boy Wonder for a spider. How big was it?"

"This big and hairy legs!" Pam exaggerated the dimensions and description for dramatic effect.

"Must have felt at home here then!" Martha and Betty giggled.

Martha had a light bulb moment. "Oh no! Please tell me you didn't buy one from the pet shop and let it loose in here?"

"Don't be stupid!" Pam replied sharply. "What am I goin' carry it home in – an armoured truck!?!"

"Wouldn't put anything past you. So, tell us, did the Knight in shining Clipper Card tee-shirt slay the beast?"

"No, he picked it up gently and put it the garden!" Pam's voice softened as she recalled Blake's admirable act of chivalry.

"That is funny," Betty chortled. "Your young man is an arachnophile. Not really an action man?"

"Well! There was plenty of action later!" Pam laughed loudly.

"STOP!" said Martha. "Don't want to hear details. You keep that as a memory which you'll regret, but you don't listen, so no point repeating myself!"

"Is that a tinge of jealousy around your gills?" asked Pam with a wry smile.

"No!" Martha replied sternly. "This is not Romeo and Juliet. Older women are just a tick-box for young men."

"That's what Daphine said!

"So, your manager has warned you!" Martha yelled. "Are you mad? You'll get arrested for harassment or sacked which might be the best option!"

"He's just a boy!" said Betty. "You're going to ruin your life for him?"

"Not ruin - restore!" Pam replied dreamily.

"Take a reality check!" said Martha. "Is mummy gonna let you parade around town with her little soldier?"

Pam lashed out, "better than goin' out with your old man!"

Betty interrupted. "Stop it you two! It's like been back in the school playground! Please change the subject. Giving me headache!"

"Alright if we must!" said Pam begrudgingly. "Okay, did you have a nice time at the wine bar without me?"

"Ah, now we gettin' to the root of the problem," said Martha. "Wine envy!"

"Wrong there. Wouldn't have missed last night for the world. Did anyone fall down the stairs?"

"Nearly missed a step in my heels," Betty chuckled. "Wished you warned me; don't put my going out shoes on much these days. Brian tripped up on the way out. We tried not to laugh but couldn't help ourselves!"

"Bet he had the right hump?" Pam giggled as she imagined the scene in slow motion.

"No more than usual," Martha replied. "But he had Ted to talk to which was a relief."

***

CHAPTER 7

A plethora of ruby red, rose gold and champagne latex balloons covered the ceiling in the stockroom in preparation for a winter wedding. Summer started on the star shape silver foil balloons whilst Indira, Ben and Pam were serving on the tills. The laughter from the stock room reverberated around the store and could be heard over the clutter of customers, on an exceptionally busy morning; two weeks before Christmas. Pam's multi-tasking skills were at breaking point as she helped Ben rectify a mistake on his till, manoeuvred the twisted cable attached to the card machine from under her feet, and tried to placate a disgruntled customer. She failed to suppress her curiosity as to the reason for the excitement in the stockroom and became more distracted by the minute. Pam walked into a scene of Summer holding Blake's hand as he attempted to tie the balloons into groups of three. Blake saw the tears welling up in her eyes and pulled his hand away sharply resulting in the balloons rising back up to the ceiling.

"Oh, B.K.!" Summer exclaimed. "Daffy'll go mad if we waste any more ribbon!"

Pam stared at Blake and thought *'why didn't you tell me your nickname?'* She frowned and squeezed past Blake to get to the fridge. The light touch intensified the mutual attraction.

"Wot am I supposed to be mad about?" shouted Daphine as she burst into the room.

Blake blushed and apologised, "Sorry, I let go of the balloons."

"I didn't get an invite to this party." Daphine's caustic comment changed the atmosphere.

"Pam, get back on the till; it's mayhem out there!"

"Just gettin' bottle of water from fridge," said Pam, "sorry."

"Don't bring it onto shop floor!" Daphine, frustrated by the actions her staff, gave out orders with such a force that it left no doubt in anyone's mind as to the meaning. "Summer! Start bagging up! They'll be here soon. Promised we'll help bring bags over to Church Hall."

Summer struggled with the large bags in front of her face and mumbled, "I'll need a hand."

Pam responded immediately and offered eagerly, "I can help."

"NO!" Daphine shouted. "Blake, you go! Might as well finish what you've started and hopefully it'll improve your customer service skills."

"Look forward to it," said Blake.

Summer beamed with delight.

***

The frost on the tarmac sparkled and a freezing wind stung Pam's eyes as she waited outside the office door at the back of Clipper Cards.

Ben and Blake sang, *"Frosty the Snowman, was a jolly happy soul."*

Pam applauded, more to keep warm than praise for the duet. "You two make a good double act."

"When you wish upon a star!" Ben said flirtatiously.

Blake, flushed and tempted, replied to the invitation, "Man! You're far too young for me! Prefer the more mature type."

"Did you hear that Pam – you could be in with a chance!"

Summer arrived and caught the tail-end of the conversation, "Have I missed anything? Latest gossip?"

"No," Pam replied. "Ben's just joking." The red woollen scarf, with a snowmen and Santa design, camouflaged her glowing cheeks.

Twenty minutes later Indira arrived with the keys. In a rush and in a fluster. "Daffy's delayed in traffic, something about accident and lorry jack-knifed. Oh, I don't know. We've got to open ASAP. Ben, refill baskets and put by entrance. I'll open tills for Summer and Blake."

"Would you like a tea?" asked Pam.

"I'd love one but don't dare. If Daffy finds us, she'll go spare!" replied Indira in a state of panic.

"Should I help Ben?" asked Pam.

"No need," Indira replied. "Please get those calendars out, otherwise Daffy will be on the warpath, again. Then move Christmas cards along – make sure you put the right labels above 'em."

Pam enquired, "which till am I on?"

"I'll sort that out later," said Indira. "We're okay for now. The dream team are on tills this morning."

***

The display of small boxes of red and white candy canes, glittery key rings, flashing Christmas tree badges, and bags of chocolate coins, perched perilously on rolls of Christmas wrapping paper packed into four separate boxes. Each time a customer pulled out their design of choice, the arrangement tilted, and Pam held her breath. She decided to reposition the candy canes to the corner of counter but during the makeover a customer called out, "Where is he?"

"Who?" replied Pam as she dropped two boxes.

"You know, the handsome young man with that hair, you'd die for," said the regular shopper in a four wheeled mobility scooter, wearing a bright orange hooded quilted jacket.

"Oh, Blake!" Pam simpered and kicked the broken candy canes under the extra-large gift bags, hanging on the side of the counter.

"Ah, that's his name. He's a fine-looking man."

"I know," Pam reddened at the reply and realised her response was far louder than intended.

"You're a lucky lady, working with him. Well, I'm staying put, he's the one, don't want anyone else serving me."

"He's in demand; you need to reserve tickets." Pam provided an insight into his popularity.

"That does not surprise me. Does he do home deliveries?"

Pam giggled.

"You havin' fun without me?" said Blake.

"Ah, here's the man himself; now young man, help me with these boxes of cards and I'll have some stamps."

"Yes, of course. How are you today?" asked Blake.

"I'm grand now you're here."

"How kind," Blake replied. "Sorry, I didn't catch your name."

"That's because I didn't throw it, cheeky. I'm Bridget."

"Nice to meet you, Bridget. Is there anything else I can help you with?" asked Blake.

"First you can move one of those baskets away from the door. And then you can stop smiling because it's melting my frozen meals and my heart."

The over exaggerated giggling from Pam from behind the counter amplified.

"Be careful of those bags," said Blake. "You'll slip in a minute."

"Ooops!" Pam exclaimed as she pulled the back of Blake's tee-shirt.

"In training for Strictly final?" Blake teased Pam as he touched her left arm gently.

"How did you guess," Pam replied. "Practising for 'couple's choice.'"

"You'll have to teach me the steps," Blake flirted with ease.

Pam took a deep breath, and asked, "Beach Trees Bar are doin' special sparkly cocktails in happy hour, this Saturday, if you fancy it?"

He gave a radiant smile and replied, "Sounds great..." Before Blake had a chance to finish his sentence, Daphine bellowed, "I don't pay you two to chat all day. Why these broken candy canes here?"

"Sorry, it's my fault. I dropped them." Pam confessed. "I'll pick 'em up."

"Yes, you will, and you'll pay for them!" Daphine berated Pam and then muttered under her breath but distinct enough to be heard. "Thought she'd have more sense at her age."

The excess of suds stuck to the shop floor as Pam tried in earnest to remove remnants with a dirty mop.

"Not havin' much luck?" asked Blake.

"No, it's not my thing," Pam replied, "think it's punishment for earlier."

"Need boiling water," said Blake. "I'll get some but best wait until Daffy's finished cashing up. She's in a right mood."

"Cheers. We goin' straight from work on Saturday?"

Blake gave her a perplexed look. "Saturday? Ah, sorry," he replied. "Forgot to say. I'm goin' out with mates from running club. We'll all be on mineral water."

Blake's attempt at a joke fell flat.

"No problem," said Pam. "Girls are comin' around for Strictly final party. But don't forget it's still your turn to buy drinks. Can't wiggle out of it that easily."

***

Bea, a ginger fluffy cat with white stripes, stared at the shimmering gold foil fringe curtain hanging in the hall. The glare from the streetlamp dazzled and tripped the light fantastic against each strand of the screen. Bea poised to pounce, but was distracted by the command from the bedroom, "BEA! Don't pull any more down, pleese!"

Pam pulled the silver glittery V-neck top over her head and dislodged the black tinsel wig. She poked her head out of the bedroom door; the cat was waiting for attention and affection. "Good girl, Bea. Won't be long. Aunties will be here soon to make a fuss of you."

Bea adopted Pam on Tuesday 1st December. Pam nearly stepped on her as she was going to put the rubbish bin out. Bea found a comfortable spot on the door mat and did not flinch. Pam thought, *'Don't usually find a cat behind the first door of an Advent calendar.'* Bea did not have a collar, however, did not look hungry but had matted fur. Pam left water in a small Tupperware pot and string cheese on the doorstep. Bea did not move. During the night, the meowing woke Pam up. The freezing fog rested on the windowsill and the outline of Bea broke through the mist. Pam opened the door to her new house mate.

***

"Comin' in ready or not!" Martha called out as she put the key in the lock.

Pam struggled with the zip on her black glittery mini-skirt and toppled over on the bed.

Bea welcomed the visitors with a meow and started purring as Betty stroked her head.

"Have you had your tea?" asked Betty.

"No. Left shop at 6, nearly had to push customers out the door," Pam replied.

"Not you, I'm asking Bea." The cat's bowl was empty and there was a saucer of sour milk on the kitchen floor. "Poor thing." Betty sympathised with the lack of consideration for Bea and held out her hand. "Look, I brought you Whiskas – tuna, and got you a water fountain."

"Put TV on and get me a drink, I'm gasping!" said Pam.

"Yes, oh master!" replied Martha.

Bags of Twiglets, salted peanuts, crisps, and Quavers were scattered on the kitchen worktops, alongside remnants of crumbs from Weetabix. Martha found three wine glasses in a wall cupboard close to the gas hob and washed them to remove the lipstick stains on the rim.

"Where on earth did you get that wig?" asked Martha.

"Market stall," replied Pam.

"Same place you got settee?"

Pam scowled at Martha's sarcastic comment and replied, "Nah, Daffy's friend was goin' to throw it out. Thought it'll do for a while. Got cushions from Cancer Charity Shop to brighten it up, and better than sittin' on floor."

The toe-tapping theme tune to Strictly Come Dancing blared out from the new flat screen TV, positioned unevenly on the rustic, pine-effect, slim bedside cabinet, in the corner of the lounge.

Pam skipped to the bedroom. "Just gettin' more sparkle."

"Better be more classy than that gold curtain thing." Martha chuckled.

Pam returned with a half deflated, silver star shaped balloon, and contorted red heart balloon. She sprinkled pink and silver champagne glasses confetti on the floor.

"Bea might choke on them," said Betty.

"She'll be ok," Pam responded dismissively. "She's got plenty of food now."

"Cats need regular meals, unlike you," Martha quipped.

Martha balanced a tray on her lap and Bea curled up on Betty's lap. Pam sat in the camping chair with a glass of prosecco lodged securely in the drink's holder.

"Yeah! It's Jay," Pam squealed with delight. "He's my favourite!"

"I want Anton to win," Betty cheered. "He's waited long enough."

"It's Giovanni for me," said Martha, "if only!"

"I'm gonna Quickstep to the kitchen – it's chocolate time!" Pam cheeped.

"Shall I make you a sandwich," asked Betty.

"No thanks," Pam replied. "I'll have toast later."

"WOW!" exclaimed Martha as she watched the wonders of the Charleston performed by Giovanni and Georgia.

"Wouldn't it be great to able to do that," said Betty.

"We could go to dance classes?" Pam asked excitedly. "C'mon girls – be like old times."

"No way," replied Martha. "Get Casanova to go, his young, and fit enough to swivel."

"Ah, just imagine Argentine Tango," Pam held onto her fantasy.

Martha chortled, "Where're you goin' do it? All that kickin' and flicking. Security will kick you out of the club."

"I'm sticking to Bingo," said Betty.

"Well, I'm not givin' in!" Pam protested. "Still life in this old dog."

"Ooh, I'm so tempted." Martha squeezed her face tightly. "But won't say it."

"Ain't stopped you before!" Pam snapped.

"Now, now, children!" said Betty. "Behave or you'll go to bed early."

"SHUSH! Saying winner." Pam covered her eyes. "YAAY! It's Jay," she shouted and jumped up.

Pam danced around the lounge with an imaginary partner.

"You'll fall over in those stupid heels," said Martha. "I'm not drivin' you to A&E."

"Spoilsport! No fun anymore. We used to dance all night in Clubs – remember Zoo Bar?"

"How can I forget it," Martha quipped. "Men you picked up are still suffering from PTSD!"

"Oh, give over grumpy. Have another glass of wine," said Pam as she looked through her CDs.

"Ladies…. are you ready?"

The introduction to the disco classic, *'Ain't No Stoppin' Us Now"* by McFadden & Whitehead, side stepped troubled memories of her volatile behaviour which was, in part, a hangover from a dysfunctional childhood.

Martha, Pam, and Betty threw their handbags in the centre of the room and danced around them in homage to their carefree days as teenagers.

"Christmas cocktails?" asked Pam. "Prosecco, ice and candy cane stirrers, and little umbrellas of course to match Betty's sparkly red top."

"So, you'll be havin' a cosy Christmas with Blake?" Betty winked.

A sullen pout took over Pam's facial expression. "Sadly, no. He's goin' to stay with his grandparents in Norfolk."

"Never mind," said Betty, "he'll FaceTime you on Christmas Day?"

Pam hesitated and looked down. "Doubt it, but he's got me a lovely card."

"Don't know how to break this to you, hun," Martha sniggered. "He works in Clipper Cards. He probably took it from the stock room!"

Pam opened the fridge door and called out, "I'll get another bottle, yeah?"

"Not for me," Martha replied. "Best get back to Maeve, check she's alright. Maddy's okay with her but once she's on her mobile; Maeve could fall over, and she wouldn't notice. And must finish wrapping up presents for Maeve's birthday. Don't forget, 'Miss Ballroom' to come around after work and bring balloons!"

Pam felt rotten about overlooking the preparations, "thanks for reminder. I'll pluck up the courage an' ask Daffy if I can leave earlier but doubt it. Shop is chock-a-block! What shall I get her?"

Martha's anxiety raised to the surface, "Nothing! I'll buy a present with Betty's vouchers. Just make sure you turn up. Maddy's goin' out and Brian's workin' late. He's organised a really important meeting on Monday evening!"

"Where's Brian tonight? Rehearsing for the important meeting?" asked Betty.

"No, he's gone out with his work mates in Canterbury somewhere."

"Doesn't have a fancy woman?" Betty enquired half-jokingly.

"Wot!? Boring Brian," Pam mocked her antagonist. "He'd bore her to death with stories of account reconciliations and tax."

"Shut up!" Martha blurted out, exhausted from the squabbling in her home and continuous criticism from her husband. "I'm off, hopefully find some form of sanity at home."

"Love you." Pam hugged her soul mate in contrition and recognition of her relentless patience.

"You sleepin' on couch?" Martha asked Betty. "You're brave!"

Betty smiled, "no. Brought my blow-up bed; Bea will probably tear it to shreds by the morning!"

***

CHAPTER 8

The shop floor had been swept and washed, the stockroom hoovered, and kitchen area cleaned. Fixing the sales posters and labels, in preparation for Boxing Day, was the last duty of the day. Pam overbalanced on the step ladder, as she moved the boxed charity cards, but managed to grab the shelf. She thought *'we need danger money working here'* and her mind wandered back to the fun of working with Blake in the stockroom in November. A moment she cherished and yearned to happen again. In recent weeks they shared two lunch times, went to the bank, and supermarket to buy kitchen supplies, however, there was no repeat of the night together or happy hour in the pub. Blake remained friendly but restrained. Pam convinced herself he was preoccupied with preparations for Christmas with his family and search for a new university course.

"C'mon Pam," said Daphine. "Leave that to Saturday. If we don't go home soon, we'll be goin' to midnight mass."

Pam walked past the crowded pubs and restaurants. Lights flickered and laughter flowed through the snow spray window art. Couples looked lovingly at each other, friends and families gathered for Christmas Eve drinks. Pam was outside the venues and felt an outsider. She took a detour via the sea front. The waves hit the shore with stoicism and the bitter wind struck Pam's psyche.

She looked at the Christmas lights on the Pier and felt drained, and ancient: wanted to be a part of a family not apart from life.

'Don't really matter,' she thought, *'I'll get chocolate from garage and wrap present for Martha.'*

***

"I wish you a Merry Christmas, I wish you a Merry Christmas…" Pam sang off-key.

"Okay! Enough!" Martha called out from her hall. "Where's your key?"

"Must be in other jacket. Bea's on guard duty, so all safe."

"Please tell me you've given her food this morning," Martha asked earnestly.

"Sure," replied Pam. "She's been eatin' treats in Christmas stockings you and Betty bought."

"Got Yorkshire puddings, roast potatoes, and mint jelly, left; do you want some?"

"Nah, that's okay but I'll have a takeaway tub." Pam's request was rooted in the fact that she did not like eating in front of others.

"I'll get you a hot chocolate. Maeve's in the lounge, waitin' for Queen's speech. Don't disturb Tabitha, she's fast asleep in cosy chair; loved lunch in her new bowl."

"The content of the snowman mug, in red, white, and green, was topped with marshmallows and spiced up with a tipple of Baileys.

"Cheers, M. Where's Brian?"

"He's workin' on something important!"

"WOT!" Pam replied. "I'll tell him where to put his work."

"Leave him. I'm worn out askin' why. Philomina's studyin' upstairs and Maddy is on her new mobile."

Maeve looked at her mother anxiously and sat on the floor closer to the TV screen.

"It's alright darling," Martha said reassuringly, "we'll get Aunty Pam to be quiet now."

Pam mouthed, *'Bleedin' cheek.'*

The National Anthem started, and Pam stood to attention.

Martha giggled. "She can't see you."

***

"Where are your gloves?" Martha asked Maeve.

"Mummy, they are in my backpack," replied Maeve.

"You'll need to put them on sweetie," said Pam. "It's freeeezin!"

Maeve laughed. "You are funny, aunty Pam."

Ginger wagged her tail enthusiastically when she heard Maeve's voice.

"Now, be on your best behaviour for our visitors," said Angela as she patted her companion on the head.

"Happy Christmas," Maeve greeted Angela and Ginger in an excited clear voice.

Pam looked at Martha in astonishment and she nodded to acknowledge the observation.

"What an amazing house," Pam stretched her neck to look at the turret.

"Thank you," Angela replied. "Come in out of the cold or you will turn into snowmen."

Maeve giggled.

Home-made slices of Christmas cake, mini star topped mince pies and traditional gingerbread men were presented perfectly on a Royal Albert Old Country Roses 3-Tier Cake Stand. Matching teapot, cups, and saucers, placed at the top of the dining room table, by the window, looked out to the calm sea and crystal-clear sky. All pieces rested on a beautiful hand embroidered tablecloth, showcasing golden stars, holly, red candles, and Christmas roses.

"How lovely," Martha looked at her daughter who was mesmerised by the setting.

Pam asked, "could I have a mug, please?"

Martha looked horrified and glared at Pam.

"Maeve, would you like to help me find a cup? Ginger can come with us."

Martha pulled at Pam's jumper. "Seriously! Can't bring you anywhere. So embarrassing!"

"I don't wanna break a china cup; can't afford to buy another one."

Maeve's eyes opened wide, and her face brightened with happiness.

"What do you say?" asked Martha.

"Thank you, very, very much," said Maeve as she stared at the gift from Angela: An enchanting hard back book entitled 'Sea Craft' and an aviary sewing box made from 100% cotton fabric, a lid with press stud fastening, raffia covered handle and edging. The internal tray with compartments filled with an eclectic mix of cottons and ribbons. A cushion stacked with a rainbow of colours and shapes of pins.

"Please forgive me, I do not have gifts for you and Pam."

"No need for an apology. Did not expect anything after your lovely hand knitted matching scarf and gloves for Maeve's birthday." Martha replied. "We only buy Christmas presents for children; the escalating costs forced us to tighten the purse strings. However, we hope you do not mind, we have a gift for Ginger."

"Oh, she will love it," said Angela. "Look, you are a lucky girl to have such nice friends."

Red ribbon tied the handles of the personalised gift box, made by Maeve. The words 'Special Delivery for Ginger' written in admirable calligraphy, adorned the front. Enclosed was a medley of snacks, a golden blanket, and an azure collar with a white shimmery clasp.

"Thank you, Angela, for a wonderful afternoon tea," said Martha.

"You are welcome," Angela replied. "Ginger loves seeing Maeve but am afraid she is ready for another nap."

"You're so kind. We'll go an' let you put your feet up." Pam blushed as she thought her comment may be too informal.

"Oh yes, we are looking forward to the Morecombe and Wise show. Victor did enjoy watching them, especially when they sang, 'There Is Nothing Like a Dame.' I think in 1977."

"Silver Jubilee of Her Majesty The Queen," Maeve's concise contribution to the conversation startled everyone.

"What a bright girl," said Angela. "If you would like to join us for afternoon tea on New Year's Eve, I can show Maeve the Jubilee memorabilia we collected."

"Please mummy, please?"

"Okay darling," Martha replied. "We'll look forward to the special treat."

**

Shreds of Sellotape fell on the floor and remnants of navy-blue gift wrap with the number 60, emboldened in gold print, scattered across the paper. Martha sat on the floor in Philomina's bedroom; referred to as a studio by the occupant. The Tissot watch, with a mahogany brown leather strap, stainless steel case, and silver dials, seemed a limited representation of twenty-seven years of marriage. However, she knew Brian would be enthralled with the craftsmanship, history, and date display function. A sense of guilt propelled her to purchase the solid sterling silver and 18ct Gold, Cricket bat and stump cufflinks, engraved with the initials *BC* - the Edwardian Script was appealing. The credit card, used to purchase the additional gift, hovered around the limit. *'The minimum monthly payments will be okay for a while,'* she thought. The coffee mug with the accreditation VINTAGE 1955 – Aged to Perfection was a present by proxy, from Maddy.

Martha hoped she had bought a card this year.

Maeve's hand-made card, based on a design in her treasured craft book from Angela, accompanied a gift bag containing a hard back copy of the novel Mary Poppins by P.L. Travers; bought in an antique shop. The red background of the front cover design reflected the heritage. She created a bookmark, using a pastel green card, with the inscription –

Celebration to mark Daddy's 60th Birthday. You are key. 60* - not out.

Philomina hid her gift and card under the bed: she adored her father, and the feeling was mutual. Similar in demeanour, disposition, and disdain for Maddy and Maeve. The denigration, egged on by Brian's sister Penelope, directed towards her younger siblings was unwarranted.

"Will you be much longer?" asked Philomina as she paced around her room impatiently.

"Nearly there," replied Martha. "Make sure you're ready by seven. Thankfully, the manager of Bel Mare, manoeuvred reservations, so we have the table by the window. Looking out to sea is a great distraction for your dad when he's bored with girly talk."

Philomina's impassive face reinforced her disgust for trivial topics, and asked, "Is there enough room for six people?"

"Yeah, if we squash together like sardines." Martha replied, "why six? Dad insisted family only; doesn't want Pam to go."

"I've invited Aunty Penelope to stay."

"WOT?" Martha yelled. "Tonight – without telling me?"

"No need to shout!" Philomina tutted. "Be nice surprise for Dad."

"Not a nice surprise for me! How on earth am I goin' get spare room ready? Supposed to have conversation with your father weeks ago about decorating bedrooms – he keeps puttin' it off."

"For once! Can you just think of him?" Philomina cried out, "What will make him happy. Dad's been under so much pressure since being made redundant. What do you do? Demand more things – bigger house, bigger furniture, and bigger kitchen! How can you be so selfish?" He's working his fingers to the bone for you!"

"How dare you talk to me like that," Martha shouted. "I'm your mother!"

"Why don't you start acting like my mother, and not like a fifteen-year-old joined at the hip with that leech, Pam! Have you told dad how much you've spent paying off her credit cards?"

Tears welled up in Martha's eyes, sadness filled her heart, and regret filtered into her mind. Inwardly she acknowledged the sentiment but felt it grossly unfair to view the circumstances from one angle. The vitriol did not surprise Martha; her eldest daughter could not see fault in her father and wallowed in the luxury of being spoilt; materialistically and emotionally.

"I'm going out with Maeve for a while, give you time to cool off," said Martha.

"Oooh! Gotta make sure Miss Special is pampered!"

"Grow up!" Martha retaliated. "Make yourself useful; find clean bedding, towels, and hoover room. Your guest, your responsibility. It's your call!"

***

Squawks from the squabble of seagulls interrupted Pam's reflection on New Year's Eve celebrations in the centre of London. Equally loud noises but emanating from diverse sources, fireworks and singing rattled through her mind. She tucked her hands into the pockets of a brown quilted puffer jacket with a faux fur hood. Her nose started running because of the ice-cold wind however her dwindling supply of pocket handkerchiefs were in her bungalow. *'Never mind, M will have packet, I can nab,'* she thought.

'On way!' The brevity of the text called attention to Martha's angst.

"Why you sittin' here?" asked Martha. "You'll freeze."

"Good to clear the cobwebs away," Pam laughed. "Don't think spent New Year's Eve by seaside. Stood by Thames few times but bit more space here."

"Angela would have let you in." Martha looked towards the soul stirring Reculver Towers.

"Didn't wanna disturb her. Why you wearin' those old ballet pumps? Normally have your boots when it's icy."

"I'll explain later," Martha nodded her head towards Maeve which was the well-rehearsed signal to give a warning the topic is not suitable for her ears.

Angela served tea in white and navy-blue striped mugs, purchased during the week, to the relief of her guests. Maeve had her Royal Collection, longest reigning monarch cup, which she was allowed to keep in Angela's kitchen.

"Now, young lady, shall we go and get the Silver Jubilee memorabilia that I have managed to find so far," Angela could sense the excitement and eagerness on Maeve's face and the disquiet in Martha's eyes.

"Take your time, darling," said Martha. "Let Angela go first."

"Yes, mummy." Maeve beamed with joy and anticipation of the search for the treasure chest.

"What's wrong, hun?" asked Pam. "Ain't seen you this jittery for a while."

Martha whispered, "keep your voice down. Penelope is coming to the meal tonight."

"How did poisonous Pen get invited?" asked Pam.

"Philomina asked her."

"Without telling you? Takes after her dad in more ways than one." Pam felt sorry for Martha and exasperated with Philomina. Although, sorely tempted to tell Philomina everything her mother had endured, Pam concluded she would not care. "Where are you goin'?"

"Bel Mare; Ted took Betty there for her birthday. Sounds really nice, but it'll be a squash with the Pantomime Dame taking centre stage."

Pam chortled. "Spot on! But, M, it's too noisy for Maeve and you know how Pen bullies her. "Can't she stay at home; I'll look after her?"

"No, Brian will blow a fuse. He wants all his children there. If Maeve doesn't go, it just gives the others more reason to call her different and special. They're so cruel at times." Martha, depleted by the conflict, yawned, and shook her head, in search for the backup generator.

"Look mummy, look aunty." Maeve skipped into the dining room.

"Oh, that's wonderful. Did you tell Angela about your scrapbook?"

"Yes. Can I show it to Angela now? Please mummy." Maeve gently tugged at her mother's jumper.

"I cannot wait." Angela, enthralled by the ingenuity of a girl who appeared to be harbouring a vessel of solitude, expressed her enthusiasm.

"I'm afraid we must leave soon. We are going for a meal for daddy's birthday." Martha recognised the anxiety slowly take hold in her daughter's face.

"Yes, mummy. He's sixty today. It is special."

"Yes," said Angela. "You will have a lovely evening with your sisters, and mummy and daddy."

Martha hesitated and stared at Pam who was shaking her head. Experience had taught Martha to give advance notice to Maeve albeit troubling.

"Will be lovely, and we have a surprise guest for daddy. Aunty Penelope will be there, that'll be nice, won't it Maeve?"

Maeve froze and her hands trembled.

Angela's expression changed from a soft caring appearance to one of unease. "Shall I get you a blanket my dear? It is very cold today even Ginger has to wear her coat when going out."

Pam tried to construct a distraction, "I've got an idea. If it is okay with Angela, we can take Ginger for a walk tomorrow?"

"You are kind. I do find it a challenge to ice skate these days."

Muted laughter followed Angela's joke however it heightened when Ginger wagged her tail profusely and tapped her paw on Angela's foot.

"I am afraid Ginger has overheard the **W** word," Angela chuckled and stroked the wavy hair on her companion's ear. "We'll go tomorrow, there's a good girl."

***

"You took your time!" Martha's strained expression greeted Pam in the porch.

"Don't blame me," Pam protested. "Took me ages to remember everything on your list, deodorant spray for my boots, slipper socks, and polo mints for my bad breath. And yes, I did brush my teeth this morning!"

"I'll have to get you stronger mouthwash to hide smell of nicotine," said Martha.

"Right, let's face the music and dance!" Pam ribbed her closest ally in an attempt to ease the tension.

"Stop it! Just behave yourself for a few minutes and then take Maeve out!"

"Yes, Sir!" Pam stood to attention and saluted.

"Oh, there you are Pam," said Penelope. "I thought I heard your dulcet tones."

"Hello Penelope, how are you?"

"I am well. All the better for joining my dear brother's birthday celebrations last night. You would have loved it, but alas you were not invited."

'Wicked witch!' Pam thought. "Never mind, it'll be your big birthday soon!"

Penelope's face reddened and the muscles around her jawline tightened. She did not retaliate because although they were both born in 1960, Pam looked much younger and had the full support of Martha.

"Think it is time for a cup of tea," said Martha.

"What a marvellous idea. Do you have cups and saucers?" asked Penelope. "I am not comfortable with mugs. Tea tastes much better in a china cup. Come on girls, we can try to stretch the cloth on the dining room table, so it looks presentable." Philomina, Maddy and Maeve dutifully followed the request from their domineering aunt.

"Give me strength!" Martha slammed the fridge door.

Pam opened every cupboard and asked, "Where's the cups and saucers?"

"Good question!"

"Found one cup but ain't found saucers," said Pam.

"I know just the place to find one," Martha replied as she picked up Tabitha's saucer located on the floor in the utility room and rinsed it under the tap.

"You can't!" exclaimed Pam.

"I can!" Martha said defiantly, "just watch me."

Martha knocked on the locked office door. "Brian, get out here now! Can't hide in there all day."

"Be out in five minutes." Brian replied.

"No! Now!" Martha demanded her husband share the strain.

"Hello Brian, did you have a nice birthday?" asked Pam.

"Very nice," replied Brian, "nothing better than sharing special moments with family."

Even though an old hand at receiving Brian's barbed statements, Pam reeled from each verbal strike. She re-grouped and asked, "Did you like my present?"

"Yes. It's in the cupboard somewhere."

"Always room for one more mug, ain't there!" Martha smirked at the return fire and loved it when Pam was on form.

The coffee mug in question, depicting an unflattering image of an elderly man waving his walking stick in anger, with the words, '60 and GRUMPY', was taken from the damaged sale stock in Clipper Cards.

Martha directed her husband, "Bring the tray into your loving sister. Be careful not to drop it into her lap!"

"Only one cup?" Penelope cross examined the hosts.

"Yes, I thought you would like the china cup with the poppy on it and the cream saucer." Pam replied.

Martha coughed into her hand to stop herself bursting out laughing. "Excuse me, got dust in my throat."

"Not a surprise when living in a building site," said Penelope. "The condensation and mould in the conservatory will cause you all to have pneumonia."

Brian saw his wife's face turn to stone and changed the subject quickly. "Philomina gave me a fantastic present; a personalised birthday newspaper book."

"Such a thoughtful child." Penelope's saccharine praise was followed by a sour slight to Martha. "Rather unfortunate about the clash of cufflinks."

"I'll return them," said Martha, "it's okay. Brian can keep the pair you got him which I am sure he prefers."

Pam looked at Penelope in bewilderment.

"You see, Pam..."

Brian took a risk and interrupted his sister, "It's alright, honestly. Martha can tell Pam the full story later."

"She might well do, but I want to provide the finer details," Penelope demanded attention.

"I've got a headache," Maddy moaned. "Gotta lay down."

"Don't be so rude," said Philomina. "Aunty Penelope has not finished speaking.

Maddy and Philomina looked daggers at each other. Maddy bitterly envied her older sister. The money spent to fund her gap year, university course in Bristol and now Cancer Research UK PhD programme in Edinburgh, and student accommodation, was disproportionate. However, the extent of the love and respect her father had for Philomina was the most painful part of the resentment.

"My dear Maddy," said Penelope. "I told you not to have the extra portion of tiramisu last night. You will be getting as podgy as Maeve if you do not be careful."

Philomina laughed loudly at her aunt's sharp wit but stopped immediately when Pam glared at her.

"Oh, where was I?" Penelope continued, oblivious to the upset etched on Maeve's face.

"Is that the time?" Pam exclaimed. "Better be goin' Let's get your coat Maeve."

"But I have not finished; I must tell you about the cufflink catastrophe," exclaimed Penelope.

"Here's a quick summary, to save your precious breath," Martha was seething. "Pen and me bought exactly same pair of cricket cufflinks. I got them engraved with two initials instead of three, and font I picked made it look like a knot. That's about it!"

"I simply do not know how you missed Brian's middle name, it's been in the family for years, hasn't it dear?" Penelope turned to her brother, she had bullied since childhood, for affirmation.

"Is your backpack in your room, darling?" Martha asked Maeve and she nodded.

"I see her diction has not improved, poor child." Penelope's callous remarked tipped Martha over the edge. "Brian, make sure you clean the table, put things in dishwasher and drive your sister to the station before I get back!"

Pam asked Brian, "by the way, what is your middle name?"

"Bertrand." Penelope replied.

"Ah, BBC, sounds familiar?" Pam's sarcasm was not lost on her audience as she referred to his full name: *Brian Bertrand Clerk.*

***

Martha charged along the Esplanade engulfed in rage.

"If your mummy doesn't slow down, she'll be sliding along like a Penguin," Pam hoped the jovial observation would encourage Maeve to smile but she, once again, shut down her emotions.

"Happy New Year Maeve," Angela welcomed her special guest with warmth and empathy. "Ginger has been looking forward to seeing you all morning. She has been waiting on the lovely golden blanket you bought for her."

Ginger sensed the sadness and instinctively sat by Maeve's feet.

"You are so kind," said Martha.

"Can I get you a drink? Maybe, a hot Ribena for Maeve?"

Maeve stared at the floor with teardrops sliding down her cheeks.

"If it is alright with you, we can go for the **W** word now?" Pam asked. "Save us taking our coats off."

Ginger stood up and wagged her tail.

"Who taught her how to spell?" asked Martha. There was no reaction from Maeve.

Angela fastened the zip and clips of Ginger's blue coat and explained the technicalities of the harness and lead. Maeve did not lift her head.

"Would it be okay if Martha stays with you?" asked Pam.

Angela recognised the signs of domestic distress. "Of course, it will be lovely to have company."

Pam and Maeve sat on the bench in the front garden of Anchor Tale. Ginger patiently stood in readiness for her adventure.

"Are you ready to go?" asked Pam.

Maeve did not reply.

"Ginger can't wait to see the bright coloured paintings on the Beach Hutches!"

"No, Aunty Pam, they are called Beach Huts."

"I know," said Pam, "but it sounds more fun, don't you think?"

***

CHAPTER 9

A sprinkle of plain flour powdered the surface of the new kitchen table and two eggs smashed on the floor. Martha managed to grip the glass mixing bowl but knocked the jug of milk sideways.

"I am sorry mummy," Maeve cried. "It's all my fault!"

"Come here, darling," replied Martha. "We all slip up and down. Especially Aunty Pam."

Maeve smiled faintly. "Now, that's better," said Martha, "ready, steady, go - let's start cleaning."

Brian told Martha he would be working later in the Canterbury office so that allowed extra time to re-group and enjoy their time together. Martha telephoned the school in the morning to explain the distress for Maeve is intolerable and requested a meeting with the headmaster of St. Bernadette's Catholic Primary school in Sea Street. She planned to keep Martha out of school until she received a clear commitment with regards duty of care. The conflict of protecting Maeve and encouraging more social interaction, played heavily on Martha's mind.

Martha bought a new glass bowl and jug, whisk, ladle, fish slice, and crepe pan for their cooking class on Pancake Day.

Project 49*WB* progressed at a snail's pace therefore the spillage did not lessen the quality or value of the crumpled cream vinyl flooring. Brian insisted Phase 1 of the project be put on hold, and funds diverted to the removal of damp and replacement of windows in the conservatory, in accordance with demands from Penelope. Martha went, unaccompanied, to in store design consultations, viewed online kitchen range brochures and held fast to the dream of remodelling the heart of the home. *'The flexible finance options are good, eespecially the buy now, pay later option,'* Martha thought, as she earnestly tried to readjust the monthly budget to account for the payments.

"I used to cook with my mum; Granny Daisy," said Martha.

"Did I meet Granny Daisy?" asked Maeve.

"Yes, I used to bring you to Granny Daisy's house in your pram. She loved seeing you but sadly, she was not well and passed away when you were only two months old."

"Do you miss your mummy?" asked Maeve.

"Very much," replied Martha. "I think of her every day." Martha felt the incomplete grief pushing against the barricade built in her mind and pressed down on the break. "Okay darling, we have to change your clothes. Could you go to your room, please, and pick out leggings and a top."

"I need to have a bath," said Maeve.

"That's a good idea. I'll be up in a minute with nice fluffy towels."

Lost in thought, Martha went into the garden, via the stale breakfast room. She did not notice the glow of the security light nor the chill in the air. Caring for her mother from 2001 until 2008 was exhausting. Unsurprisingly, Daisy's health deteriorated after the death of her husband, Jack, in 2001. Her two sons had left home; therefore, Martha bore the weight of responsibility in physicality, psychologically, and financially. Martha, Bobby, and Alfie inherited equal shares of the family home. The expectation of a life changing amount diminished after the survey raised the issue of dry rot. Subsequent costs to treat the fungi and replace windows reduced the overall profit significantly.

Regrets and anger hit Martha intermittently. A baby to nurture, two older daughters to pacify, and a husband to placate, tested her resilience. She cleared her mother's house and was left to bid farewell to her childhood home in isolation. Lambent light flickered, sporadically, during the seven years of caring for her mother. They volunteered at the local community centre. It helped Daisy to socialise and remain mobile. A vast range of classes, events and opportunities boosted their energy especially when Daisy was able to go to Ballroom lessons, in the main hall, which were pleasant and baffling. The Men's Shed offered a safe space to share interests and a hive of activity and trips out. Brian dismissed, what he considered, a pointless pursuit. On the third floor the art studios held out an invitation to tranquillity and creativity. Martha first met Muiris (pronounced More-rish) Joyce as she admired the modest art gallery. His jet-black hair and striking blue eyes caught her attention as they entered a conversation about the different portraits, brush strokes and his mastery of calligraphy displayed in all its glory in his bespoke range of greeting cards. Although not strikingly handsome, as promoted in the media, he had an air of mystic charm. He was not brazen like her dad and did not share the characteristics of a 'cat on a hot tin roof' like her husband.

Their paths crossed on several occasions throughout the years. Muiris lived in a flat in South Croydon, owned by a cousin, working abroad. A convenient location and provided an opportunity to attend the college of Arts in London, for part time study, and indulge his passion to visit art galleries, British Library, and fringe theatres. He was ecstatic when presented with reduced price 'Monday Tickets.' Martha did not think Brian would notice the trivial entry, on her credit card statement, when he completed the domestic expense reconciliation. Anyway, she thought M.J. deserved a benefit in kind without obligatory tax.

Daisy's motherly instinct rang an alarm bell in her mind, but she clung to the hope that Muiris would only be a passing ship to calm the waters of the tragedy Martha held in the recesses of her heart. Martha suffered a miscarriage in the 7th month of pregnancy on 27th July 1992. Brian refused to see their son, Ben, and cold-heartedly delegated the hospital arrangements and grief to Martha. Depression followed and an end to her ability to retain an employment contract. The trial separation resulted in strengthening the bond between Philomina and her dad. Martha took refuge in Pam's flat temporarily and the strain on the marriage was inevitable. Maddy was born on 30th September 1999. Daisy, Pam, and Betty shared the concern about bringing another life into the broken remains of a marriage. They concluded Martha's age of thirty-nine was one factor i.e., a last chance for a son that Brian coveted. No one wanted to share their worries with Martha, especially after the loss of her baby. Maddy brought a new wave of happiness for the Clerk family. Brian and Martha welcomed the perceived freedom from torment, and they promised Maddy she would always be the baby of the family.

***

The manager of the community centre organised a celebration for Daisy's 65th birthday; a sign of gratitude for volunteering with Martha, and Brian's help at the job club: explaining tax codes and national insurance rates. The more mature members appreciated the guidance in relation to Inheritance Tax and savings in retirement. Brian attended his mother-in-law's party, much to everyone's surprise.

Muiris created a charming birthday card with adequate space for all the staff and volunteers to sign. A bouquet of flowers and gifts presented to Daisy. Martha received a hand-crafted pastel green gift box: inside - a framed small portrait of her standing on a stone bridge arching over a stream flowing smoothly; her reflection glistened in the water, ripples reflected the inner beauty trapped by the responsibilities she shouldered. Muiris' friends, in a Céilí band, accompanied him during his version of the song 'Galway Bay.' The lyrics and serene tone permeated Martha's heart and her face glowed with a joy long forgotten. Brian interpreted Martha's emotion as a reflection on her mother's age and ill-health. Daisy tapped into the depth of connection between these soul mates. There was not a dry eye in the room, except Brian, when Muiris dedicated the song to Daisy and Martha; "May true happiness find you and be a close companion for the rest of your days."

The build up to their affair was as entrancing and precious as the physical act which inevitably started in a moment of weakness. Muiris announced his plans to move to Amsterdam and Martha allowed herself to follow a shooting star, albeit a brief cruise off to an exciting new chapter, but reality dropped the anchor. The final curtain fell on the soulful bond with Martha who was flattered by the attention from a young man and awestruck by his artistry, in June 2007.

Martha did not tell Muiris about Maeve. He was a free spirit, not yet; maybe never, ready for parenthood.

The conversation did not take place between Brian and Martha. He tolerated Maeve; supported her financially but his indifference infected Philomina and Maddy.

***

"Mum, Mum, MUM! Mobile. It's Pam. When you gonna change that naff ring tone?" The discordant shout from Maddy startled Martha.

"Honestly, you're getting grumpier than dad. What's wrong with *'Boogie Wonderland'* it's a disco gold.

"Hi, M, everything okay?" asked Pam.

"Yeah. Maeve's made lovely pancakes for you. Pop in for a cuppa." Martha replied.

"She's such a sweetie. Would love to, but Daffy's givin' me lift to Canterbury."

"You doin' overtime in other store?" asked Martha.

"Nah! Much more exciting: buyin' outfit for Valentine's night. So definitely no eating!"

"Boy wonder takin' you out? Didn't know they did Happy Hour at chip shop!" Martha mocked but worried this would be another let down.

"Stop it! Just jealous," said Pam. "I'm takin' him out; surprise, booked table at Bel Mare. And you know what year it is?"

"Yes, it's 2016. What's that gotta do with candlelight spaghetti for two?"

"Keep up!" Frustrated and anxious that her confidante had not understood the significance of the announcement. "It's a leap year and I'm goin' pop the question."

Martha, face ashen, dreaded the fallout from a reckless proposal and shrieked, "NO! Stop and think. Call me later, don't care what time it is. Don't make a fool of yourself. He's just a boy! There's no way he's goin' to say yes, and doubt he'll even go to restaurant."

"Bet he does!" Pam smirked and ended the call.

"What's wrong Mummy?" asked Maeve.

"Nothing, darling," said Martha, still shaking. "Aunty Pam sends her love and is so grateful you cooked pancakes. She's just getting over excited about Valentine's Day. But more importantly, I've warmed up fluffy blue towel in tumble dryer. Let's get you washed and ready for bed."

"Mummy, will you be going out on St. Valentine's Day?"

Martha sighed, "No darling, mostly for young people."

"Do they love each other for ever?" asked Maeve, fascinated by the concept of one day for romance.

"Sometimes. Tricky to find time to love when we are busy."

***

CHAPTER 10

"No more red heart balloons left!" Daphine shouted from the stockroom door to the three members of the team, overburdened with a surge of customers, commotion, and a relentless taskmaster.

"PAM!" Daphine bellowed.

"Yes, comin'" Pam replied and locked her till, and shoved a bundle of plastic bags back on the shelf under the counter; all of which had fallen on the floor shortly after the doors opened.

Daphine stomped around the stockroom. "Take your break now! Make it quick. Ben should've been here ten minutes ago."

Ben tapped on the back door tentatively. "Phew, thank goodness it's you," Ben whispered.

"Daffy's been askin' about you," said Pam. "Hurry up 'n' sign in. Where's your backing singer?"

"Who? Oh, Blake. He's got few days off. Daffy ain't changed rota on wall."

"What time do you call this?" yelled Daphine as she pushed past Ben to get to the safe.

"Sorry guv," Ben answered with an attempt to crack a joke. "Had pile of Valentine cards to open."

Daphine berated her employee who was still wet behind the ears. "Firstly, I ain't your guv. And secondly, you're washin' shop floor tonight!"

"It'll ruin my nails," Ben's cheeky comment brought about a slight smile from Daphine.

During the verbal duel, heavily weighted in Daphine's favour, Pam searched for new messages on her mobile.

"Put that back in your locker!" Daphine's order alarmed Pam and she complied with the instruction, but the anxiety heightened as Blake had not responded to her texts. "Put those box cards out, tidy display and then take over from Indira."

***

Pam twisted, stretched, and tussled with her new glittery red skin-tight dress until it covered her slight frame. The four-inch stiletto angle strap sandals elongated her gangly silhouette.

The bright red super-stay 24-hour lip colour added tint to a face that looked pale and drawn. A 1980's big hair style achieved by using a mix of dry shampoo and extreme hold spray which pushed back her brassy coloured hair, dispersed into split ends, a consequence of excess chemical mixtures, to disguise her raven colour; deemed bad fortune by her mother.

Bea ran into the kitchen as Pam liberally sprayed strong perfume on her wrists and neck.

"Sorry Bea," Pam called out. "I'll come out in a minute to refill your water fountain."

Bea sat beside her empty bowl and miaowed loudly.

"Okay, okay, here's your favourite biscuits. We can share tuna sandwich tomorrow. That'll be nice."

Pam sprayed perfume near the cat litter tray and thought *'Must clean it an' ask Martha for money to fit cat flap.'* The solitary card on the kitchen worktop showed the greeting, *Happy Valentine's Day from the cat. With lots of love from Bea.* The personalised card, posted through the door accompanied by a bar of chocolate, was Martha's anticipatory step to ease the pain of the inevitable hailstorm. Pam toppled over to stroke Bea. "You're such a sweetie. Now be a good girl an' I'll introduce you to Blake later, but you'll have to sleep on the settee."

***

A rousing rendition of the well-loved song *'Nel blu dipinto di blu' ('Volare')* whirled out to the seafront. Pam stepped in time with the infectious beat and went into the Bel Mare restaurant. Cheerful chatter, clink of champagne glasses, and the tantalising smell of aromatic pasta sauces added to the appealing ambience.

"Buona sera, signorina," Renato, the waiter dressed in white jacket and black bow tie, sang the greeting with a beaming smile.

Pam proclaimed with vivacity, "Hello, I've booked a table."

"For how many?" asked Renato.

"Two!" Pam replied curtly: embarrassed and offended anyone would think she would be a *'table for one'* on Valentine's evening. "The reservation is in my name – Pam Docker."

"Bella!" Renato showed her to the table, snug in the corner, with a restricted sea view.

Pam picked up the red rose on the table. "He's already here?"

"Mi scusi. Who is here?" Renato hoped the manager had not double booked. "La rosa for you, signorina, a gift from us."

"Merci. Sorry, that's French. Don't know what it is in Italian?"

"Grazie," Renato smiled, only too pleased to offer an Italian lesson to a beautiful single woman.

"My boyfriend will be here in a minute," said Pam.

"He's a lucky young man; so, signorina, would you like the prosecco now?"

Pam's patience sounded strained, "no, thank you. I'll wait. He's name's Blake and he's late for everything."

Pam repeatedly checked her mobile but there were no new messages. She viewed the posts on Facebook; boasting of bouquets of flowers, platinum solitaire diamond rings, and photos of couples captured in their ivory tower.

Conspicuous abandonment surrounded Pam. A convenient stopgap: her mobile, prevented eye contact with the fellow guests. The WhatsApp status for Blake showed as offline as did his Facebook account. She telephoned him but the call went directly to voice mail. Her mobile landed on the Italian terracotta and marble floor at an awkward angle and cracked the screen. "DRAT!" Pam exclaimed. She leaned down to pick up the pieces and the content of her handbag fell to the floor.

"Signorina, please let me help you," said Renato.

"I'm so sorry!" Pam nodded to the couples on the surrounding tables. Her natural blusher glossed over the cosmetic powder bought specially for her hot date.

Renato gently reminded the customer of the restaurant regulations. "Mi scusi, signorina, no smoking in restaurant."

"No. Sorry, of course not." The comment flustered Pam and she thought, '*must give up.*'

"Please, let me get you a drink. What would you like?" asked Renato.

"Prosecco. Oh no! I'll wait and share bottle with Blake. But I'll have spritzer now if that's okay?"

"Of course, signorina." Renato observed the signs of rejection and tried to lighten the mood. "Your friend is wrapping your gift; bows and ribbons are very tricky!"

One more call to Blake, on her shattered mobile, resulted in the same outcome. There was no reply to the five text messages. After forty minutes Renato asked, "Would you like to order signorina?"

"No, thank you. Grazie," Pam's elementary Italian language skills did not hide the sadness. "I'm leaving. How much is the bill?"

Renato responded with an empathetic smile, "Un regalino. A gift."

The humiliation etched on her face and feeble footsteps aged Pam. Red heart shaped balloons glistened in the candlelight. *'They didn't look so pretty in the stock room'* she thought.

"Please, signorina, take the chocolates?" Renato placed two, milk chocolate praline pink foiled hearts, in her palm.

"Thanks," Pam tried to stay afloat on the sea of shame, "I'll have to come back here again."

"I look forward to seeing you next time," Renato's flirtation was well rehearsed. "Arrivederci. Bella signorina."

Pam did not feel the biting wind and ignored the goosebumps on her arms. Cigarette ash dropped down through the gaps between the wooden slats on the bench seat. No new messages and no hope frazzled her brittle public persona. Clumpy eyelashes and tears jumbled together. The green, white, and red serviette, stuffed in her handbag, substituted the travel tissues usually carried by Martha.

***

Fractures in her family and failed relationships haunted Pam. An introduction to boys in the Whitgift Centre, Croydon, distorted the need for affection to the realms of heartless action. The awkward distasteful encounters, devoid of emotion, became an automatic reaction for Pam.

Her mother had little interest in her daughter and did not question why she arrived home so late from school. The senior Physical Education teacher, Miss Littlewood, noticed the frequency Pam requested to go to the toilet and sharp pains in her lower abdomen. Initially interpreted as an excuse to avoid lessons, but concerns increased when personal hygiene embarrassed Pam and bullies goaded her but there was not the usual forceful retaliation. Martha and Betty tried to diagnose the condition by reading books in the library; frightened to ask their mothers in case they thought they had an infection or associated with Pam's habits. The naïve and mistaken analysis resulted in the purchase of treatment for cystitis in a chemist with Martha and Betty's pocket money, and the three friends were convinced they found the solution. Pam did not receive pocket money therefore relied on a Saturday job in Woolworths, to buy cigarettes and clothes. Her miserly disposable income did not stretch to the need for extra sanitary protection products and knickers, so she followed the shop lifting techniques used by the gang in the Whitgift Centre. Regular sore throats, fever and issues with her menstrual cycle eventually led Pam to seek help from Miss Littlewood who made an appointment at a sexual health clinic. The untreated Gonorrhoea resulted in infertility. The mentor at the clinic educated her on the appropriate contraception and importance of regular cervical smear tests. Miss Littlewood arranged discussions with Pam; the discretion and empathy of the teacher moved Pam to reflect on her lifestyle and consider consequences. Unfortunately, the stability was short lived.

***

Martha's mother, Daisy Burtin (nee Taylor), and Pam's mother, Gillian Docker, shared their teenage years in Croydon. Martha's grandmother, Florence, felt sorry for Gillian because it was widely known how scathing comments pervaded her childhood home. Florence invited Gillian to her home for much needed meals and respite.

Daisy and Gillian first met at the community centre; groups gathered to make decorations for the celebration of The Coronation of Her Majesty Queen Elizabeth II.

Daisy's creative skills far exceeded those of Gillian however the bond between them set during the shared experience. Daisy took on the mantle of the big sister to Gillian who was four years younger. Their friendship born of the deep disquiet about Gillian's wellbeing, grew into a framework of co-dependency.

Family and neighbours squashed into Florence's house in South Croydon, excited to see the small box, in the corner, broadcasting the spectacular ceremony and events on 2nd June 1953. Daisy and Gillian helped make sandwiches and squash.

The two friends became more involved in events at the community centre organised by the volunteers and full-time staff. They also enjoyed rock 'n' roll music, learned to jive, and fancied Teddy Boys. Florence granted her daughter permission to be fond but not foolish.

Excitement filled the air but not Florence's mind when the engagement between Daisy and Jack Burtin was announced on 2nd May 1957 - Daisy's 18th birthday. Jack took advantage of the fact Daisy's mother was a widow. Florence's husband, Tommy Taylor, was killed during World War II when Daisy was only five years old. Florence did not remarry and focused her attention on her only child. The rebellious outburst did not wholly surprise Florence. 'Just like her dad,' she thought as she reflected on their tender marriage bitterly cut short by brutality as he battled for his King and country.

Jack jumped at the chance of a ready-made house in South Croydon, courtesy of a loan from his soon to be mother-in-law. He knew Daisy's mother would overlook the objections when she had grandchildren.

Jack wanted the easy life; he could not contemplate living in a chaotic house that Gillian endured with continuous arguments and an abusive stepfather.

A modest celebration of commitment started with a wedding service in St. Gertrude's Catholic church and an afternoon tea in the adjacent hall. Uncle Henry, Florence's older brother, took on the mantle of giving away the nervous June bride. The bridegroom gave a rousing speech and his wife's natural blusher deepened and burned. Robbie, the best man, sailed closed to the wind with his speech and it ended abruptly when Father Michael dropped his plate of sandwiches on the floor: the definition of the words had hit the boundary of decency. Jack asked Robbie and his band to play a few songs with the caveat the volume and movement of the lead singer be restrained. Robbie applauded Gillian's jive and recommended she cool down outside. They found a space, in the shade, to share a cigarette. She resisted his forceful advance for a kiss, and he hit back with the taunts, "Oh, I see, you're a good girl? No fun, just boring?" Although tempted by his dark shiny Teddy Boy quiff and mischievous character, Gillian respected Florence's standards. Most importantly, it was her best friend's wedding day and that took precedence over a quick thrill. *'Anyway,'* she thought *'I am goin' to wait for my Mr Right, just like Daisy.'* Her mind, temporarily, crossed the shredded thread between reality and delusion.

Gillian missed Daisy more than she imagined. She helped by babysitting Bobby, born in 1958, and Alfie, in 1959, but sensed a tense atmosphere in the family home. Granny Florence welcomed the two new members of the family with love and relief after strenuous deliveries necessitating extended stays in hospital. Jack, proud to be a father of two handsome boys, was not enamoured with the excessive demands on Daisy's time. He felt he had lost his wife and adopted a nanny who often slept in the spare bedroom to ensure the boys did not disturb the breadwinner's sleep.

Florence, Daisy, and Gillian organised days out with the children to alleviate the stress however exhaustion impacted them all so the trips had to be abandoned.

***

CHAPTER 11

Colourful costumes cascaded down The Esplanade, and the architectural frame of Anchor Tale set a classic stage for the children, animated by World Book Day. They rushed home to tell stories about all their adventures.

Ginger waited patiently by the front door. "You will get cold sitting there. Come on, let's go into the kitchen." Angela's companion walked unusually slow along the hall with her head down. The faint sound of Maeve's steps re-energised Ginger; she turned around and started wagging her tail. "You are a clever girl," Angela claimed proudly.

Angela invited Martha and Maeve in, and Ginger could hardly retain her happiness.

"Hello, how are you?" asked Martha. "That smells scrumptious."

"I hope you are feeling brave," said Angela, "have not cooked a quiche for a couple of years. Maeve, would you like a Ribena?"

There was no verbal acceptance from Maeve. She fixed her eyes towards the floor and moved her head as a sign of acceptance.

"Yes please," Martha replied, "how kind of you to remember. Please can I have a cup of tea?"

Martha hugged Maeve and smiled faintly towards her host. Angela acknowledged the request with a nod, the empathy in her eyes replaced words. Ginger sat close to Maeve's feet.

"It's okay, darling." Martha tried to comfort her distraught daughter, after she had endured merciless taunts because she did not wear a costume. Maeve declined her mother's requests to design a costume and Pam's offer to bring home strands of ribbons and bows from the shop. The shyness prompted her not to wear fancy dress, but the subsequent bullying caused distress. "Let's get your book out to show Angela."

Maeve took two bites of the quiche, to be polite, but did not eat the home-made fairy cake with an anchor decoration on top.

"That looks an interesting book," Angela commented. "What is the title?"

Maeve patted Ginger on the head, took a deep breath and replied, "Harper and the Sea of Secrets."

"Sounds an interesting invitation for a delightful read. Shall I get the chocolate finger biscuits and we can read it together?" asked Angela.

Maeve responded, "Yes, please."

"Why not get your notepad and pens out of your backpack, and we can make notes."

Martha explained, "I'll just help Angela bring the plates into the kitchen."

Ginger remained with Maeve as a source of comfort.

Angela whispered, "The school cannot allow this to continue."

"I know," said Martha. "I am at my wits end. I had a conversation with the headmaster, and he promised the situation would improve and how they take their responsibilities seriously."

"Have you contacted the school governors?" asked Angela.

"The plan was for Brian and me to go to a meeting, but he cancelled it at short notice which did not go down well, to put it mildly."

Angela's sympathy for a frazzled mother prompted the next question, "Would you like Maeve to stay here for a couple of hours to give you a brief respite? A chance to have a conversation with your husband?"

"You are kind, but when Maeve is this distraught, she can be quite unpredictable; best she is in familiar surroundings." Martha's weary face broke into a lighter expression. "Also, my friend Betty is staying tonight, so need to get the guest room ready. We will read a couple pages of the book, if that is okay, and then go home? Ginger most definitely has a calming effect."

***

"She ain't stayin' again?" Maddy bellowed.

"Who's she? The cat's mother," Martha replied.

Maddy moaned, "Poison Pen! She does my head in."

"You're getting' more an' more like Aunty Pam every day," said Martha.

"She ain't my aunt." Maddy's scathing attack riled her mother.

"Really? Don't mind callin' her your aunt when you want something or somewhere to hide when you've got a hangover."

"WHATEVER!" Maddy slammed her bedroom door shut.

"Make sure you finish your course work tonight and CLEAN YOUR ROOM"

There was no reply.

The course of direction for Project 49WB diverted to the guest bedroom and priority placed on the exacting standards set by Penelope. Martha closed the made to measure white shutters resting against the new triple-glazed window, checked the thermostat setting on the new horizontal triple column traditional radiator, and straightened the duvet on the king size bed with an ultra-luxe Posturepedic mattress. The deep pile carpet fitted neatly into each corner beneath the walls decorated in non-toxic paint. The total cost of the refurbishment reduced the renovation fund for the rest of the house, apart from Philomina's bedroom which she called, and expected everyone else, to call a studio.

***

"Remembered my key this time," Pam shouted.

"Who invited you?" asked Martha.

"Well, I've had friendlier welcomes. What's got your knickers in a twist?"

"Nothing, tell you later," said Martha. "It's not a sleepover, unless you wanna share bed with Betty?"

"Fine with me." Betty declared her agreement from the living room whilst acting as an impromptu cushion for Tabitha.

"You've got enough space to house an army!" Pam teased her friend but misjudged the mood.

"Just a slight exaggeration, as usual. Do you want a drink?"

Pam replied cheerfully, "Yeah. It's wine o'clock. What's for tea? Can't beat good old fish 'n' chips! Even though it is Thursday. Used to be a Friday night treat. Do you remember chip shop by South Croydon station? Delicious! And that was just the owner!"

"It's like a disease," Martha groaned. "Can you talk about anything else but men for a minute!"

"Alright hun, just jokin.' Thought you needed cheering up?"

Martha retorted, "next time, bring balloons and party poppers from shop!"

"Not workin' there anymore," the bravado burst, and the Pam's hyper pitch flattened.

"I'm sorry," said Betty. "Cutbacks, I guess?"

"Something like that. Best get my busking boots on again."

Martha, caught off guard but not totally surprised, said, "When did this happen?"

Pam's face reddened with embarrassment. "Monday."

"And you didn't tell us. What is the matter with you?" Martha snapped. "Please tell me you didn't get the sack!"

"Keep your hair on. No, of course I didn't. Just didn't get picked to stay on. Only kept one temp this year."

"Might be for the best," Martha replied, "before you get arrested for harassing younger staff. You can wave goodbye to gettin' job in another shop, Daffy will gossip with other managers."

"Where is Blake?" asked Betty.

Pam's subdued body language foretold the explanation, "London, Royal College of Music. Daffy said something about undergraduate or Bachelor of Music? Don't know."

Martha sniggered, "That's a bit different to a card shop!"

Pam muttered, "His mother's arty, paints things at seaside. They live in posh house near Hempton Inn. She's brilliant playing piano and encouraged him; should I say, bullied him to practise his musical skills again. And she made him get part time job after he dropped out of first university - give him taste of the real world, by the sound of it."

Betty's curiosity got the better of her, "did he contact you after Valentine's Day?"

Martha stared at Betty and shook her head slowly.

"Nah!" tears welled up in her eyes and she started to shake.

"I'll get you a top up!" said Martha.

Betty steered the conversation into a different direction, "How's Bea? I've got some of her favourite food, bring it around tomorrow?"

"Yeah, be great. She loves you."

More drinks, chatting, and giggling ensued during the evening. Three friends drawing from a mixture of memories.

Pam stalled and cried, "I miss him."

"Oh, you big softie," said Martha. "Never learn. That type always leave – they're free spirits." Martha hugged Pam and understood the heartache because it was how she felt after Muiris left. But Martha retained a genuine deeper connection and a cherished daily reminder when she looked at Maeve.

Pam deteriorated in emotional resilience and physical appearance, after only eating a small plate of chips.

Betty smiled cheerfully, "look at you, lady of leisure, and already done in. What are we goin' do with you?"

"Must be temp work around. Someone must want you." Martha quipped. "Just joking!"

"I'll meet Prince Charming," Pam responded with determination. "He'll rescue me."

"From what? The seagulls" Martha chuckled.

"As long as he doesn't look like Adam Ant," said Betty.

"Don't take the mickey out of song and video," Pam replied before singing, *"Don't you ever, don't you ever,"* she stuttered and searched her memory bank, "oh yes, that's it; *Prince Charming, Prince Charming, Ridicule is nothing to be scared of."*

Martha placed a cushion beside each ear, "Tabitha can sing better! You're ruining dreams of my idol. Remember watching Top of Pops? Couldn't wait for Thursday evenings."

"Bet you remember dance?" Betty looked at Pam and hoped the challenge would soften the emotional bruising after the recent fall.

Pam stood up and hummed the tune. Martha grabbed her arms and pulled them in different directions. "Looks like a wrestling match not a dance!" said Betty.

Pam slumped into the cosy chair, "I'm worn out!"

"Stay the night, old girl," Martha laughed. "If you feel sick, stay down here. You'll scare the life out of Brian when he gets back but what does that matter. And don't disturb Maeve, she's had a really rough day."

Betty asked, "what about poor Bea? Has she got water?"

"Yep, she loves the water fountain, and I changed her litter tray today."

"Wonders will never cease!" exclaimed Martha.

"But she needs a cat flap." Pam looked at Martha earnestly begging for attention and money.

"I'll get you money next week, can't have poor thing locked up like a prisoner."

***

CHAPTER 12

"Hola! Welcome, come in – more the merrier." Rhythmic steps from the exuberant Salsa instructor, Hilario, encircled Pam, waiting by the entrance to the annexe of the Irish Catholic club. Latin American vibes of the song *'Cuba'* set an imaginary scene of an upbeat sultry, summer evening, however, the cloudy sky, grey walls, and broken stone step, dampened the mood.

The tinny sound rattled Pam's mobile and diverted attention to the text:

'Sorry, need talk to hubby. No salsa for me' ☹

She rushed a reply, *'I'm nobby no mates & grabbed by crazy teacher. Help!'*

Last text read, *'You'll find someone. Kee.ep dancing*!'

Pam thought, *'Won't let her forget this in a hurry. She can talk to Brian any time. How can she leave me on my own?'*

Hilario called out, "Señorita, bonita. Put your jacket on the chair and change into your Latin shoes. Join us when you're ready."

"These are my dancing shoes" said Pam apologetically. She pointed to her black patent ballerina shoes with silver Cateye Crystal diamanté wedding bridal shoe clips, bought from a market stall as a pick-me-up after losing her job at Clipper Cards.

"Fantástico!" exclaimed Hilario.

"Okay, watch me." The instructor demonstrated basic steps which the class almost followed in different styles and directions. After a combination of practice steps there was an announcement, they all dreaded, "Now, are we ready? Here's where the fun starts. Join up with a partner and you'll switch when I say *'Buena!'* Okay? Let's go!"

Pam froze with fear and looked towards her feet. "Good evening, we best start, keep up with music," said a mature gentleman, dressed in a starched white shirt, navy blue tie, and black polyester trousers, black (and dark brown) leather reversible textured belt, and highly polished black patent shoes.

"Yes, of course," said Pam. "Don't know what I'm doin' so will follow your lead."

"I come each week, so you'll be fine." Pam stumbled and stepped on her partner's shoes more than the floor. "Hope you've got thick socks on?" said Pam.

"Didn't feel a thing," he grimaced. "Excuse me, forgot my manners, my name is Anton Rennard. Good to have you in our class." "Cheers, uhm... thank you. My name is Pam."

"Nice to meet you Pam, briefly; time to move on. Don't worry, we'll be back together soon."

Soon? Pam thought, *It's like the Magic Roundabout without Dougal.*

"Buenos Noches," said next partner, dressed in a mauve ruffle tuxedo shirt and light blue trousers and Cuban heels. "Hi," said Pam. "Just to warn you, I've got two left feet."

"No worries, Señorita, hold on tight we'll have good time. Especially with turns!"

Pam strived to pull away from his vice like grip and in the tussle their feet entangled, and he trod on her toe with such force that it broke her shoe clip in half. "OUCH!"

"Are you okay?" asked Anton.

"Think so, my toe's not happy," Pam replied, "I'll sit down for a minute."

Anton moved a chair towards her and said, "Can I get you a drink?"

"White wine, will be great, thanks."

"Am afraid, no alcohol," Anton replied. "But there is tea or orange squash."

'This is getting worse by the minute,' she thought. "Squash will be great." Pam examined the red lump on her toe and took the clip off the other shoe, and thought, *need danger money.* The phrase immediately drew her back to her time with Blake. *'Imagine if he could Salsa, snake hips and gorgeous hair. WoW!'* Her trance like state was interrupted by Anton, "Your lucky night, got biscuits."

"Lovely," Pam tried to sound enthusiastic, "can't beat sugar rush!"

Anton held out his hand, "Ready to try again?"

"Yeah, as long as I can keep away from the elephant in the room."

Anton laughed at her quirky sense of humour. The remaining dances were awkward but injury free. Pam insisted on staying with Anton giving the excuse he had great deal of experience and patience. Once past the embarrassment of sweaty palms and bodies moving in different directions, Pam relaxed into a few steps that resembled Salsa. There was a break and Pam said, "I'll go wild an' have a cup of tea this time."

Anton returned from the kitchen with disappointing news, "Tea, but all the biscuits have gone. "Never mind, got bar of chocolate in my bag, somewhere. Do you wanna bit?"

"No thank you. You'll need all the energy you can get for last part of evening."

Pam feigned a smile and thought *There's more!* "Don't worry," said Anton, "this is free style; partner free."

"That's music to my ears," Pam quipped.

Pam warmed up and enjoyed the last ten minutes. She stood behind Anton and tried to keep up with his style and precision. Frequently he turned to see if she was okay and encouraged her to keep going. A round of applause ended the class and a big sigh of relief for Pam.

"Did you enjoy the class?" asked Anton. "Yeah, was okay," said Pam, "after foot stomping or was it tap dancing on my toes."

"You did well for first time," said Anton. "See you next week?"

"Yeah, sure." Pam's foot started to swell up and she stumbled knocking into a pile of chairs in the corner. "Will you be alright?" "Think so," Pam replied. "Will hobble home."

Anton mumbled, "Can I walk or hobble with you to your home?"

She appreciated the offer of help from Anton but wished it was Blake, "May be wise. Not sure if I'll manage in dark an' it's been raining."

Anton held out his arm, as a gesture if Pam wanted to steady herself.

"What do you do for a living?" asked Anton.

"As actors say, 'I'm resting."

Anton tried to empathise, "I understand. It's tough to get a new job at our age. I am sorry, did not mean to be rude. Please forgive me."

"No, you're right," said Pam. "What's word? Dynamic better known as young. Can't win. Want you to have work experience but look like Peter Pan! What's your job?"

"I am an accountant. Work in Canterbury, been there for over ten years."

"Didn't know accountants could Salsa, don't usually go together," Pam laughed. "Where do you practise, in the car park?"

"There's not enough space, always full."

"Where's your car now?" Pam was curious and cautious. She did not want an awkward moment. There had been plenty who said they needed to go to the toilet just to get a foot in the door.

"Don't need it, I live near here with my mother," Anton announced proudly.

"That's nice," Pam had not intended to be that patronising. "Thank you for your help, I'm okay now. Only over the road."

"Would you like to go for a drink one evening?" Anton asked sheepishly. "I leave the office at 5p.m. sharp, so it would not be too late."

"Can't this week, gotta help my friend with babysitting, she's so busy. I'll probably see you next week."

"Looking forward to it," Anton was heartened by what he perceived to be a positive response. "Good night, Pam."

"Night, thanks for a squash." Pam blinked slowly and thought, *No! Why did I say that?*

Pam discreetly walked out of Martha's front garden, back onto the Esplanade. The curtains appeared to be closed but she did not see Maeve peeking out of a corner from her bedroom window. Pam wanted to avoid the wrath of Martha and needed time to come up with an excuse as to why she misled Anton as to where she lived.

***

"Hello! Special delivery for Señorita," Martha shouted as she opened Pam's front door.

"Not funny!" said Pam. "How could you leave me at the old – timers' Salsa class? Thought there'd be hot Latinos."

"What in Wishym Bay? Are you serious!" Martha chortled. "You've had too much chocolate. Anyway, here's money for cat flap."

"Cheers hun!" Pam hugged Martha. "Do you wanna coffee, got chocolate biscuits?"

"Make it strong, an' don't want sour milk."

"Oooh! Bit touchy ain't we?" Pam said mockingly.

"I'm shattered," Martha replied. "Appreciate help with gardening but don't usually do it in the dark!"

Pam's face reddened and she dropped a spoon on the floor. It was time to face the music. "I can explain. Wait a minute, who grassed me up? Bet it was Maddy?"

"No, not this time. Maeve was looking at the moonlight shining on the sea and saw you. What on earth were you doin'?

Pam hesitated and anticipated the onslaught, "Didn't want him to know where I lived?"

"WHO'S HE?"

"It's all your fault, anyhow." Pam protested and searched for sympathy. "You abandoned me with that crazy teacher and then Señor Big Foot - look at bruise on my toe, thanks to you! So, Anton saved me and ended up dancing with him."

"When was last time you missed chance to bring a man back with you? What's wrong with this one, too old, over twenty?" said Martha.

"Ha! Ha! Very funny. He's alright; bit odd, lives with his mum, works in Canterbury, wears a tie and he's an accountant."

"Not exactly, goin' be on crime watch with that description, is he?" Martha chortled.

"He don't drink," Pam moaned, "he's just a bit, you know, strange."

"So, let's get this straight. Poor bloke thinks you live at my house. If he's a bit clingy, so to speak, he'll be outside my home waitin' for you. What if he works with Brian?"

"They'll make a nice dance couple," Pam giggled. "He's a good teacher."

"If he turns up, I'm givin' him your mobile number and address. You can sort it out! I've got enough on my plate!" Martha's patience was stretched to breaking point.

"It'll be fine," said Pam as she kissed Martha on the cheek. "Whilst you're here, could you do me a favour?" "What now? I'm frighten' to ask," said Martha.

"Take a few photos, that's all."

Martha frowned and said, "Of what, the cat?"

"No, don't be silly. It's for dating website."

Martha slumped in the settee, "You're a glutton for punishment!"

"Cheers, hun, just put my lippy on!"

"Don't spend money on new clothes and cigarettes," Martha instructed her impetuous friend. "It's for Bea!"

***

Bea's muddy paw prints, caused by her morning adventures in the neighbour's garden, left their mark on the kitchen floor, and she knocked over the water fountain in search for a drink. "Get you water in a minute," said Pam, engrossed in searching through dating website. Pam patted the cushion and Bea jumped up; the soggy fur did not detract from her determined search for her Prince Charming. The filter by age group caused alarm and she thought, *'No! I can't. Why do the older ones look the same? I ain't that wrinkly?'* She tried to look at her reflection in the screen of the laptop balanced at an awkward angle as she sat crossed leg on the settee.

"What do you think, Bea?"

Her accommodating feline friend tapped a paw on her arm, as a reminder for the need for food and water. "Time for a break, doin' my head in. How 'bout tuna? Got some left in tin." Bea ran into the kitchen, meowing in anticipation. Pam tried to fix the water fountain, but it fell apart in her hands. She took a small plate from the sink, put it on the floor and tipped a cup of water on the surface. "That'll do for now," she stroked Bea. "Aunty Betty will get you a new one."

Pam's eyes strained and her heart yearned for fulfilment. She did not notice the cup of coffee had fallen on the floor nor the cat fur on her pink heart print fleece dressing gown. Bea took refuge on the duvet in the bedroom. The like notifications raised her hopes until the profiles were reviewed. She thought, *'must be more to their lives other then, "Enjoy cuddling up in front of TV with bottle of wine."* There were no action man profiles in appearance or character. *'Where have all the real men gone?'* she asked herself.

The location of Samuel caught her eye. *'Wouldn't need to get a train or taxi'* she thought. A positive point because it cut down on expense. *'Couldn't possibly ask him to stay on first date? But, why not'* she thought, *'only live once!'* Pam giggled and suppressed the memories of degradation after the one nighters left without even saying goodbye. In desperation and unrealistic optimism Pam repeatedly used the same tactics. One of the men said, "It's a numbers game. Keep goin' darlin. You'll strike it lucky one day!"

Samuel's profile looked promising: interests showed - sport, cinema, Italian food, and fishing.

'Fishing?' she thought, 'well, no one's perfect.' The description showed he worked for the emergency services. There was a mutual like and the heart notification ignited a spark of euphoria. The initial messages were about everything and nothing, including the weather which did not amuse Pam. He asked if she could take a selfie and send it to him. She delayed responding; '*Maybe a bit odd*' but was pleasantly surprised when he sent his selfie first; date and time stamped. A redhead was not usually her type, but he had a crew cut which watered down the copper colour root. Pam changed into a red long-sleeved tee-shirt, showing a slither of cleavage, fluffed her hair and applied the pièce de resistance – red lipstick.

"Bea, come on, there's a good girl," Pam shook the box of biscuits. The inclusion of Bea in the background may deliver the message of a caring nature and Bea's colouring would surely score some points.

Pam zoomed into his photo and although the background was blurred it looked familiar. The street view search on the internet verified her suspicion, it was the library. She said out loud, '*I wonder?*"

***

Squeals of delight from the children quickly followed by cries of, "Be careful!" from overprotective parents emanated from the Fire Station during the Family Safety Day. Billy took his turn to '*jump on board*' whilst an impatient queue waited their turn. A fire helmet covered most of Delja's face, but she smiled broadly as her high-spirited mother took photos, as she stood next to one of the Firefighters, who along with the team were encouraging the adults to book a Fire Safety visit to their homes.

"Pam! PAM!" shouted Summer. The bouquets of balloons fluttered in the wind, and she tightened her grip on the ribbon. Two large bags in her other hand were scraping the floor.

"Hi, how are you?" said Pam. "Silly question, let me help."

"You're a star!" Summer replied.

"Does Daffy know you're here?" asked Pam. "You ain't done a runna with bunch of balloons?"

"I wish. No, she sent me here. Clipper Cards, responsible members of community and caring, or somethin' like that?"

Pam untied the bags, arranged the balloons, and adjusted the strands of ribbon, "Like old times."

"Yeah," replied Summer. "Sorting out orders, but scenery much better here; these firemen are hunky, aren't they?"

"Hadn't noticed," Pam winked. Summer chortled and said "Liar, liar pants on fire!"

They both giggled loudly attracting attention of two of the firemen.

"Can we help you ladies?"

Summer blushed, "I'm from Clipper Cards."

"Your tee-shirt gives the game away!" said Phil, a tall, dark, handsome Station Manager.

"Cheeky!" Summer replied. "Oh no! Ain't got balloons on sticks for children. Daffy will have right hump! Won't be long. My mate will sort out these bags."

"And what is the name of your mate?" asked a tall and broad-shouldered redhead with a familiar smile.

Pam and Samuel chatted casually about the Family Safety Day. The event provided a good distraction. Some of the families thought she worked at the Fire Station.

Pam used the line, "No, I'm just volunteering."

"Didn't know we have public helping out today?" Phil asked Samuel.

"No, not exactly Guv," he replied hesitantly.

"We can't use these days for speed dating events. It's tempting, but it's a big NO!" Phil set out the boundaries in an authoritative manner befitting to his seniority.

"Sorry. Not planned. Bit embarrassing really." Samuel looked at his colleagues laughing at him.

"Always are, Carrot!" The Station Manager used the designated nickname to fast track the resolution. "Ask her to leave, nicely. Don't want complaints on social media!"

***

Samuel agreed to meet Pam at the Sea Gull Café – opposite The Seaside Museum.

They enjoyed chatting about the open day and Pam's job in Clipper Cards "I come bearing gifts!" said Samuel.

Pam tried to mask her excitement and exclaimed, "Wow! My lucky day. Two for the price of one!"

Samuel laughed at her oddball sense of humour, "don't get too excited. But a life saver!"

"A smoke detector and a carbon monoxide detector!" Pam sounded downcast. "Not the most romantic gifts but have been meaning to buy them for months. My mate keeps on at me, she gets really angry when I smoke in bed."

Samuel reinforced the warning, "She has every right to be angry. Statistics show that during a fire more people die from smoke and gas inhalation than from burns. Smoke alarms save lives! Remember, it's not only your house up in flames; think of your neighbours."

"But I need something to keep me warm in bed!" Pam's mouth dropped open and thought, '*NO! NO! I didn't say that! Why am I so stupid?*' Her face and neck glowed with embarrassment.

Samuel turned the situation around by cracking a joke, "There's always the fluffy cat? What's his name?"

"Her name's Bea. She'd wake me up," said Pam.

"You must research effects of smoke and the importance of a carbon monoxide detector. That can be your homework before we meet again?" Samuel said flirtatiously.

"When do I have to hand it in?" Pam could not conceal the eagerness to meet him again.

"Monday evening, okay?" he replied.

"Yes. But can't get these fitted before then!" Pam's anxiety dampened her mood.

"No problem. I'll call around before we go out. Won't take long," said Samuel. "We can go to Bel Mare. Lovely Italian restaurant."

Pam failed to think of a good excuse not to go there. "Yeah, heard it's really nice."

***

"Alright, hun?"

"What do you want?" Martha's brusque manner prompted Pam's playful response, "Love you too! Need to borrow your little black dress."

"You can't wear that to an interview?" said Martha.

"Well, not going for an interview," Pam paused before falling into the well-trodden pit of desperation, "well sort of; interview to be a wife."

Martha gasped, "Give me strength! Who is it this time? Not Anton?"

"No, he's so yesterday! This is Samuel."

"Where did you dig 'im up from?" Martha snapped.

"Don't be nasty. He's a respectable fireman."

"You've got a date with Fireman Sam? I don't believe you!"

"Didn't think of that, D'OH!" replied Pam. "He don't like being called Sam."

"No wonder! How did you meet him? Don't tell me, you put Bea up a tree and called the Fire Brigade to rescue her!"

"No need to be catty!" Pam replied and they both laughed. "Met on dating website. He's so handsome and taking me out for a meal this evening. Can't wait!"

Martha, well versed in the routine, and the consequences, played along, because she knew, the more she objected, the more irrational Pam's behaviour. "Thought it was odd, weren't a squeak from you yesterday. Guess you were doin' your nails and hair?"

"Yeah and removin' hair. Wax strips from market narf hurt! Red rash all over place now."

"Told you not to buy them!" Martha directed her gullible friend, "Go to beauty salon, quicker an' don't get red bits, well, a few but don't last long."

"Ain't got money for luxuries, Bea's food costs a fortune."

"Costs Betty a fortune, not you!" Martha's cutting retort reinforced the endless pressure on her time. "If you want dress, come over now, gotta go to Maeve's school at lunchtime."

***

Samuel gently kissed Pam on the forehead as she curled up in the warmth he left on the duvet.

"Don't go!" she pleaded. "Nice 'n' cosy here."

"Have to. Duty calls! See you soon."

The beam on Pam's face was as broad as the door frame.

"BEA! You can come to bed now. Where are you?"

Bea was eating the biscuits Samuel had put on her plate mixed with water. He changed the litter tray, out of sympathy for a cat that tolerated the somewhat lack of care and checked the cigarette butts in the old BBQ were safely extinguished.

The pulsating light from the smoke detector, firmly fixed on the hall ceiling, shone through to the bedroom. Pam's mind replayed the pleasures of the night, on a loop. She felt re-energised by the temporary fix to satisfy her craving for affection; to make her feel loved.

The content of the text received during the evening, was familiar to Pam. She had seen the words numerous times i.e. *'It's not you, it's me.'* The tears swelled up in her eyes and the lump in her throat tightened to prevent the inner tormented scream from bursting through the façade. She threw a sock at the smoke detector but had the sense not to strike it again because she could not fix it.

***

Green, white and orange bunting had become entangled in the paper garland, pierced by rusty drawing pins, pushed into the suspended ceiling tiles; still discoloured by remnants of nicotine, clinging onto the past when smoking was permitted inside the Wishym Bay Catholic Social Club.

Cheers and cries of *'Sláinte'* filled the area by the bar when another pint of Guinness was poured to celebrate St. Patrick's Day. The CD player was turned up to maximum volume and the tune of *'If You're Irish Come into the Parlour'* leaped over the welcome mat towards the hilarity brought about by Martha, Pam, and Betty's attempt at Irish step dancing.

"Not sure what you're on there ladies, but I'll have some too!" Timothy, the barman, shouted.

"That's me done," Betty gasped for breath. "And me," said Martha. "Quick, get that booth; if I don't sit down soon, I'll fall down!"

"What do you wanna drink?" asked Pam.

"You sure you're alright?" Martha smirked. "Did you raid piggy bank? Because your credit card is maxed out."

"Could you shout that a bit louder?" Pam looked shamefaced. "It's alright, sold my red dress on Wishym Bay friends Facebook page."

"In that case, I'll have a pint of Guinness," said Betty. Martha and Pam looked surprised at this outburst of rebellion because Betty was not a heavy drinker. Even though they dabbled as teenagers she stopped before Martha and Pam over-indulged.

"Go on then," make that two pints," said Martha.

"I'm goin' have double whiskey," Pam announced. "No, you're not," said Martha. "I ain't carrying you home. Remember last time? You an' whiskey don't mix."

"You such an old grump these days," Pam complained. She missed the care-free ladies' nights and dancing to dawn. Her selective memory overlooked the terrible hang overs, stomach pains, and ridicule from men in the night clubs. Her reputation preceded her therefore she was an easy target for cruel remarks e.g., "Don't worry about cost of taxi lads, its B&B guaranteed!"

"Okay," Pam surrendered, "it's three pints of Guinness. Anything to shut you up!"

"Would ye like to squeeze in there darlin'?" asked Séamus, a club member, who had been propping up the bar since it opened.

"Why not," said Pam, "looks nice and cosy."

"Now tell me, young lady, those words on your head true?" Séamus chortled.

Pam shook her fluffy green headband boppers with the words, *'Get lucky with me.'*

"Might be," she replied. "But it'll cost ya!"

"What would that be?" asked Séamus. "My Leprechaun's still lookin' for the pot of gold."

"Ah, we won't disturb him," Pam teased. "Three pints of Guinness will be great!"

"That's more like it. Do you have a thirst? The Irish Dancing wears out the best of them." Séamus winked and enjoyed the company; in a crowd but the loneliness weighed heavy on his shoulders.

Séamus told stories about the good old days in Galway, and they laughed at all the different theme related costumes around them.

"I'm parched," said Martha, "what is she doin'?" "Who's she with?" asked Betty.

"Goodness knows. Thought she'd have a night off after Fireman Sam!"

"What a shame," said Betty. "He's handsome and got a decent job. What happened?"

"Ain't got a clue. Gone the same way as the rest of them," Martha replied. "Maybe she's destined to be on the shelf. Knowing her it's got be highest one an' she 'll keep fallin' off and shriek for help." Martha and Betty laughed in unison.

The two female singers gave a rendition of the song 'Galway Bay' which hushed the lively audience. Although the melody was mesmerising the performance did not have the protective passion and tender timbres of Muiris. Delicate drops of fluid memories danced on her cheeks as she was immersed in the past.

"Now we'll have none of that," said Padraig as he handed Martha a white linen handkerchief: ironed to perfection.

"Thank you," Martha said in a faint voice before looking up. "Oh, I'm sorry didn't see it was you. How are you?

"I'm grand," replied Padraig. "But it's you we need to be worryin' about?"

Martha patted her palms on the tears in hope it would soak up the sorrow. "I'm fine, it's just my age. Never know when it'll strike next. Anyway, on a happier note, this is my friend Betty."

"Nice to meet you, Betty," said Padraig. "Where's your drink? You'll have to raise a glass for St. Patrick."

Betty smiled and said "Hello. Our friend is the bar. You can't miss her with those green fluffy head boppers."

"Well, she'll be at the bar all evenin' if I don't rescue her from Séamus, the Eejit!" said Padraig. "He'll watch your back until he's blue in the face an' got me out of a few scrapes over the years, but he's full of blarney. But before I go on my mission, where is the beautiful young Galway girl?"

Confusion filled Betty's complexion and she was intrigued by the question.

"Is that Maeve? My youngest daughter?" Pam tried to deflect the tension. "She's at home with her dad."

"Surprised he's not here enjoying a pint of the black stuff?" asked Padraig.

"He hates Guinness and Irish music; come to think of it, anything Irish!" Martha's pent-up rage rose to the surface and breached the emotional defence barrier.

"More fool him!" said Padraig, perplexed by the scenario, but wise enough not to push beyond the boundary he had unintentionally marched on.

"Mrs Clerk! How are you?" asked Father John O' Clery (O Cleirigh), the Parish Priest in the Roman Catholic Church: Our Lady of the Assumption, in Brightfield Road.

"I am well Father. How are you?"

"In good health, thank God," he replied. "Well, there's a bigger congregation in here than in our Sunday services. Will ask the manager what the secret is?"

"It's the black stuff!" Pam replied. Martha's face turned to stone, and Betty shook her head.

"The communion wine is quite nice," said Father Cathal *(pronounced as Ka-Hal)* Cusack.

Pam chuckled.

Father O' Clery's jaw muscles tightened, and his fixed stare showed the annoyance. Through pursed lips he said, "Cathal, let me introduce you to Mrs Clerk, and it's Mrs Cooke? Is that right?" Betty nodded. Father O'Clery looked at Pam, "and, it's, give me a minute, I'll remember. Sure, that's it, Mrs Docker?" Pam replied, "nearly, I'm not married. Nice to meet you Ka-Hal. That's a nice name, how do you spell it?" Martha kicked Pam's ankle, under the table. "OUCH!" Pam squealed." "Are you alright, can I help?" asked Father Cathal.

"No, it's okay, just a touch of cramp," Pam replied. "You're very kind."

"Father Cathal is very busy," Father O'Clery chastised his apprentice. "He is our new curate, and there is always lots to do." Father Cathal, humbled by the firm reminder of his duties, smiled softly.

"How is Maeve?" asked Father O'Clery, "we have not seen her for a while."

"She's not been well, I'm afraid," Martha responded apologetically. "She's blessed with creativity; it helps her so much when she's at home. Look at this lovely scarf she made me and the bags for Betty and Pam." Martha proudly presented a knitted green scarf with orange and white buttons stitched onto each end piece. One golden felt heart was sewn in the middle with the letter *M* in blue – representative of the word mother, however for Martha the chosen letter was etched on her heart. A sprinkle of green felt shamrocks, in various sizes, decorated the handmade linen tote bags. Circle wooden key chains, tied to the woven orange wool handles, had minute pots of gold meticulously painted on the outer sides.

Father O'Clery complimented Martha on how she nurtured Maeve, "Now, that's a gift that will take her far afield and back home again. Contact the office; we'll discuss the school, and we will find the right path." "Thank you, it will be such a relief," said Martha. "We'll see you Sunday."

"Now, that is good news. Look forward to seeing all of ye?"

"I will not be able to go," Betty replied. "Ted, urhm, my husband is coming to get me tomorrow – only one ladies' day, at a time, at my age."

Pam jumped to her feet, out of the reach from Martha, and announced loudly, "I'll be there!" Her left knee caught the side of the chair and she lurched towards Father Cathal.

"Don't be breaking your shin on a stool that's not in your way!" said Father O'Clery.

***

The clatter of the stiletto heels echoed around the pews in the church and raised up towards the staggering tall roof.

Martha pushed Pam and mouthed, "Sit there!"

"I can't genuflect in these shoes?" Pam whispered.

"Just sit down!" Martha's hushed tone highlighted the humiliation as other members of the congregation turned, tutted, and said "Shush!"

Maeve followed her mother as they all managed to squash into the same pew. She then knelt on the hassock to pray for *Aunty Pam.*

"When does Cathal talk?" asked Pam.

"Please, just stop!" Martha replied. "You'll get struck down."

"Now ladies, how lovely to see you all," said Father O'Clery as the congregation started to leave the church. "It was a lovely service," said Martha. "You liked it didn't you Maeve?"

"Yes," replied Maeve. "Especially the words from the Bible."

"Well, your wisdom is greater than your years," said Father O'Clery. "Now, you be a good girl, and look after your mammie."

"Oh, mummy is okay. I need to look after Aunty Pam."

Howls of laughter filled the porch. Martha gave her daughter a big hug. "Can you help, please darling? Ask Aunty Pam if she can bring you to the shop to buy a pint of milk."

"The red milk, mummy?" asked Maeve.

"Yes, that's right," Martha reassured her daughter who liked to know precise details. "Then we can go to say hello to Bea, if you want?" "Yes please! Bea is pretty, but, I think, a bit hungry."

Martha waited until Maeve distracted Pam from talking to Father Cathal and waved to them both.

She went back into the church to light a candle for her mother. *'Miss you so much Mum,'* she thought, *'didn't mean to break your heart, I love him, and he's love for me is a treasure I'll never find again. Maeve is beautiful and she would love to have known you. I will do everything I can to protect her.'* Martha started to leave but turned back to light a candle for her soul mate – Muiris. Their lives were intertwined physically, albeit too briefly, but the powerful force of the emotional connection strengthened her resolve; to hold onto the flicker of hope, he would return.

Martha smiled faintly and held on tightly to the claddagh ring impressed into the palm of her left hand. She read the words on the card, resting on the collection box *"May peace and plenty be the first to lift the latch to your door, and happiness be your guest today and evermore."*

***

CHAPTER 13

A soft synthetic Aquafine watercolour brush glided along the shell of the blown goose egg with precision and purpose. Colours specifically selected and each line leading to the next phase of the fine art. Sky blue faded into strands of long grass. Intense yellow daffodils with bright golden trumpets, stood tall, encircled by the drooping flowers and petals of bluebells; deep in thought and chiming to the sounds of spring – new life and hope for brighter days.

A drip of yellow paint landed on Ginger's head. "I am sorry!" Maeve cried. Ginger, not perturbed by the accidental highlight in her hair, wagged her tail.

"There is no need to worry," said Angela. "Ginger likes a wash, and we have gentle baby shampoo in her cupboard, which will remove her new hair tint in no time at all. Deep down, she likes the fuss, so probably knocked your chair deliberately."

Maeve relaxed and smiled, "Please can I give Ginger a biscuit, to say sorry?"

"Yes, she will love that," Angela replied, "after the visit to her personal beauty parlour, she will return as clean as a new pin." Maeve giggled. Ginger, filled with excitement, walked to the utility room.

Maeve softly touched the Easter card with her fingers to test if the paint had dried. On the front, a church, set in the backdrop of a watery sun light at dawn, amidst a field of long grass, home to tulips, grape hyacinths, and daisies. No people; no agenda - simply nature. Her innate skill in calligraphy intertwined the letters M and D inside the card.

Ginger scampered into the kitchen with the energy of a puppy and proudly displayed her freshly groomed head, face, and ears. "Oh, Ginger! You do look pretty," said Maeve.

The gifts were gathered after a craft morning which Maeve dearly loved. The larger white wicker basket: pistachio green silk ribbon and Pandora cherry blossoms attached to each end of the handle, was for Martha. The decorative egg, nestled in wood wool, rested on top of a bed of miniature chocolate eggs individually wrapped in foil.

The smaller brown basket with thin strands of azure blue ribbon interwoven around the edge, held Cadbury mini eggs treat size bags under three painted wooden eggs: a presentation for Philomina, Maddy and Brian. Quick-drying, water resistant ink was etched into the wood with the ultra-fine tip of a Sharpie pen. Watercolour paint in shades of brown, orange and beige spread evenly over the surface area, but the black pen lines cracked through the top layer.

Maeve explained, "they will not like the eggs, but Tabitha will play with them. She does not eat eggs but likes tapping her favourite treat blue ball, and always finds ways to get the biscuits – she is very clever. Aunty Penelope does not like Easter eggs, she says Easter is silly and a waste of time and money."

Angela felt pity for the adult in question, "how sad. She is missing the blessings which are directly in front of her eyes." Angela tuned into Maeve's sense of foreboding about her aunt's visit on Easter Sunday, "shall I ask your Mummy to bring you here to spend time with Ginger? Maybe Aunty Pam can join us for tea."

"Oh no, Daddy will be very angry. We all must be at home when Aunty Penelope is there."

Angela changed the conversation in an attempt not to deepen her high level of psychological distress which was clear for all to see but convenient to ignore. "Your mummy will love the posy of flowers you made. Such beautiful colours."

"Thank you," Maeve replied. "I tried to match the colour of the posy The Queen had on Thursday. During the Royal Maundy Service, The Queen distributed Maundy money to 90 men and 90 women – one for each of The Queen's 90 years. A little early. Her Majesty's actual birthday is on Thursday 21st April."

Angela admired a young mind filled with fascinating facts but, at times, was trapped in an isolation cell when the surrounding noise and nonsense overwhelmed her.

***

Martha methodically filled the dishwasher and put the large roasting tin in the sink to soak. She learnt the art of effective multi-tasking from her mother and after managing four children, three juveniles and one adult i.e., Brian, she acquired her P.H.D. in house management.

"Look mummy, look mummy," Maeve eagerly pointed to an original copy of the publication "*Our Queen's Year*" - a 64-page tribute to Queen Elizabeth II's Silver Jubilee. A unique souvenir, encased in a protective, hand tooled, leather book cover. A cherished first wedding anniversary gift to Angela from her devoted husband, on loan as a special treat for Easter. Maeve promised profusely to safeguard the memorabilia and return it on Easter Monday. Brian gave the excuse he was too busy to look before Sunday lunch. Philomina and Maddy complained, "It stinks!" Penelope ignored Maeve.

"It's lovely, darling," said Martha. "Can you bring the book to your room please. I'll just finish, and we can sit down and look together We have to take care of Angela's special memory."

"Mummy, if I help you, we will be able to go to my room sooner?" asked Maeve.

"You are so kind," Martha replied in earshot of Philomina.

"Ah, so sweet," Philomina sniped, "domestic bliss!"

Martha chastised her eldest daughter, "instead of being spiteful you can help rather than just standing there!"

"Dad and Aunty Penelope want coffee," Philomina fished for her mother to complete the boring task.

Martha's caustic reply set the scene for reprisal. "That's nice, you know where everything is. Don't let me stop you!"

Philomina slammed the cupboard doors, banged the cups on the kitchen surface and dropped the sugar bowl. "STUPID

THING!" Philomina shouted. "What you grinning at?" Her rancour directed towards Maeve.

Martha glared at her eldest daughter and gripped the tea towel tightly to help release the tension rising from within. "You're makin' two cups of coffee, not a soufflé. Get over yourself and get back to your aunt."

Martha hugged Maeve and they took it in turns to rinse the cutlery and place in the cage basket. Maeve made sure the knives and forks were in separate compartments.

Boiling hot black coffee soaked through the thin pages after Philomina nudged the book off the table; the pages slipped out of the cover and fell onto the pile of sugar.

"What have you done now?" asked Martha and then she saw the rumpled torn pages entangled in the gluey mess. She tried to shield Maeve's eyes, but it was too late. The scream was followed by uncontrollable sobbing.

Martha pointed to the hall and told Philomina, "Get out!" She held Maeve tightly and encouraged her to take slow deep breaths. "It is okay, mummy is here. It will be alright, please do not worry."

Brian looked shamefaced as his sister sharpened her venomous tongue and said, "You need to control that child. She is spoilt!" What is all the drama about this time? Was there a spoon out of place in the dishwasher?" Philomina chortled and wallowed in her aunt's wicked sense of humour and replied, "I don't know; something about that stupid smelly book."

"What, the one you threw on the floor!" said Maddy.

"Do not be so childish Maddy!" Penelope sneered. "Philomina is not going to waste her time on inconsequential bric-a-brac. Maeve is far too precious and needs discipline not mollycoddling. Why is Martha rewarding such abnormal behaviour?"

The speed of the words moved up a gear, and Penelope's diatribe continued, "Just do something about her! A son would have more strength and resilience. If only your wife could have given you a son – to play cricket and inherit the family name. Never mind when Philomina has a handsome husband, I am sure she will persuade him to keep her surname. Their son will be your heir."

Penelope overlooked or purposely ignored the fact that Philomina never had a boyfriend. Friends stayed for sleep overs, and no one dare question why they were always female and her social media accounts reflected the same picture.

Martha ushered Maeve up the stairs to shield her and start packing a suitcase.

"Where are you going Martha?" asked Penelope. "You must prepare the afternoon tea for your family." Martha ignored her and turned towards Brian, "Get that woman out of my home and I don't wanna see her back in here again. DO YOU UNDERSTAND ME!?!"

"Just about sums it up doesn't it." Philomina lashed out. "It's your home! What is Dad, a lodger?

He has worn himself out for years and what happens? We end up in this dump because you want to live by the seaside." Philomina knew her aunt would back up her criticism.

"Yes, well said. At least my dear niece offers the support my darling brother needs."

Maddy picked up her mobile and declared, "I am out of here. You're a bunch of losers! This ain't a family it's a farce. Pam is right about you," she pointed at her aunt, "you really are a poisonous pen!" Maddy slammed the front door with such a force the frame rattled.

Brian called out to Martha, "When will you be back?"

"When I'm ready!" Martha guided her distraught daughter towards Pam's bungalow.

***

Pam took a deep breath, and the imminent conversation almost tugged her back out of the gate, but Ginger barked sounding the alarm of an unexpected visitor. *'Drat'* Pam thought.

"What a nice surprise," said Angela, "is all well?"

"Yes, uhm, sort of, uhm, not really," Pam stuttered and stumbled along the words she rehearsed but could not make their way to her mouth in a coherent manner.

Angela asked, "Would you like to come in for a cup of tea?"

"No thank you, it's okay, well not okay but don't want to disturb you," Pam realised that a one-word answer would have sufficed. Although tongue-tied she persisted, "Just come to say how sorry we are about your book."

"Yes, Martha telephoned me to offer an explanation and profusely apologised." Angela replied.

"It was a precious gift from Victor however forgiveness was a gift he gave to many."

Pam pleaded, "we really don't know what to do and hope you can forgive us. Maeve can't stop crying and asked me to give you this." The handcrafted card had a drawing of a broken heart on the front and inside the word SORRY in bold blue ink. Pam continued, "We know the book cannot be replaced, but is there anything we can do or buy for you?"

"We can have tea and cake tomorrow and a nice talk. Do you think Maeve will come?"

"I'm not sure, she is so frightened, but Martha will do her best to encourage her."

"You can mention that Ginger would love to see her and does not have any of her favourite biscuits left in her tin. Maeve may wish to bring a new box of treats for Ginger?"

The tense lines on Pam's face eased, "That's a good idea. Poor Maeve, she gets bullied in school and at home which is the worst. Don't get a bit of peace."

"Yes, it is incredibly sad, but we will find a way," said Angela.

***

Seagulls conducted their board meeting on the pebble beach in Whitstable. Top of the agenda was breakfast – spoils from the fishermen and snacks from the fleeting tourists.

Maeve held tightly to Angela's hand as she eagerly advanced into a day out with her mentor. An adventure and a rare full day away from her mum.

Although gripped by anxiety, Martha welcomed the invitation by Angela. Maeve had all the contact telephone numbers in her notebook, adorned with wild meadow flowers cover design, safely tucked into a corner of her backpack. Maeve insisted on taking the navy-blue Kids travel carry-on bag a.k.a *'just in case,'* containing mini bottles of still mineral water, two bananas, cereal bars, Foxes glacier mints, hand towels, and water fresh hand & face antibacterial wipes. She told her mum that the necessary provisions would be too heavy for Angela so had to take the supplies on wheels.

"Where would you like to go first?" Angela asked.

"There is so much to see," Maeve replied as she tried to absorb the new surroundings with a slither of unease, but it was soon dissolved by an undiluted happiness of a day out with Angela.

Two souls separated by age but unified in anticipation of brighter days.

"Can we look at the beach huts?" asked Maeve. "Lovely colourful stripes! Must have taken a long time to paint them so neatly."

"Yes," replied Angela, "lots of patience and good at arts and crafts just like you."

Maeve blushed in appreciation of the compliment. "Aunty Pam calls them beach hutches. She is silly but I love her."

Angela was taken aback by Maeve's openness in sharing her feelings without a hint of a stutter.

"She is not really my aunt, but I wish she was," Maeve conveyed a sense of melancholy.

***

They strolled along the serene sea front surrounded by the fresh spring breeze. Most of the children had gone back to school after the Easter break but Maeve was too traumatised to return to the classroom. During the intermission in caring for her youngest daughter, Martha went to St. Bernadette's Catholic Primary School and demanded to see the headmaster. The private protest had to be kept from Maeve because the distress would escalate to new heights.

"Would you like to go to the book shop?" asked Angela.

"Yes please," Maeve replied.

Maeve strode along the pavements buoyed up by the opportunity to explore more shelves of stories. Floral fabric Easter bunting flags adorned the frontage, but Maeve was intrigued by the description of *Antiques and Collectables* under the shop name Leaf Trá.

The trove of books was divided into petite rooms with charismatic decorative features. Maeve was enthralled by a vintage hand knotted rug in the reception space: boasting a geometric oversize centre medallion. The colours and shades included: cherry red, sky blue, mallard green and blush rose.

"Welcome," said Petra Leaf, the owner – steward of a family run business going back five decades. "How can I help you?"

"Hello," Angela replied. "Well, it is as stroll down memory lane for me and an introduction for this young lady."

Petra leant towards the youngest customer of the day and asked, "What is your name?"

Maeve moved closer to Angela's coat with a double-breasted bodice - made from Harris Tweed in mottled colourway of greens and subtle browns. She proffered a faint reply, "I am Maeve, and this is my guardian, Angela. She is very nice."

"Kindred spirits," Petra sensed the connection. "Are you looking for a special book Maeve?"

"Oh yes, books by Cerri Burnell and lots of different crafts, please."

"If I may say, they are excellent choices," Petra replied. "We will try to help. We have an arts and craft corner. You can create some wonderful designs from this large book, which has been waiting especially for you."

"Yes, please!" Maeve shrilled with delight.

"Would you like a drink?" asked Petra.

Maeve look at Angela for approval and she gave a discreet nod.

"Ribena please," Maeve replied.

"Coming right up!" Petra capered into the kitchen.

Maeve settled into the chair and started working on her next expression of an innate gift inherited from a dear land across the Irish Sea.

"It is a good idea to have a craft corner," said Angela. "My mother brought me here. There used to be story and reading room. My father helped children who found the three Rs a challenge. He wanted to volunteer more frequently but was immersed in the duties and responsibilities of a teacher.

"We need assistance even more now," said Petra, "if we can get the children to turn their mobiles off for ten minutes, we may stand a chance!"

They both laughed and concurred that for some, technology overshadowed basic literacy skills.

"I love this book!" Maeve called out. "Can I buy it please?"

Angela caught sight of the title, 'Vintage 1940s Cookbook, 250 Classic Cake Recipes.'

"Mummy and daddy gave me pocket money and I have savings. I promised daddy to write down each debit."

Angela smiled and continued to be astounded at the vast range of Maeve's intelligence. The reasonability of the sale price prompted a positive reply. Angela held the book whilst Maeve returned to her impromptu art gallery.

A mist of reminiscence led Angela into an emotional epilogue, using the format of inhibited grief.

The song '*Book of Love*' featured in the film *Shall We Dance?* played in her mind. In February 2005 Angela invited her cherished her husband to an evening at the 'flicks' to celebrate the 29th anniversary of their engagement. It would prove to be their last visit to encapsulate a story committed to celluloid.

Victor proposed on Whitstable beach with a chill chiming from the clear blue sky. A mid-19th Century diamond engagement ring in 18ct gold with a flower head surrounded in Platinum was presented in anticipation of acceptance.

The inheritance from Angela's maternal grandmother was willingly passed to Victor after he respectfully asked Ernest Oyston for his daughter's hand in marriage. A precious family heirloom kept secret from Angela not out of malice but out of her parents' desire she would find love as deep as the ocean.

Angela tripped backwards in surprise hence hindering her reply but once composed she gave an unequivocal, "YES!"

"We should include those steps as we share the first dance on our wedding day," said Victor.

Their smiles matched the crystal-clear devotion to their lifelong commitment.

Tears glistened on her cheek: like rain drops they germinated the new seeds of hope.

"She really has a gift for arts and crafts," said Petra.

"Sorry, ah, yes," Angela's words stumbled along a hazy path. "My apologies, miles away.

Yes, Maeve is a special girl, blessed with many talents that not everyone wishes to see. Last Wednesday, she surprised me with a gem of a gift for my birthday: a painting of a beautiful bouquet of spring flowers cushioned by white and pink gypsophila (baby's breath).

"What a lovely drawing. Who is that for?" asked Angela.

"It is for mummy," Maeve replied. "I have made a post card for Aunty Pam. Daddy thinks post cards are silly and too expensive. We can use this one. I have postage stamps in my rucksack. He will not be angry now."

Angela was alarmed at the use of the word angry in relation to a minor item. She deemed it to be an abrupt response from a father to his considerate daughter. Angela detracted away from the negativity and focused on lightning the mood. "Beach Hutches, nice and bright. Aunty Pam will love it!"

Memory Pillar, a treasure chest filled with artifacts from a bygone era, was the next stage of the adventure for Maeve. "This is magnificent," Maeve proclaimed as she looked in wonder at the array of antiques on display in an extremely long and narrow shop.

"I am sure we will find a beautiful one for your mummy," said Angela.

"Can I help you, ladies?" asked Mr Hérit.

"Yes, please," Maeve replied. "We are looking for a photo frame for my mummy."

"Très gentile Mademoiselle," Mr Hérit replied and politely nodded to Angela who was overjoyed at Maeve's growing confidence and clarity of communication.

"Merci Monsieur," said Angela. "Voici le beau dessin."

"C'est magnifique! Qui est l'artiste?"

Angela gently gestured towards Maeve.

"Well, there is no time to lose, we will have to find a marvellous frame for the masterpiece!"

Mr Hérit's theatrical voice whorled towards the vaulted ceiling and returned with equal tempo.

***

"Can we sit in the corner by the fire please?" asked Angela.

Maeve was subdued by the number and volume of other customers in Tudor Tea Thyme, a 17th century tea room, run as a family business since 1974.

"Yes, of course," replied the waitress. "Make yourself at home and I'll bring you a menu."

Angela understood Maeve's need to find a safe space in a crowded restaurant therefore this was an ideal place to rest their feet and review the progress on their outing.

"Would you like to share a quiche with me?" Angela knew not to pressure Maeve on the topic of food therefore the suggestion of sharing proved to a comforting alternative.

"Is it as nice as the one you made?" asked Maeve. "You have a good memory," replied Angela, "I am sure it is very nice."

Maeve ate the quiche, slowly but surely.

"I do not have wrapping paper for mummy's picture frame," said Maeve.

"Why don't you fit your drawing in place now and we can buy a gift bag in the Beach Corner card shop, after we finish our tea?" said Angela.

"Aunty Pam worked in a card shop; it was very busy!"

"This shop is tiny in comparison. A sharp corner with a soft centre." Angela reassured Maeve with her empathetic description. Maeve held her drawing; a sunset in Wishym Bay, burning shades of orange surrounded the sun which rested on the sea. The evening sky cirrus clouds, arranged in diagonal strips, waited for the final curtain to fall.

The mid-20th century Rococo style brass picture frame with an ornate easel stand complimented the dramatic scene.

"Monsieur Hérit found an enchanting frame," said Angela.

"Yes, I hope mummy loves it. Monser, oops," Maeve started to worry. "What is the correct word?"

"The word is Monsieur. But it is fine, a good effort, "said Angela, "we can call him Mr Hérit."

"Thank you. I will practise before our next visit," Maeve replied. "Mr Hérit was very helpful and funny. Is Trá a French word?"

"Not that I am aware of," Angela replied, "cannot remember learning it during my French lessons, although that was a long time ago. Ah, the name of the bookshop; Trá is an Irish word and in this context means beach. For some a *beach is an absolute haven and has a wealth beyond description when you love it.*"

Maeve was mesmerised by the poetry of Angela's response although the aroma of the apple crumble with hot custard pivoted about her sensory input. The waitress kindly set out the three vintage *Pyrex* cottage rose pattern bowls, one each for Angela and Maeve with the remaining piece placed in the centre of the table to facilitate sharing the dessert.

"Please can I have two extra serviettes?" asked Maeve.

"Yes, of course," replied the waitress.

Angela was perplexed but intuitiveness restrained her inquisitiveness.

Maeve set out her proposed plan. "I can use them to wrap Ginger's gift. They only have white serviettes, but I can draw a flower on the top. Do you think she will like that?"

"Yes, she will be very happy with the drawing and the gift," Angela replied.

Maeve placed the antique brass oval dog name tag in the serviettes folded into an envelope shape and sealed it with a double-sided sticky dot: an item from the stationery supply in her rucksack.

"How thoughtful of Mr Hérit to search for a tag in the bits and bobs box?" said Angela.

"Oh yes. Can we put Ginger's name on the tag, please?"

"I will bring it to the jewellers in the High Street," said Angela, "they should be able to fit all the letters in."

"How did Ginger get her name?" asked Maeve.

"Born from a story steeped in happiness and sadness," Angela replied. "Shall I share it with you whilst you have your Ribena?"

"Yes please!"

"I first met my husband, Victor, in October 1975. We were on Poppy collection duty at Whitstable & Tankerton station."

The prologue was stalled by Maeve's question, "Was Mr Bentley there with Bobby?"

"Oh no, my dear, they are too young but are devoted to their charitable mission now."

Angela paused to have a sip of tea and continued, "during one evening shift the other volunteers had to leave earlier than expected. We stayed and gathered up all the boxes and money tins. Unfortunately, it was difficult to see in the dark – the hexagonal lampshade above me was not working. I tripped over an uneven piece of concrete but thankfully Victor reached out and broke my fall. My face beamed red with embarrassment – it was so bright it lit up the pavement. He was polite and caring. We returned to the hall which was the centre of operations and had a cup of tea. Victor served in The Royal Navy."

"Was Victor a captain of a ship!?" asked Maeve.

"No, but he had an important job and was very brave." Angela reflected on the courage of Victor and other members of the armed services throughout their lives. The strain of the Falklands War in 1982 took its toll on Victor's health.

"Did you and Victor go to the Leaf Trá bookshop?" asked Maeve.

"Victor had to return to the naval base. We agreed to write to each other until he returned on leave for Christmas."

"Did Victor live near the beach?" Maeve asked.

"Well, his parents lived in Wishym Bay," Angela replied

"In Anchor Tale?" Maeve tried to place all the pieces of the jigsaw together. Angela was not perturbed by the questions, rather the opposite; she embraced the flow of words and was thrilled to see Maeve breaking free from the constraints of angst.

"Yes, in the same house but Victor chose the name Anchor Tale."

"Did you have Christmas dinner with Victor?" asked Maeve.

"No, Victor's parents had set out the plans for Christmas. They liked to preserve tradition, and I respected their rules. We met a couple of times for tea and cake during his break."

Maeve was enraptured as the romantic story unfolded. "Did you come to Tudor Tea Thyme?"

"Yes, it was our favourite place," Angela swallowed slowly, determined not to get deeply upset in front of Maeve, especially in unfamiliar surroundings. "We also went to the cinema."

Maeve's excitement burst out slightly louder than anticipated, "WHICH FILM!?" She blushed and looked down to the floor, "I am sorry, mummy says I should not shout."

"That is okay, we need to consider the other customers, they may not be interested in the film." Angela and Maeve smiled in unison and in recognition of the boundaries.

"*Follow the Fleet* starring Fred Astaire and Ginger Rogers. Victor took me to The Oxford Cinema in Whitstable."

"Did you enjoy it?" asked Maeve.

"It was wonderful," Angela beamed as she was transported back to the first *official date* with Victor. She was nervous but not fearful of him being forward. Angela was engrossed in the music and the stunning steps of the zestful dance scenes. However, she felt the warmth of Victor's eyes as he looked with affection and protection for her wellbeing. The magnificent music raised spirits and she allowed herself a few taps along the pavement whilst humming a few notes to the song, '*Let's Face the Music and Dance*' as Victor walked her home.

"They are very good dancers," said Maeve. "Mummy likes watching their films. Aunty Pam likes dancing but she needs more lessons."

Angela appreciated the cheeky comment but choked back the tears of heartache with a cough. "Oh my, such a dry throat after storytelling, I need another tea. Would you like a Ribena?"

Maeve pondered. "So Ginger is named after Ginger Rogers?"

"Yes, a tribute to a dreamy evening," Angela replied. "I adopted her eighteen months after Victor passed away in 2005. She was only six months old, a rescue dog, therefore not a playful puppy at the beginning."

"Are you sad?" asked Maeve.

"A little less sad now but I miss Victor every day."

"Mummy is sad sometimes," said Maeve. "She cries and says love never dies; it moves to a different part of your heart."

"Your mummy is wise." Angela perceived the broken seams of grief in Martha's past.

***

CHAPTER 14

"I'll buzz you in!"

"Thank you," said Pam. She pushed the front door, but it did not budge. Pam pressed the button again.

"You not in?"

"No, sorry, the door is stuck!" Pam replied using the entry phone.

"I'll be down in a just a sec."

Pam tugged at her black skirt and checked for marks on the heels of her shoes.

"This door, honestly, drives me crazy! I'll have to call Robert again. Never mind me, come in. Just up the stairs on your right."

Alarm bells started going off in Pam's head, but she could not escape because the front door was stuck.

The minimalist design of the office was interspersed with elaborate bouquets of fresh flowers in hand cut crystal bud vases with the 'Romance' design, featuring a matt hand cut heart blended into the glass, elegantly rounded off with 3 carefully placed genuine Swarovski crystals.

There was one desk and a laptop in the compact reception.

Pam overheard the telephone conversation from the bottom of the stairs.

"Please get here as quick as you can otherwise, I'll have to climb down the side of the building if there's an emergency. Maybe a handsome fireman can save me. Could be my lucky day!"

Pam stood frozen with dread as to what might happen next.

"What a start! Take your jacket off, make yourself at home."

"It's my suit jacket," Pam replied, "I normally keep it on in the office."

"Oh, might change your mind later, gets quite stuffy in here. Mine'll be off soon. Anyway, come into my boudoir. I've got a new red Nespresso Vertuo coffee machine and biscuits but am afraid no George Clooney."

Pam looked around the spacious and lavishly decorated office of Marty Rhys, owner of the dating agency - PierInn2, starkly juxtaposed with the grey, clinical reception.

The alluring flower carved chaise longue with its deep plush buttoned back, upholstered in soft light gold woven fabric, sat in the sunlight under the bay window; dressed in light purple ball fringe curtains held with gold twined tie backs and topped with a Bordeaux styled pelmet.

Pam thought, '*Please! Please! Don't ask me to sit on there!*'

Marty invited Pam to sit in the equally comfortable, but far less challenging, leather office chair on the other side of his solid mahogany desk holding a mixture of beautiful, scented flowers in a matching vase to those in reception. The desk calendar, in six languages, supported by a sturdy red plastic stand with a slide mechanism and marker to indicate the current date i.e., Wednesday 13th April, seemed out of place, but somehow suited the quirkiness of the eclectic décor.

"That feels better," said Marty after taking a few sips of coffee. "Let's start again. Take Two!! Good morning and welcome to PierInn2U. Lovely to meet you."

Pam stuttered, "Yes, it is. Uhm. No! I mean, it's nice to meet you too. Sorry I'm a bit nervous."

"No need for nerves. I'm a big softie, but only after the first cup of coffee!" Marty chuckled. "Betsy at the Temp Agency told me you would be here today. Good you arrived before the door jammed. That would be the first test of the day!"

'*TEST!*' Pam thought, '*no one mentioned a test!*'

"Finish your coffee and we'll have a chat," said Marty, "and have the extremely chocolatey milk chocolate shortcake biscuits – they're scrummy."

Pam held the Espresso cup tightly after she left the stainless-steel saucer on the edge of the desk. "I'll save the biscuits for later, if that's okay? Had a big breakfast to boost my energy." Pam hoped the fabrication of the truth would not cause suspicion. Her breakfast composed of half a slice of toast with jam.

"Oh yes, most important and my favourite meal of the day, apart from the Linguine allo scoglio, in Bel Mare restaurant. Delizioso! The waiters are so friendly. Have you been there?"

"A couple of times. It's nice," Pam replied, hoping the focus of the conversation would shift to her CV.

"Anyway, best stop chatting. I have a client meeting at 11:00. Keeping everything crossed door will be open before then. Betsy says you have admin experience, worked in The City?

Pam hesitated, "yes, for Barclays Bank. I left in 2015 so am little rusty."

"No problem; we'll find the '*oil can*' to remove the rust." Marty improvised the character, the *Tin Man* in the film *The Wizard of Oz* and they both laughed.

"Here is my CV." Pam placed the document covered in a plastic wallet contributed by Martha.

"Thank you. I am sure it is fine," Marty replied nonchalantly.

"Betsy has your details and I have spoken to Daffy, oops, I'll be in terrible trouble, should say Daphine."

Pam's faced burned red with embarrassment and her line of sight diverted towards the flowers.

"There is no need to worry, we can overlook a minor indiscretion. We've all been there. Daffy showed me a photo of the young man - absolutely stunning, and, that hair, exquisite!"

There was an awkward silence.

"Right, let's start at the very beginning. Maurice typed some procedure notes. He's usually here two days a week but he's got a few relationship problems lately. Me and my big mouth! I shouldn't gossip. I've only got a couple of meetings today so we can go through the basics. In the meantime, just answer the phone in your most bright and bubbly voice and take messages. You'll be fine. Welcome aboard!"

Marty returned to his office and as he swept past, Pam sat in the Dress Circle of a theatrical production and delighted herself in the spectacle. The light scent of aftershave drew attention to the stylish costume; a dark single-breasted suit made of extra fine merino wool fabric with thin lavender pin stripes, a matching left hand pocket square arranged in four points – straight edge, complimented by a soft lilac shirt. Shimmering under the spotlight and taking centre stage was a silver tie with varying shades of lilac stripes and swirls. Shiny slicked back short black hair cut to precision. A manicured moustache was as magnificent as his eyebrows - shaped to promote warm brown eyes and long tinted eye lashes. The star of the show sparkled as did his whitened teeth and black patent shoes.

"Anyone in?" The voice called out from the top of the stairs.

"Yes, good morning," Pam looked up at the tall, dark, and muscular man. He carried a carpenter's old time wooden toolbox. "Marty, I mean Mr. Rhys is on the phone at the moment, can I take a message?"

"No, it's okay, I'll wait."

Pam looked confused, "if you don't mind me asking, how did you get in the front door?"

"Well, that's the beauty of being a master craftsman, can get through anything."

"Sorry, you're Robert?" asked Pam.

"Yes, Robert Niski, that's the name on the invoices, but people call me Bob the builder – wish they'd think of something bit more original."

"Like handsome man. NO! Sorry, I meant handyman."

"I'll take the first option any day of the week," said Robert. "You're picking up this dating agency work quickly!

Pam smiled nervously and thought, '*Stupid! Just think before opening your mouth. Why don't I listen to Martha's advice?*'

***

"GOT KETTLE ON YET?" Martha shouted as she put key in Pam's front door.

"You're such a task master!" replied Pam. "Got bread and jam?"

"Yes, otherwise won't have anything to eat," said Martha. "Bought chocolate biscuits for treat and food for Bea."

"She's so spoilt!" the green-eyed monster rattled within Pam.

"She's so tolerant!" Martha retorted. Bea jumped down from the blanket on the settee in anticipation of an alternative to bites of tuna sandwiches.

"Duvet Day?" asked Martha.

"No! Savin' my energy for later."

Martha hesitated but felt compelled to ask although realised it was a waste of her breath to object to the latest craze in Pam's tumultuous life. "Go on then, tell me what is happenin' later?"

"Can I borrow a leotard and leg warmers?" asked Pam. "Must have some hidin' at the back of your wardrobe."

"Yeah, in 1980s! Who wears leg warmers?"

"I joined the gym at beginning of April, you know, one next to cinema?" Pam prompted but there was not an immediate response. "First session with personal trainer this afternoon."

"Was it an April fool's joke?" asked Martha. "Wait a minute, how can you afford a personal trainer?"

"Special rates!" Pam winked at Martha.

"Alright, what's his name?"

"Sean Dekker, but he's called Sean-Paul, you know like the singer," Pam replied, and Martha shook her head.

"He's really fit! And he sings," Pam's sale pitch did not fill Martha with confidence and the repeated vicious cycle pulled away from the starting line.

"Couldn't care less if he's number one in the karaoke charts. Don't get entangled with Sean -Paul or whatever he calls himself. You're no gym bunny!" Martha tried the direct and sharp attack in desperation. She knew the inevitable rejection would hurt far more than strained muscles.

"He's goin' to Jamaica in July, for his cousin's wedding, never know, play my cards right or do enough gym classes and could have a free holiday out of it!"

"Give me strength!" Martha rubbed her forehead.

"He can get us into shape for the Race for Life" Pam tried to put a positive spin on the topic.

"What race!?" Martha exclaimed.

"You know, mentioned it while back. Getting forgetful in your old age," Pam quipped. "Anyway, not to worry, have signed you up. Be great fun!"

Exasperated with the suggestion, Martha asked, "I've got enough on my plate? Hope you're dragging Betty along?"

"Yep, she ain't getting off that easy. You two can toddle along at the back and I can sprint to the finish into the arms of my fit young man!"

"Puhh ..lease. Come down from that candyfloss cloud," said Martha. "Alright, if it keeps you quiet for a while, it'll be worth it. Good to raise funds for such a worthy cause."

"Wait til' you see the costumes - ordered them online!"

"Well, you can unorder them!" Martha retaliated as quick as a flash. "Official tee-shirt with leggings - that's my costume. Take it or leave it!"

Pam protested with a well-rehearsed pout. "Spoils sport! Such a frump. Thought sea air would blow away some of those grouchy cobwebs."

Martha handed Pam a white envelope, "here's money you asked for. It's for work clothes, right?"

"Of course," Pam replied, "really appreciate it. You're a star! Gotta keep up with Mr Glam.

"Who?"

"My boss," Pam explained. "He's like a model."

"How old is he?" asked Martha. "Surely, can't be that young to own a business?"

"Marty's 40 in July. He's party is in Whitstable Castle. Wow! Before you start lecturin' me. He's not interested in ladies in that way."

"Blimey Pam. Talk about old school! You can say he's gay – if that's what you mean. Ain't a crime. You better get up to speed with your diversity and inclusive training or you'll be out on your ear!"

"It'll be okay. Don't worry!" Frustration crept into Pam's voice, but it had to be restrained because she needed the zero-interest and zero repayment loan. "Only been there two days. Find my way round soon."

Martha teased, "he don't realise how lucky he is!"

"Shut up!" Pam poked her tongue out at her ally who she increasingly leaned on and relied on.

***

"Good morning, PierInn2U, Pam speaking, how can I help you?"

"Good morning! You are a new voice?"

"Yes, I am the new receptionist," Pam replied, "only started last week."

"If I may say, you are making an excellent start."

"Thank you, you're so sweet, NO! I mean, you are kind. Sorry! Can I take a message?" asked Pam.

"I take your flustering to be flattering. A nice start to my day. Please ask Marty to call me."

"Yes, of course. Could I have your name please and number?"

"I was hoping you would ask that! My name is Alexis Vasilantonopoulos and my mobile number is 07965 241777."

A scattering of indecipherable letters and numbers found their way onto Pam's notepad. "That is a lovely name," said Pam. "Could you spell it for me please?"

"I was born in Greece. It has a certain 'je ne sais quoi' but is a conversation stopper. Not many pronounce it correctly the first time or any time!" he laughed.

"Do excuse me, it's a bad line, and haven't woken up yet," Pam grimaced at her reply. *'Stop being silly -too much detail – just concentrate'* she thought.

"Up all-night partying?" Alexis provocatively made enquiries. He played her like a 'bazouki'(mandolin), and Pam danced to his tune which increased her stress.

"Sadly not," said Pam, "watched Eastenders on my own. Well, not really. Bea was sitting on my lap!" *'Just stop talking!'* she thought.

"Bea is very lucky!" Alexis teased.

"Yes. She's great company but her fur is all over my bed." Pam crossed into Flirtation Drive without using the Highway Code.

"I find silk sheets are easier to clean!" He sensed her embarrassment and stifled his laughter.

"Okay!" said Pam, "let me get a new biro, Always the way, run out just when you need them."

After three attempts at spelling his name correctly it was agreed the message would just be 'Alexis called!' "Good morning, good morning. Sorry for being late," said Marty. "Had to take Bouquay to my sister's. She isn't well. That's Bouquay not my sister! Couldn't leave her alone. She's got her favourite blanket, treats and lead but doubt if there'll any walkies today. Keepin' fingers crossed."

"Ah, poor thing. NO! I mean, poor Bouquay. Hope she's better soon." Pam cleared her throat and continued. "There is one message from Alexis."

"Alexis?" Marty looked perplexed.

"His surname is, uhm, excuse my pronunciation - Vaseline…"

"Oh, Alexis Vasilantonopoulos," said Marty. "Glad he called again. Daffy recommended us to him. She'll be askin' for commission." The confusion on Pam's face prompted Marty to explain, "He's the cousin of Summer Panayiotou. Did you work with her?"

"Yes. Summer's great fun," said Pam, somewhat annoyed she had not been told about the single cousin. "I told him we'd find him the woman of his dreams."

"You need to amend his record on the database," said Marty.

"Oh, I am so sorry. I thought, uhm, I mean. He sounded so.."

"Flirtatious?" said Marty. "Daffy warned me, he's mischievous. He'll be a star attraction!"

***

"Happy Birthday to you! Happy Birthday to you!"

"MUM! TELL HER TO STOP!" shouted Maddy from top of stairs. "Doin' my head in!"

"Wouldn't happen to be a hangover?" Pam smirked. "Anyway, what's wrong with my singing!? I could join the church choir?"

"You could not!" Martha snapped. "What is this? A competition to see who can make most noise?"

"What a lovely happy family home!" Pam's sarcastic comment heckled the band playing in Maddy's head and weighed heavy on Martha's shoulders.

"Alright to have a coffee?" asked Pam.

"Yeah, sure. Great idea. I'll have one," said Martha before calling out to her middle daughter, "do you wanna coffee? Aunty Pam's making them, and she's got biscuits!"

"Where's Philomina?" asked Pam.

"She's in Edinburgh," Martha replied. "She wants to be with her friends on her birthday.

"Friends!? Geeky university students more like it!" Maddy's bitterness towards her older sister's academic success continued to eat away at her. "Oh yeah and there's her special friend, Rune."

"Cheers, Maddy," said Martha. She subsequently looked directly at her confidante. "I'll tell you later."

Martha continued, "Face timed this morning. She's happy received our cards and presents."

Maddy pointed at Pam, "she ain't got your card. It's in kitchen!"

"Been busy, mixed-up dates," Pam muffled her apology out of resentment because she knew Martha bought and sent the card from Maddy.

"Busy doin' what?" Maddy chortled.

"Working!!" Pam stared at Maddy - her empty promises to find a part time work resulted in added strain for her mother.

"You gettin' on alright?" asked Martha.

"Think so, lots to learn. Made a few mistakes but Marty is patient, thankfully."

"You'll be fine," said Martha. "As long as you don't offend anyone and don't take client care to the extreme."

"What me! Wouldn't do that?" Pam winked. "Keep it polite and professional."

"Where you workin'?" asked Maddy.

"Receptionist for Dating agency, PierInn2U, near toy shop."

"Is it legal?" Maddy smirked. "Thought they'd gone out with the ark! You must fit right in. Waste of money. Just go online like normal people?"

"Some people still like to talk to another human instead of a screen," said Pam. "Marty offers a bespoke service. He's clothes are gorgeous, an' you should see his office? As Craig would say, "*A-MAZ-ING*! So, so, tempted to lie on, err., what's it called? Long settee, but probably fall off, ain't got sides and looks really expensive?"

"Chaise longue," said Maddy with a look of total contempt.

Martha, surprised at Maddy's pronunciation asked, "how do you, know that?"

"Do listen to some lessons at school," Maddy replied and looked at her mobile. "Gotta go!"

"Go with empty cups to kitchen first," said Martha. "I'm not your waitress!"

"I ain't a skivvy" Maddy snapped as she chucked the cups into the sink.

"How's Mick?" asked Pam. "Not brought him home for afternoon tea yet?"

Maddy stomped towards the front door and shouted, "Whateva!"

"Who's Mick?" asked Martha.

"It's okay - she just fancies him! Be bored by next week!" Pam tried to put the lid back on the can worms she had just forced open.

Maddy stood in the hall, out of sight but within ear shot. She sighed with relief however had no intention to thank Pam. It worked to her advantage, and she could weaponize it. *'Aunty Pam keeping secrets from Mum. Tut! Tut! That'll disturb the co-dependency, even for a jiffy'* she thought. Pam and Maddy had similar characteristics and weaknesses. But stubbornly and naively believed her mantra, *'My life will be completely different. I'm tougher and not going to make same mistakes and end up as a spinster!'*

***

'E.T.A. in 5 - Birthday Granny' Martha's text message did little to enthuse Pam to move from under the cosy duvet until she realised the full ashtray was still on the rustic, pine-effect, slim bedside cabinet. She shrieked, "Bea, move. Please MOVE!" Bea lazily jumped down from the bed and meowed for food. "In a minute, wait a minute!" Pam panicked and threw the contents of the ashtray into the garden and tried to cover it with cat litter. "Bea. Wait! Must wash my hands. Aunty Martha will be here soon!"

"She's here now!" Martha chuckled. "Bea, what's she been up to? C'mon Bea, spill the beans! No need to waste your energy, I can smell the evidence. Pam, when you gonna learn, it takes a bit more than a few squirts of Impulse body spray to disguise old ash. Talkin' of old, Happy Birthday Granny!"

"Ha! Ha!" Pam retorted. "Surprised Mrs Perfect Housewife has time to visit old friend. Anyhow, why you callin' me Granny, it's you're birthday in July an' we'll both be in the fifty-six club!"

"Don't remind me. I'll give you a birthday hug an' all out aches an' pains will go away!"

Pam was comforted by the affection and acceptance of her weaknesses.

"Go on, sit on settee, an I'll get breakfast or what us poor underlings call lunch!"

Pam yawned and stretched, "cheers. Ain't much in cupboard."

"Now there's a surprise!" Martha teased. "Lucky, I stopped off at Tesco. Look Bea, got your favourite biscuits, save you munching another tuna sandwich. I'll clean your bowl, that'll be a nice change."

"Wot you witterin' on about?" Pam groaned.

"Be careful. Don't bite the hand that feeds you!" Martha chortled. "May I show you the menu madam. Chef specials are toast an' strawberry jam with chocolate buttons for dessert. Would you like to taste the coffee first?"

"You on extra strong sweeteners or somethin' else?!" Pam grumbled. "I'm goin' get my slippers."

Martha did not make a comment about the crumbs falling over the sofa nor attempt to sweep them up. *'Don't say anything'* she thought *'turn a blind eye – it's her birthday.'*

"Maeve's made you a card an' fairy cakes with extra chocolate on top." Martha tried to lift the weight on Pam's shoulders.

"Say thanks will ya, she's so thoughtful. I'll have cakes later."

"Blimey, must be bad, if you're not eatin' cakes. Okay, what's his name?" Martha asked.

"Don't always have to be about men!" Pam snapped.

"You sure you're alright? Headache or grumpy granny syndrome?"

Pam looked dejected, "No.oo. No more work at PierInn2U! Maurice's been to marriage guidance or relationship counselling, whatever you call it! And he's patched things up with his better half, so he's refreshed and back to take his P.A. role from dizzy temp!"

"Right, stop feeling sorry for yourself. I'm not goin' to your pity party. Go an' have a bath, I'll tidy up an' you can come 'round to mine. We can have mid-week pizza and Maeve will love singin' happy birthday to you. Betty said she can make it next Friday, yes, it's Friday 13th but don't matter, we can go to wine bar. But in the meantime, we'll find you another job, even if it's volunteering for a while. Least it gets you outta bed!

***

The sprung door brass bell chimed around the shop, devoid of customers.

"Hello there," said Iris Stone, manager of the Cancer Research UK Charity Shop. "Great you could come into today at short notice. Haniah's had an emergency."

"Hope she'll be okay soon," said Pam.

"Her niece is in a Hospice. She battled through years of treatment, but her body is too tired. So sad. Her children are distraught. Their father passed away last year."

Pam's eyes brimmed with tears and was lost for words. Frightened to say something inappropriate and frustrated by the nonsensical extent of pain and loss imposed on one family.

Iris empathised with the dilemma facing Pam and said, "there are no words. We'll support Haniah the best we can. Think she finds coming in a temporary distraction." Iris took a deep breath, "Okay, right, best get on. We're only taking on volunteers at moment. Might be part time work later in the year."

"That's okay," Pam replied. "I've worked in a shop so when I saw your sign in the window last week, thought could help out for a while. Nice to chat to people."

"I might need you to work out back, some days; not much chatting there, I'm afraid, unless it's with the odd mouse or two!"

"Happy to muck in!" Pam's smile was subdued by the thought of mice as work colleagues.

"You can work on till today - I'll run through a quick do's and don'ts. I have to dress shop window, promotion for 'Race for Life' Should've got full stock in by now but there's been mix up with delivery. I don't know. Better off when we had horse and cart!"

"I've entered that with my friends. Can you keep 3 tee-shirts when they arrive, please?"

Iris sighed with exhaustion. "You'll have to remind me - brain like a sieve these days."

Pam tidied the rails closest to the till and re-arranged the jewellery in the glass display cabinets which had to remain locked after a spate of shoplifting.

Pam looked up as the bell tinkled and quickly tried to hide behind the card rack, but it did not turn as expected. Her agitation and awkwardness caused the stand to topple. A steadying hand reached out to stop it falling to the ground.

"Thank you so much," said Pam. "Don't want to wreck the joint, I mean, shop."

"You're welcome. Ah, hello again. Didn't know you work here?"

"It's my first day. Sorry do I know you?" Pam forced wrinkles on her forehead to falsify facial features to add gravitas to the red herring.

"Sorry, shouldn't have assumed you remember. Dog walking? Tangled leads? We had to free poor Ginger from corner of bench."

"Oh yes, of course. Got memory of a fish! How's, uhm, sorry forgotten her name."

"It's Bud and he's happy at home listening to Classic FM. It should be the Alan Titchmarsh show by now. And my name is Monty"

"Oh right, that's good." Pam bluffed her way through a conversation she did not want.

"I've brought in some donations. I have a gift aid card. Manager usually helps but she's busy. I'll wait and browse."

"You can leave the bag behind counter, if you want, she won't be long."

Pam peeped through the gap at the top of the white weekend bag filled with women's white polo shirts and blouses in various pastel colours; clean, ironed and neatly folded. Pam did not dare to ask the question rising to the surface. Something stopped her and unusually the filter mechanism in her mouth kicked in.

"PAM! Found a couple of Race for Life tee-shirts in back. Have a look, check the sizes and while you're there put the kettle on."

"Hello Mr Haye," said Iris, "how are you today?

***

The unmistakable 'potato-potato-potato' sound from the Harley-Davidson motorcycles rumbled across the sea front.

Pam, dressed in tight black leggings, black sports bra tucked tightly under a white cropped tank top with thin straps and a cut out on the back, ran towards the pedestrian crossing.

"Hello darlin' Are you late for something?"

"Just practising – keeping fit." Pam tried to catch her breath and look casual.

"Look pretty fit to me, special event?

"Race for Life, Sunday 26th June. Starts at 11. Be good fun and need the support."

"Cheers. Won't join in but be nice to watch if they're all like you."

"Cheeky!" Pam blushed and wiped the beads of sweat from her forehead with the palm of her left hand. "We're usually here weekends."

"Hadn't noticed!" The pretence from Pam's lips scrambled the delivery but she hoped they would not notice.

"Tell you what, meet you tomorrow and we go for a drink, take weight off your feet. Be alright with that? And then I can take you for a ride. Would you like that?"

"Yeah, sure, sounds fun. My feet will be pleased."

"I'll definitely be pleased. I'm Danny, what's your name?"

"Pam."

"Right Pam, see you tomorrow." Danny smiled broadly and winked as he lit up another cigarette.

"Yes, it's a date." '*NO!*' she thought '*Stop being so obvious*."

***

"You been smokin'?" asked Martha.

"No! It wasn't me."

"Who was it then?" The penny dropped. "What's his name? Surely, super fit Mr. P.T. don't smoke?"

Pam did not reply and asked, "Do you have leather trousers I can borrow?"

"Leather Trousers!?! Who do you think I am? Firstly, how could I afford them and how on earth could I fit into them without looking like an all-in wrestler? What are you involved in now?"

"You know the bikers by the sea front?"

"No, should I?"

"Well, Danny, asked me to go for a drink tomorrow," Pam giggled. "He's so good looking."

"And who are you going to be Sandy? Have a day off!" Martha's sharp reprimand introduced the questioning: "You must have black jeans? They'll do. You're not a biker chick. What if Sean sees you?"

"Bit of jealousy won't hurt," replied Pam in rebellion and in denial.

Martha did not rise to the bait and asked, "Do you wanna come in? Cooking roast potatoes and Yorkshire pud."

"Cheers. Better not, gotta watch my weight." Pam sensed Brian's disdain as he sat in the living room peering over The Sunday Times.

"Hope he's got a spare crash helmet if you fancy a whizz along the sea front and there's no other traffic on the road especially when you fall off!"

"Cheers for the encouragement. Love you."

Martha waved and called out, "Love you more!"

***

Strong rays of sunlight warmed the pebbles on the beach and bounced the light back up to the start line. A cloudless sky made a perfect backdrop for selfies as the runners assembled.

Lyrics from '*Busy*' by the artist Sean Paul rang out and hoots of laughter accompanied the attempts at twerking and twisting. "Don't even think about it!" Martha stared at Pam.

"You're such a spoilsport!" Pam moaned. "Sean is smashing the decks!"

"Can you translate that for me?" asked Betty. "I'm not down with the kids. Put on '*The Twist*' by Chubby Checker."

"Well, you old frumps can stay there, I'm joining in for a fun warm up. He'll make sure I'm okay and teach me some moves."

"Make sure your tutu doesn't get caught up with his headphones?" Martha giggled, "Bum bag – that weren't in video of '*Busy*' but never mind. You can show yourself up, oops, meant, show us what your made of."

"Where did she find that tutu? asked Betty. Thought we're all wearing tee-shirts and black leggings.

"From charity shop. She couldn't resist it, anything to stand out from the crowd. Although by the looks of DJ Sean, he's not impressed. That ain't a cool look for someone trying to attract the younger ladies. The sunglasses are shading her from the sun and reality. But do you think she'll listen to us."

"Nope." said Betty. "We'll just do some basic leg stretches."

Pam's exaggerated giggle could be heard over the top of the music. Her antics embarrassed Sean and he moved alongside a lady with long blond hair tied in a high ponytail with silk pink ribbon set out artistically. He held her hand to show off his skills as a dance instructor. Her hourglass figure moved rhythmically and mirrored his style. They soon drew the attention of the crowd. Pam envied the popularity, youth, and talent of the lady in the spotlight. She stomped off to the start line and chatted animatedly with a group who had co-ordinated fancy dress outfits. Her solitary appearance stood out, but her quirky humour made them laugh.

The escalating 'potato-potato-potato' sound from the Harley-Davidson motorcycles caught the attention of some of the runners and organisers who were startled by the group. "Good luck darlin'" Danny shouted. "Show 'em what you're made of!" Pam hollered, "Well, you know all about that!"

"I didn't hear that," said Martha as she covered her ears.

"Come on Betty, we'll go to the back with the walkers, Give us a chance to catch up, whilst speedy Gonzales breaks the world record for embarrassing comments."

"I'll order you drinks," said Pam. "By the time you finish, I'll be on my third spritzer after cool down with Sean."

"Blah, Blah, Blah," said Martha.

At the 2K mark, Pam stopped to regain her breath and have a bite of her finger tuna sandwich squashed into the corner of her bum bag. There was no desire for breakfast as she wanted to look slim and trim for her personal trainer. Unfortunately, the Seagulls tried to join in the snack break. They flew over her head and squawked in protest as she stuffed the remaining bread under her tee shirt.

"GO AWAY! GO AWAY! HELP!" Pam screamed as she waved her hands above her head. "Stop making so much fuss – makes them worse," said Danny.

"My Knight in shining armour. Shining Harley-Davidson is much better," Pam smiled with relief. "Are you staying – buy me a drink to celebrate?"

"Love to but we gotta go. See a man about a dog or is that seagull," Danny replied.

"See you another day?" asked Pam hankering for a positive response.

"Maybe, you never know your luck," Danny winked and said, "Go on – get back in the race. Never know might win first prize."

Pam stopped at the next water point and felt despondent. She dragged her feet.

"Don't give up," the group shouted in unison. "Come with us. It's great fun, good cause and can't let them down!."

Sun burn attacked Pam's nose and shoulder blades. She ordered ice with her Spritzer and found a corner of a bench to sit on. Sun sparkled on the water and reflected towards the shore. The *'I did it on medal'* was not an adequate consolation for the resentment as she witnessed Sean, ecstatic, as the lady with blond hair, tempted him with her *99 ice-cream*.

"There you are!" Pam exclaimed. "Thought you'd got lost."

"No. Best to take it easy, Ted wouldn't be chuffed it I pulled a muscle," Betty replied. "I've gotta run a house, not like you – a lady of leisure."

"Do you mind," Pam bantered with her long-term friend, "I volunteer at charity shop, keeps me busy for now."

Martha laughed, "But don't keep you outta of trouble, does it?"

"That'll never happen," said Betty, "always up to mischief."

"Yeah," said Martha. "What's the word? Ladette? Gift of the gab!"

"Blimey! I ain't that bad," Pam stared at them open-mouthed. "Right after those insults, you can buy me a spritzer and supersize it!"

"Is that man waving at you?" Martha directed her question to Pam as she flushed and looked down. "Another fan waiting for your autograph?" Betty teased.

"Looks as if he has a gift bag?" Martha asked as her curiosity was increasing by the minute. "I'll call him over."

"NO!" Pam shrieked.

"He doesn't look dangerous," said Betty, "and doubt if his dog is vicious."

" For goodness sake! " Martha turned in frustration and walked towards the lone spectator. "Sorry about this, she's not ignoring you; just dizzy after the run - so unfit! I'm Martha and that's our friend Betty."

"Nice to meet you. Pam talks about you a lot," said Monty. "I do not want to interfere but promised to buy a new lead for Ginger. Am afraid Bud stepped in front of me and we all ended up entangled in a bench. It was quite comical, but it damaged Ginger's lead."

"Thank you." Martha replied and could not resist asking, "So have you met Pam taking Ginger for a walk a few times?"

"Yes," replied Monty, "and we had a chat in the charity shop. Quite a feisty character but her humour brightens any day."

"Her bark is worse than her bite. Pardon the pun," said Martha. "I am not a comedian like Pam. Nice talking to you. You're welcome to pop in for a drink and biscuits - of course. There's enough space in the conservatory for Bud to stretch out."

"Thank you, that sounds a nice idea," Monty smiled. "Might take you up on your kind invitation. Bud loves all the fuss. That is a lovely big house Pam has on the Esplanade and it is great you live so close, near the garage, I think she said."

The muscles on Martha's jaw line tightened as she gave a restrained response, "Really!?!"

***

CHAPTER 15

Towels and tights fell out of the white laundry bag as Pam rushed into the launderette.

"Let me help you, s'il vous plait. That is, okay?" asked the young student. His shoulder length brown hair pushed back away from his face in the same casual style as his five o'clock shadow. Not slovenly but with an alluring demeanour.

"They always say, don't wash your dirty laundry in public," Pam tried to alleviate an extremely embarrassing situation with a joke as usual.

"Pardonnez-moi, I do not understand, my English is not too good, but I am learning."

"You speak better English than me." Pam then asked a tirade of questions, "Am I too late? Is there time for a quick wash? Shuts at 1 p.m.? I've forgotten my washing pods, wonder if they've got some? Have to use those for sensitive skin otherwise I'll go all patchy."

"Parlez un peu moins vite, please."

"What?" Pam tried to find 'Google Translate' on her mobile, but the battery had run out.

"Slow?"

"Ah, yes, sorry," Pam blushed. "Must wash my clothes today and it shuts at 1 O'clock."

"You're alright love," the assistant interrupted, "open until two on Sundays."

"Thanks, sorry, get so confused these days, must be the sea air." Pam hoped her feeble excuse would mask the fact that she had been to the launderette each Sunday for the last few weeks.

"Déjà vu? Yes?"

"Think so. Can't remember," Pam's pretence was holding strong, but she slipped on the final spin. "You're usually here earlier." She had to think of a distraction. "My name is Pam, nice to meet you."

"Je m'appelle Pierre Laver. Nice to meet you. Enchantée."

Pam, mesmerised by his gorgeous green eyes and desirable masculinity, stuttered, "Didn't recognise you without your glasses."

"Ah, yes, trying contacts? I do not see you with pretty dress. You wear jeans? Pardon, is this rude?"

"Oh, no! It's good, very good." Pam smiled and gave him the thumbs up. *'What are you doing?'* she thought.

"My jeans need a wash."

Pierre did not notice that there were no jeans in her laundry bag.

***

"At last! Where've you been? Why didn't you answer your mobile?" Martha's frustration boiled over.

"Been to launderette." Pam dropped the bag of revitalised clothes on her bedroom floor.

"Ooh la la!" Betty exclaimed. "You went to the launderette in that dress?"

Pam gave the excuse, "my jeans need a wash." But she knew Martha would see right through her fibs.

"So why are your jeans thrown on your bed?"

Pam called out to Bea as a distraction. "Forgot to bring 'em."

"And the truth is?" Martha asked sharply.

Betty's instinct kicked in quicker on this occasion. "And his name is?"

Pam knew she was cornered and replied reluctantly, "Pierre Laver."

"You've gotta be havin' a laugh," Martha chortled. "Do you know what laver is in English?"

Pam, tired of the teasing, whispered, "No.

"To wash. Even for you, that's classic" Martha laughed, and Betty joined in the banter, "the owner is French?"

Martha had repeatedly seen Pam's expression for decades and she asked, in anticipation of another quick high followed by a painful thump as she hit the floor of reality once the bubble burst, "how old?"

"Don't know. Bit rude to ask?"

"What does he do for a living?" asked Betty.

Pam murmured, "he's still studying."

Martha's face reddened, "Which University?"

"Hasn't started yet. He's nearly at the end of a gap year." Pam waited for the inevitable fall out.

"NO! Absolutely not." Martha shouted. "I've watched you get entangled with a mixed bag of men but not this time. Ain't being a cougar, it's cradle snatching!"

"You're such a drama queen," Pam snapped. "We're only havin' a laugh and helpin' him practise his English."

"Poor bloke. What's his family gonna think when he goes home with a cockney accent?"

Betty tried to diffuse the tension, "when is your washing machine going to be fixed?"

"Have called the man a few times, but think it'll be next month."

Martha butted in, "right, I don't care how much it costs find a new plumber this week!"

"Alright!" Pam moaned. "Like being back at school. Anyway, why you here?"

"We're goin' for a drink," Betty replied, "early celebration for Martha's birthday. I can't get here on Tuesday. We've had a lovely Sunday roast, thanks to Martha. Ted and Brian are talking about football or some sport, so we thought we'd go out for a couple of hours? We tried to contact you."

"Cheers, but'll give it a miss this time. I'll curl up on sofa an' have Weetabix and need to find the charger for my mobile."

"Yes, you do that," said Martha. "I'll give you a call later and will come around after Betty has left. You better be in here on your own."

"Why don't you just put a tag on me!" Pam's reply had a sharp edge.

"I'll see you soon, take care of yourself." said Betty. "I've changed Bea's litter tray and given her fresh food and water." Pam hugged her friend in appreciation and need for comfort.

"Have a good time. Don't get too drunk. Martha's gotta save herself for Tuesday. We'll chat later about outfits, make-up, and venues for our ladies night!" Pam smiled cheekily at Martha. She recalled the all-nighters at the clubs with rose tinted glasses. Youth had dissipated physically but mentally she was still a teenager and occasionally could persuade her lifelong friend to re-join the carefree days and fearless attitude because they were undeniably indestructible.

***

"M, how are you hun?" Pam asked in her most grovelling pitch.

"Alright, bit tired, nothing new. Are you okay, not in trouble?"

"No, thought give you a call to see if you're well."

Martha, seasoned in the routine, inquired, "what do you want?"

"Ouch, that's harsh," Pam replied. "Nothing. Just need to ask a favour."

"Go on," said Martha.

"You know tomorrow is your birthday?"

"Yes, all day," Martha enjoyed dragging out the awkwardness.

"You ain't makin' this easy," Pam stuttered. "You know we're supposed to go out. Is it alright if we cancel?"

Martha sniffled and play acted, "Go on, desert me, I don't care. Thought you loved me.

Two-timer." Martha reverted to the habitual question, "what's his name?"

"Renato," Pam surrendered the name immediately in hope it may soften the blow. "I'll call him, say can't go. He won't care, plenty other fish in the sea.

"Where did you meet him?" asked Martha. "Let me guess, *Molo Gelati* near the bandstand?"

"Ha, ha! Yeah, I was practising my duet with Sidney the seagull when our eyes met over a Knickerbocker Glory," Pam hid behind her comical shield. "Not quite so glamourous, Marty arranged it. I want to keep in his good books as there may be more temp work in September. And the thing is, Renato only gets one night off a week, he works in Bal Mare."

"At least you'll get a discount in the restaurant?" Martha laughed.

"No. Just goin' to wine bar. "He'll have a big lunch and I'll have extra toast and biscuits. He's fed up being in any restaurant. So sorry M, will make it up to you." "You certainly will," Martha quipped. "It'll be lovely to have quiet night in with Maeve. Maddy is staying over with a friend and Brian is workin' late so it's just what the doctor ordered."

Pam did not give into the temptation to mention Maddy's liaison with Mick, because she was in the middle of a delicate negotiation.

"You ain't seen Pierre?" Martha asked sternly.

"No, promise, pinky promise!" Pam crossed her fingers behind her back.

"Have a nice time with Renato. Don't spoil it. Just leave it at the front door. That's your door not mine! No more random men inspecting my house. Yeah?"

***

"Mummy, mummy, these are for you!" Maeve proclaimed with a burst of exuberance. Martha, delighted with the transformation in her character and clarity of speech although slightly too loud, smiled and said, "Thank you darling, that is very kind, but you gave me a card this morning?"

"These are special; Angela helped me." Maeve looked up at her wondrous mentor.

Martha expressed her gratitude because she had extra time to catch up with housework.

"Thank you so much for bringing Maeve home."

"You are welcome," Angela replied, "it gives us a chance to look at the Beach Hutches. Maeve likes all the assorted colours."

"Oh yes, there are new ones to look at today," said Maeve, "I know there are really called Beach Huts, but Aunty Pam likes to call them Beach Hutches."

Maeve nodded at Angela, and they knowingly shared the non-verbal mutual caution that Aunty Pam should not teach Maeve too many witty words.

"Would you like a cup of tea?" Martha asked.

"That is kind, but I better get back to Ginger, to give her tea and calm her down after all the excitement this afternoon."

"I hope Maeve has not been wearing you out?" Martha looked concerned but Angela radiated happiness "Oh no. I look forward to our time together."

"Thank you," Maeve hugged Angela. "I will bring my reading book tomorrow and finish the writing page."

"What shall we have for tea?" Martha asked as she helped carry the gift bags into the kitchen.

"Mash with sausages, please," Maeve's response had a postscript, "Aunty Pam says, Bangers and Mash."

"Can we open the cake, Mummy?"

"I am full, can we have the cake tomorrow?" Martha finished putting the plates in the dishwasher and then opened the vintage Tupperware round cake container with a carrier handle, and she remarked, "You have been busy, there are so many cup-cakes."

"Yes," Maeve replied, "we can keep them for other days. We can share with daddy when he is at home and save two for Aunty Pam. We can put extra chocolate on for her."

As the night time routine began, Maeve enjoyed her favourite *'Matey Bubble Bath'* and placed the rubber duck, named Hope, in the middle of the foam These were not an option when Maddy was at home because she mocked her for throughout the evening and the next day.

Refreshed and relaxed, Maeve folded herself into a long-sleeved vintage soft cotton white nightgown. "Come on, my angel, let's get you tucked up nice and cosy into bed."

"Oh, but mummy, you have not opened your surprises in your bag," Maeve keenly pointed to the door and her longing eyes prompted Martha to return to the kitchen. Whilst there, she put the dish washer on, checked the back door was locked and filled up the Tabitha's water fountain. Her house manager and caring motherly duties merged with an extraordinary ease but was often belittled by her husband and two eldest daughters.

"This one first, this one first, please," Maeve's excitement filled the room and Martha's heart because she witnessed a side of her daughter's character often overshadowed by torment.

"I'll open the envelope carefully, do not want to ruin the colourful design," Martha said as she revealed the gallery of decorative handwriting inside the card. "Beautiful, just beautiful."

"Angela allowed me to use Victor's fountain pen. It is very special, and she showed me how to use the ink bottle."

Martha did not want to focus too much on Angela's late husband therefore introduced a different view from a brighter corner. "I hope you did not spill ink on Ginger?"

Maeve giggled, "No, not this time. Ginger had to stay in her beauty parlour, I mean utility room, because she likes to jump up to look at the drawings. I think she wants to help but her paws are far too big to hold the pen."

The calligraphy was an artistry far beyond her years. The words 'Happy Birthday Mummy. Thank you for looking after me. A posy of love for you.' The letter M was distinctively different with swirls and curls wrapped around the text. Tears welled up in Martha's eyes but her expected spill of emotion took flight as Maeve's outburst startled her. "There's another gift in the bag, mummy!"

"I am so spoilt," said Martha.

A hand-crafted book filled with pages of drawings. It was bound with blue silk ribbon.

"Sweetheart, you are so clever! Look at these wonderful pages of drawings and paintings."

"Angela tied the ribbon, it is pretty. She is very clever. I hope I can be like her one day?"

Martha hugged her youngest daughter, "be the best of you and you will bring happiness to everyone who takes the time to love you. Now let's look at these pretty pictures."

Each page brought to life by paintings of flowers e.g., tulips, bluebells, dahlias, daisies. A single poppy filled the penultimate page, and the finale was a drawing of a small stone bridge over a rivulet in ancient woodland.

"Do you remember mummy?" Maeve asked anxiously.

Martha searched her memory bank vigorously; she did not want to upset Maeve. "I am sorry, please remind me."

"I will give you a clue, Pooh Sticks. Does that help?" asked Maeve with empathy.

"Yes, I remember now," Martha sighed with relief. "We were on holiday in Wales, enchanting scenery and you won!"

Maeve chuckled, "Your stick got trapped on a thorny branch. We had fun. Daddy stayed in the lodge. Where were Maddy and Philomina?"

Martha had to quickly think of reasonable excuses for a fractured family, "daddy had a bad headache; he had to sleep, Maddy had a grumpy teenager day and Philomina was in Edinburgh."

"Where is Aunty Pam?" asked Maeve.

"Uhm," Martha had to think on her feet because this was a question out of the blue. "With a friend." Martha hesitated, there was no point in making up a story because Pam would blurt out the pieces. "A boyfriend."

"Does she love him," Maeve was keen to find out why Pam was not married.

"No. Just friends having a nice evening together." Martha explained and hoped the description would quench the thirst for knowledge and asked, "we can read a bedtime story together, would you like that?"

"Yes, please mummy."

"You choose one," said Martha as she sat on the edge of the bed next to Owen, the barn owl, a plush character, and loyal companion who enjoyed a rare evening out of the vintage 1950s deep brown suitcase, with brass fittings, hidden under the bed. Free from Maddy; she revelled in hurling him against the wall.

Maeve looked through the bookcase chock-a-block with words of education and escapism from pain. "This one; Monsieur Hérit found it and sent it to Angela."

"Monsieur Hérit?" asked Martha.

"Do you remember when I told you mummy? His shop in Whitstable is a large treasure chest where you could get lost in memories. He is kind and funny; we laughed when he told us stories. Angela said I like books and he thought of me."

Martha, relieved there was not a connection to Pierre Laver, replied, "How kind. Ah yes, that is where you found the photo frame?"

"Can we go there one day with Aunty Pam?" Maeve asked with exuberant expectancy. "I do not think daddy will be with us?"

Martha managed Maeve's expectations in consideration of her wellbeing, "I'm afraid daddy is too busy, but Aunty Pam will love it and buying you an ice-cream." Martha sincerely hoped for Monsieur Hérit to be a mature man without chiselled features. It was bad enough listening to the latest addition to Pam's top ten but to put temptation in her path would be too much to handle.

"Can you read the story, please mummy?" asked Maeve as she yawned after an exhilarating afternoon. "The title *Grá* (Love)"

"Okay," Martha replied, "but I am not good at performing all the different voices."

Martha opened the delicate pages ruffled at the edges after decades of stewardship.

'Bridget and her daughter Mary finished the lace tablecloth with a grapevine and butterfly design.

"Now, what have we've got here," said Harry, the owner of the family business, manager of the shop, Craft Cravan, in Mainguard Street, near Eyre Square in Galway and head of the steady family of three who lived in the cosy flat upstairs. "That'll be sold in a flash," the proud husband and father announced.

"Come on young lady, we have to finish cooking the hearty stew," said Bridget. "Daddy needs a good meal after a hard day's work and before he meets Uncle Páraic (Patrick)."

"Mammy, when do we start on the wedding veil for Kathleen," Mary called as she finished drying the dishes.

"Now!" replied Bridget. "It won't be doing itself. She'll be in tomorrow asking Daddy more questions."

Bridget and Mary carefully set out the pattern and delicately started to sew the edges.

"Daddy will be walking you down the aisle soon," said Bridget beaming.

Mary blushed. "Mammy you know Niall is studying in Dublin. He will be a grand teacher. The letter he sends are like poetry."

"Keep them safe, he will be distracted when he's providing for you and the babies," said Bridget. "I'll give this to you now, treasure them. They were Nana's."

Mary opened the round musical jewellery box with flowers and a butterfly painted on the lid. Inside a Claddagh ring, two hands clasped a heart holding a ruby and a crown magnified the heirloom.

Mary cried with happiness. "Mammy, I can't. This costs the world."

"No, darling, our world is worthless without love." Bridget stroked Mary's hand and explained, "The crown represents Loyalty, the hands Friendship, the heart Love." Tears were wiped from their eyes not out of sadness but out of gratitude for a family filled with love.

"Now, you keep those safe with the letters from your fiancé."

Mary placed the antique gifts in the top drawer of her dressing table and read a letter from Niall as she looked in the mirror. "Dear Ily (a sweet name for I love you), I look forward to seeing you soon. Patience is the key to our future. Commitment sews our spirits together. Your heart beats in time with mine. Niall.x"

"The drawings are lovely," said Maeve. "They are a happy family. Can we cook stew?"

Martha tried to decipher the mixture of questions and answer appropriately, "Yes, it will be good fun to cook stew. I think it takes a long time so we will have to get an early start once we have all the ingredients. The artwork helps to understand the story, and the family are blessed with joy."

"Did your mummy read you bedtime stories?" asked Maeve.

"Yes, sometimes. She was busy." Martha felt a little melancholy.

"Did your daddy read bedtime stories?"

Martha answered with a definitive, "No." And she coughed lightly, "He looked after your uncles and met his friends. Too late for night time stories."

"Did he go out with special friends like Aunty Pam tonight?"

"No, my sweet, not like Aunty Pam. Your granny loved your granddad very much. She was his special friend," Martha hoped the explanation would satisfy Maeve's curiosity.

Martha brushed her daughter's black shiny hair until her eyes slowly closed.

"Sweet dreams," Martha kissed her forehead and prayed for a soothing sleep and for a resolution with regards the issues at the school. Martha refused to send Maeve back until the headmaster took the required action. Angela kindly gave lessons and Pam help with physical education as they walked with Ginger along the sea front.

Martha checked her ring box hidden under the shoe rack inside her wardrobe. Brian would not waste time looking around the bedroom and Maeve would not search in the bedroom without asking permission. Maddy occasionally looked in her jacket pockets for spare change to fund the next purchase of alcohol; thinking her mother was too naïve or too old to notice the difference. The claddagh ring was wrapped in the same pink tissue and she held in tightly before placing it back in its sanctuary.

Martha returned to the kitchen and felt guilty about the times she complained about 'boring' Brian and gossiped with Pam and Betty. But she was extremely grateful that he did not cause the disturbance her dad did when he returned from the pub. Her older brothers thought it was amusing and sometimes joined in with the singing. Pam hid under the covers with her teddy bear, 'Basil' who was an incredible comfort and an accomplished listener. Occasionally the loud noise turned aggressive, and her mum patiently made him coffee as she bore the brunt of the verbal abuse. Her brothers ran to their bedrooms when the volume turned up a notch and the air filled with blue language. Her dad was certainly a 'Jack the Lad,' a cheeky chappy with his mates and a ladies' man when the opportunity presented itself. Domesticity was a burden; did not suit his bold spirit but deep down knew he had to stay. The love for his wife was not romantic or visible but his devotion to provide for his family was deep rooted in old fashioned tradition. He regularly thought of leaving but where would he go? The house in South Croydon was the best of a bad lot and Daisy was a brilliant cook and his clothes were cleaned and ironed each day. Would be a tough act to follow especially with the fancy ladies who were more dedicated to their looks than housewife duties.

Martha cried discreetly, although there were turbulent moments, intermittently, during her childhood, she missed her mum and dad. How lovely it would have been for her children to have Granny and Grandad to share more Christmas, Easter, and birthday celebrations. Martha surveyed the large house, desperately in need of repairs as Project 49WB progressed at a snail's pace, with regret for moving but with resilience to battle on.

***

CHAPTER 16

"Come on! You're such a wimp!"

"I'LL GIVE YOU WIMP!" Martha shouted. "Ain't climbing up that slope with Maeve just to save five minutes. We're not in *SAS: Who Dares Wins*. We'll walk on the path and meet you in the park."

Pam's skirt caught on rose thorns, and she regretted taking the supposed quicker route. She tried to show off to Maeve and relive her youth when she ran around with Martha during their summer holidays.

Maeve look concerned, "aunty Pam, you have thorns and twigs stuck on you. Does it hurt?"

"Only hurt her pride," Martha chuckled. "Hope your skirt didn't cost too much coz there's a nice big hole in the back. Nice flowery knickers! Thank goodness you're not wearing the narrow ones."

"Thanks M, could you speak a bit louder. Don't think people in Wishym Bay heard you," said Pam. "Is your Mum embarrassing you Maeve?"

"Oh no, Aunty Pam, I think you are funny," Maeve replied without a hint of maliciousness. "I have safety pins in my rucksack and plasters just in case you scratch your finger."

"There's nothing like being prepared but Aunty Pam is never prepared," Martha nodded at Pam who stuck her tongue out in a silent protest as Maeve busily rearranged the items in her rucksack.

"Any more repairs?" asked Martha impatiently. "Can we now please go into the park before the sun sets."

"Just need to top up my lippy," teased Pam. It was met with a short, sharp reply, "See you there!"

Maeve was enthralled by the history of Reculver towers and looked intently at each information board. "Mummy, can I write notes please?"

"Yes, darling. I will sit on this bench and watch where you are," Martha replied with a hint of anxiety because more visitors arrived at pace.

"Looks much better," Martha quipped, "new trendy colour range? Invisible?"

"Least I make an effort," replied Pam, "when I remember make-up bag. Borrow your lip seal?"

"It'll cost ya!" Martha joked.

"Will this do?" Pam puffed up with pride as she pulled two mini bottles of white wine and plastic cups out of her threadbare black faux leather rucksack.

"What are you doin'?" Martha goggled at Pam in dismay, "don't you think I've got enough on my plate beside gettin' charged with drink driving and what a great example to Maeve. Her mother drinkin' a bottle of wine on a day out. Not in a restaurant or in a pub garden like civilised people but sittin' on a park bench!"

"Talk about over exaggerating," Pam grumbled "only half bottles and we've got cups. Sort of picnic; a liquid break. Maeve knows we're only jokin' around and bout time you got a new car, have a bump, and claim on insurance!"

"Just listen to yourself. Did you have a few extra double chocolate cookies for breakfast or is your brain mashed after the latest Romeo?" Martha, drained by Pam's non-sensical ideas, said, "we ain't got enough money to finish decorating the kitchen never mind a new car. Old Fiesta will have to keep going another couple of years. It'll be okay, don't go too far."

"What about Brian's new car, how much did that cost?" Pam protested at the inequality in Martha's life.

"He had to spend a bit of his redundancy on what he wanted," Martha justified the imbalance, "boys and their toys. Keeps him occupied when he ain't working."

Pam responded with sarcasm and steely hatred, "Bet Princess Penelope approves of the arrival of his executive Jaguar on her gravel drive."

"Don't remind me," Martha remarked with total contempt "it's Poison Pen's birthday next month. She probably wants a garden party or a state banquet. It won't be in my home! Ain't talkin' about her any more - not ruining our day with trivial trash."

Maeve waved at her mum and smiled broadly.

"Things any better at her school?" Pam asked hesitantly.

"No! Worn out tryin.' Had meetings with headmaster even Father O'Clery spoke to him but nothing. Mind you, she's doin' much better out of school. Summer holidays startin' soon but can't keep her at home in September, I'll have authorities on my back."

Pam interrupted with a well-rehearsed comedic timing, to lighten the load, "Maeve has the best P.E. teachers money could buy. Ginger and me are great motivators and improve her vocabulary."

"Like Beach Hutches?" Martha smiled again.

Maeve studiously continued to add historical facts in her notebook, adorned with wild meadow flowers cover design, and patiently waited in a queue, unlike a few rowdy boys pushing forwards.

Martha stood up and frowned with the intention to pull the boys away.

"Hold on," said Pam in an unusual sober assessment, "give her a chance."

Maeve assertively kept her space in the queue and held a serene expression.

Martha turned towards Pam, astonished at the transformation in Maeve's character albeit not consistent.

"Mummy, can I draw the two towers?" Maeve asked without distraction or distress after her encounter with her hostile peers.

"You can draw a picture of me?" asked Pam in her best jovial tone followed by a protective enquiry, "do you want me to speak to those boys?"

"No thank you, Aunty Pam, they are just silly and did not make any notes," Maeve replied. "I can draw you at home by the sea with Ginger, she will make an excellent model."

Martha chortled. "Well, you did ask!"

She looked at her watch and said to Maeve, "It is nearly lunch time, so can you sketch, please. Aunty Pam can take some photos, can't you Aunty Pam." Martha nudged Pam who was distracted by a teacher counting all the pupils in his care.

"What? Yes, wait a minute, can't find my mobile! Hope I ain't lost it," Pam panicked as her mobile was her life, so she thought, and told everyone who would listen. "Must've dropped it in your car?"

"I'm not goin' back to the car park just to look for your mobile which is probably in the same place as your lipstick!" Martha snapped.

"I know." said Maeve, with an unrecognisable mischievous expression, "Call your number, and Bea will answer."

"Thankfully, I remembered my mine," said Martha, "and portable charger."

"Please take photos, mummy," Maeve asked as clouds slowly moved across the towers limiting the visibility of the idyllic reflections in the sea.

"Yes, of course and when I've finished, Aunty Pam would love to take pictures of you and me?"

Pam knew it was a demand more than a question and intervened, "and then we can start on the selfies!"

"No selfies!" Martha dampened Pam's over enthusiasm.

"We need one of those silly selfie sticks things, otherwise you'll get the top of your head and my nose."

"Okay!? I get the picture!" Pam laughed. "Be alright to put 'em on Facebook later? Fun to show our day out, won't it?"

Martha replied as quick as a flash. "No! Next question."

Martha, acutely aware Maeve was not interested nor comfortable with social media, unlike her two older sisters who were addicted to the number of likes, followers and watching endless videos on YouTube. She did not want their day out to be an endurance rather than an experience.

Maeve veered the conversation to a different direction, "Mummy, can I come here with Angela?"

"Such a nice idea, but we need to consider there are uneven surfaces."

Maeve's reply surprised and embarrassed Pam to a level she could not jump from. "Can we ask Monty? He can help Angela and he likes talking to Aunty Pam."

Grinning like a Cheshire cat Martha said, "Really?" Followed by a few lines of the song '*Summer Nights*' from the film Grease. "Tell me more, tell me more. Like does he have a car?"

"Your mummy is being really silly now, let's go for lunch," Pam held Maeve's hand, more to support her footing and escape the embarrassment than to assist her honorary niece.

The cafe near the Caravan Park wore age admirably.

"Can't believe it is still here!" Pam gasped. "It ain't changed."

"The prices have changed, unfortunately," Martha replied before taking the orders for lunch, "what's everyone having?"

Maeve replied, "I will have my sandwiches in my rucksack, thank you. Do you want to share with me, Aunty Pam? I know you usually share with Bea."

Pam thought, '*is there anything this young girl misses? She must have CCTV installed in my home.*' "Bea has been telling T.A.I.L.S."

"No, Aunty Pam, the correct spelling is T.A.L.E.S. You are funny." Maeve giggled.

"She's not funny, she just can't spell!" Martha stared daggers at Pam: their telepathic communication signalled, '*stop encouraging my daughter to spell and pronounce words incorrectly!*'

"Very kind of you, sweetheart, but I am sure mummy will be only too delighted to share her lunch with me?" Pam's statement overtook the misinterpretation.

Pam found a table located outside in the best sunbathing spot. Maeve untied the fine cream string wrapped around the brown sandwich paper.

Pam sung the words, "Brown paper packages tied up with strings, these are a few of my favourite things." Maeve covered her ears. "Aunty Pam, we can ask Angela to teach you to sing, she used to be in the church choir."

"Ginger likes my singing," replied Pam, "the best talent judge of all. Do you know which film the song is from?"

"Yes, Mary Poppins," Maeve's face lit up but quickly saddened, "I gave daddy, a hardback copy of the novel Mary Poppins for his 60th birthday, but he did not like it. I rescued the book for my bedroom collection."

"Your daddy overlooks the gems in front of his eyes," Pam replied as she gently touched Maeve's arm.

"Cheese and tomato toastie – acceptable for you, my lady?" Martha bowed in front of Pam.

Pam asked, "Do I have a choice?" and received a blunt response, "Nope!"

"No sugar for my coffee?" Pam complained.

"Patience, patience," Martha replied as she pulled two sachets from her jacket pocket.

Pam pointed at Martha, and re-enacted grassing to the teacher, "silly mummy forgot your drink. What would you like?"

"You are kind, but my carton of apple juice and bottle of spring water are in my rucksack. Mummy said I may have another drink later."

Martha looked at her playmate, turned tell-tale, with a smug smile.

Maeve placed one of her navy-blue paper serviettes adorned with small golden crowns on her knees, and the other on the table after she wiped the surface with her water fresh hand & face antibacterial wipes. She looked towards the sky, "A lovely sunny day, just like the Royal Wedding on 29th July 1981 but it was a Wednesday not a Friday."

"Who got married?" asked Pam, "can't remember. How old was I then? Twenty-one. Can't believe it! What has happened to all those years?

Maeve conveyed history with glee, "His Royal Highness Prince Charles and Lady Diana Spencer. A beautiful big dress but a little wrinkled once unveiled from the Glass Coach. Lady Sarah Armstrong-Jones, the chief bridesmaid, helped smooth the train which was 25-feet long.

The minutia of detail and vocabulary confounded Martha and Pam.

"'A fairy tale - The Prince and Princess on their wedding," Martha almost quoted the actual words of The Archbishop of Canterbury. An attempt to strengthen the bond with her daughter.

"A sad end to the fairy-tale," Maeve's gaze sunk to the floor.

"Yes, darling, very sad," replied Martha, hoping the memory would not blight her daughter's mood. "Shall we think of happier moments and how we can enjoy today?"

Pam clowned around, "I know, ice-cream! If your mummy behaves, I may even buy her a 99. What do you think?"

Maeve's frame of mind lightened and replied, "Double 99 for mummy. Please can I have Black current ice-pop?"

"Comin' right up, madam." Pam skipped to the cafe, showcasing all the fun at the seaside. The return trip, quite literally was a trip, resulted in one ice-cream unintentionally decorating the path with a white scatter rug: not a complimentary colour scheme. The customers roared with laughter and shouted, "YAAY!! Encore! Encore!"

"What are you goin' to have for dessert?" asked Martha rhetorically. Pam resorted to the predictable pout.

Martha responded, "Okay then, we'll share! But I'm havin' the flakes."

Maeve placed her serviettes over the ice cream as it sloped towards the grass verge and took tissues out from her ruck sack.

"Please do now worry, sweetheart," said Martha, "the waiter is here with a mop."

Pam's pupils dilated as the young, stunningly handsome man with a tan smooth complexion, crystal blue eyes and scintillating blond hair, attended to the spillage with vigour.

Martha recognised the signals and pinched her arm.

"OUCH!" Pam squealed "What was that for?"

Martha shook her head and mouthed "No." An impassioned plea for Pam to put a stop to her fantasy.

Pam's face reddened and frowned, but accepted, in the presence of Maeve there should not be this type of distraction.

"Let's go an' have a look around the Caravan Park?" Pam suggested and hoped her fellow tourists would agree.

"We haven't got a booking," Martha replied, "we can't peep into windows. They'll call the police."

"On go on, M, let's see if our caravan is still here?"

Martha tut-tutted and replied, "Don't think it would have survived the wear n' tear and rust of 40 years."

"Dunno?" said Pam, "you ain't done so bad!"

"Maeve, what are we going to do with Aunty Pam?"

Her young mind pondered the question. Abundantly astute on their day trip, Maeve replied, "I know! Aunty Pam can go in first and if anyone calls the police, they will take her away?"

Martha burst out laughing, "Get out of that one, Aunty Pam."

"You're ganging up on me now, it's just not fair!" Pam shuffled her feet in frustration.

Pam suggested, as a compromise, at the first sign of trouble, they would leave immediately. Not running but a quick march.

An empty space replaced their bygone holiday adventures. Pots of pansies, freesias, and sky-blue asters rested on the freshly mowed grass. An eclectic mixture of garden gnomes guarded the white rectangular plastic table and matching four chairs: one with a wheelbarrow, another sitting on a sphere holding a welcome sign, a patient fisher and a gentle soul reading a book.

"What have they done?" Pam shrilled.

"It's called progress. Keep up," said Martha.

Maeve, fascinated by the background of the summer holidays, asked Pam, "Did your mummy stay in the caravan?"

"No, Aunty Daisy, well, not my real Aunty," Pam chuckled as she used Maeve's description, "Your grandmother took your mummy and me on holiday a few times. Not every year otherwise she would have worn herself out. One week was far more than enough with the terrible twins!"

"You speak for yourself," said Martha. "Didn't your mum come here for her 16th birthday?

Mum told me about holiday with dad to get rest from my rowdy brothers.

Your Aunt was there. Uhm, what was her name? Can't remember. Anyway, think she paid for your mum as a birthday present?"

"Yeah." Pam replied. "Think Gran paid something; she didn't have much money but would've spent her last penny to get my mum from under her feet for a week."

Increasingly confused by the different relatives, Maeve asked Pam, "Did your daddy stay in the caravan?"

"No, sweetheart, he was too busy." Pam veered carefully away from a delicate topic she did not want to impose on Maeve. "Your daddy is busy too, but he always has time to eat your yummy cup-cakes."

"Hello ladies, can I help?" asked the Caravan Park manager.

"No, uhm, I mean, thank you. We're okay," Pam stumbled through a reply. Martha took over to explain clearly, "Please excuse us, we apologise if we are making a nuisance. We are taking a walk down memory lane, we used to stay here for our holidays. We think this is where the caravan used to be."

"What year you talkin' about? I've been in charge for nearly 40 years," said the manager.

"Early 1970s," Martha replied.

"I'm not that old, but look ancient after dealing with all the customers, present company excepted, of course." Laughter broke the awkward conversation.

"My old man was manager then. I learnt the trade from him, followed him around everywhere, used to drive him mad. He didn't take any nonsense from punters, much tougher than me."

"Sorry, forgot to introduce ourselves, my name is Martha, this is my friend Pam and my daughter Maeve."

"Good to meet you, my name is William but call me Bill, everyone else does. Dad made a few changes before his retirement; only had two years putting his feet up, bless him, before he 'checked out.' Thank goodness it was quick, he hated hospitals. Blimey. I'm rambling, been up since five, fully booked for summer holidays, getting everything ready. The band were rehearsin' this morning, scared the seagulls and I've got a splittin' headache. Where was I? Oh yeah, dad made a bit more space, people complaining they were in each other's slippers. Kept this area, the gnomes are popular, we usually get a few new ones each year and a few take aways if you get my drift. Some will take anything if it's not nailed down. So, I'm afraid ladies, you've missed the boat, so to speak."

"Thank you," said Martha, "we won't keep you."

"No problem. Tell you what, take the weight off your feet and I'll get my grandson to bring you drinks. We'll stretch to crisps if you're lucky. White wine? Not for little one, don't wanna start her gettin' into bad habits."

Pam's face lit up, "Cheers!" Martha responded, "soft drinks for me and Maeve, please."

Bill set off but turned to say, "think I've got old photos in office, if I find them, will bring them out to you."

"Please do not trouble yourself," said Martha to be polite, and hoped it would not dig up rotten roots, difficult to explain, and painful to prune.

"Mummy, please can I draw the caravan with the chimney?" asked Maeve enthusiastically.

"Yes. We'll be watching, please do not go out of our sight," Martha pleaded with her daughter.

"Be careful, there may be a giant gnome on the other side," Pam chuckled but Martha nudged her, not amused, and worried her daughter's anxiety may take over.

"Do not be silly Aunty Pam," said Maeve with an amiable expression, "gnomes are tiny. You have a big, giant, imagination." Martha laughed loudly, Maeve smiled, and Pam eventually surrendered to the banter.

Pam sipped the chilled wine and Martha used the multi-colour striped flexible straw to drink from the bottle of Diet Coke. Maeve enjoyed her 7UP through the blue and white striped bendy straw. Martha expressed her apprehension, "Hope she'll be alright with a fizzy drink, she doesn't normally have one."

"Oh, stop worrying," said Pam, "she's tougher than you think. She's a very lucky girl to have a mother who loves her to pieces."

Martha welcomed the compliment, "Great I can spend time with her. Busy is an envied status symbol these days, and welfare of children is moving down list of priorities, beneath anti-social media. Good old days weren't that bad, were they?"

"Yeah, sometimes," Pam said with a heavy heart. "Didn't know what to tell Maeve about my dad. Do you think it was alright?"

"Best we can say for now," Martha felt sympathy for her *'fidus Achates' (faithful friend and devoted follower)* who was never told the name of her dad. "Maeve knows your mum passed away a long time ago, so told her your dad passed away few years later. What can we say? She ain't asked more questions, but she looked confused earlier, so I know she'll draw a family tree. She's curious, not in a nasty way, but likes to understand."

"Know how she feels," said Pam. "We'll have to make up a name and keep to the same story and tell Betty. Maeve is super clever so will notice gaps or differences. Horrible to lie to her but will explain in a few years."

Martha nodded in agreement, "Maddy and Philomina are not interested, and Brian wouldn't care if he was the 7th Marquess of Wishym Bay."

"Ooh! What would that make me?" asked Pam. "Posh!" Martha replied.

Pam smiled to hide her sadness, but Martha could see straight through the pretence.

Bill found a few black and white photos which included one of Aunt Ena, Gillian, Jack, and Daisy. They had two caravans with a low white picket fence between them.

"He's a good-lookin' chap," said Bill, "with the two beauty queens. One at the end looks as if she's sucking a lemon."

"That's my aunt, Ena," Pam explained, "and there's my mum." Martha pointed to her dad and mum.

"Here I go again," said Bill, "puttin' my foot in it. She don't look like any of you so thought she was photo shooting?"

Pam sniggered, "it's photo bombing. She weren't a real aunt, long story, won't bore you to sleep."

"Ain't got time for sleep," Bill replied, "my grandson can get you a copy, he's a whizz on techie stuff, I can't even use the remote with these fancy channels, films and sports and goodness knows what else. Better when we only had three channels, and the National Anthem at end. None of this all-night news on the TV. Good old days."

***

The wedding suit fitted comfortably, and Jack's ego inflated as his hands gripped tightly around the waists of his wife Daisy and her best friend, Gillian, who eagerly anticipated the evening out for her 16th birthday.

Daisy wore a princess styled knee length pink dress; Gillian squeezed into a shimmering ice blue pencil dress. Ena, annoyed Daisy dared to wear the same colour, adjusted the contrasting purple sash belt on her sleeveless, silk, wiggle, pencil style dress and sharpened the outfit with kitten heels. She paraded a diamond ring, falsely promoted to be the engagement ring she craved. Ena refused to accept the status of spinster. Marriage and children passed her by and therefore envy darkened her connection with the beautiful, easy-going, delightful Daisy. Rank resentment ripped through her reasoning because Daisy had scuppered her plans as a self-appointed matchmaker. The aim was for Jack and Gillian to be married and Ena liked to get her own way, no matter who she trampled on in the process.

Gillian, filled with elation, grabbed the offer to go to the seaside for her 16th birthday especially with her best friend. Daisy enormously appreciated her mother's willingness to care for her sons, Bobby, aged eighteen months and Alfie, six months, who exhausted her from tip to toe. Jack, frustrated, his wife had deserted the marital bed for their two children, welcomed the opportunity to rejuvenate his marriage and claim his right as a husband.

Gillian's mother begged Ena to take her out of the house for longer than a week, but it did not fit into the coercive jigsaw.

Ena Able adopted the title of aunt to detract attention from the disturbing link with the family.

***

Albert Burtin, Jack's father, was engaged to Ena in 1935 and succumbed to her demands to marry. He bought the silver-plated engagement ring, with a tiny Cubic Zirconia stone, a poor substitute for the 'stunning rock' (diamond) Ena wanted. He asked her mother's permission because her father was detained at Her Majesty's pleasure i.e., in prison. Albert booked the Croydon Register Office. He did not dare ask the priest of the local church because Ena had a widely publicised reputation. He felt trapped but obliged to fulfil the promise made to Ena's mother who was wilted by paying the bills and hiding her husband's wayward behaviour from her family in Dublin.

Albert turned up late for the ceremony on Tuesday 13th August 1935 and Ena's heart sank with anxiety but her determination to get married strengthened her resolve. He apologised profusely to the Registrar. Ena's mother read the signs of trepidation.

'Why isn't he smiling?' Ena thought, 'Probably just nerves?'

The Registrar started the proceedings. Albert exclaimed, "Can't do this, can't do it."

Ena screamed and slapped his face repeatedly, until Stanley, the only other witness who was a lifelong friend of the beleaguered bridegroom, pulled her arms down.

"YOU COWARD! CALL YOURSELF A MAN, YOU'RE PITIFUL!

"Sorry" he whispered and repeated, "can't do it." He looked at her mother and she nodded, not out of anger but acknowledgement her predictions throughout the years, 'no one will put up with her' had come to fruition. Her eyes looked towards the exit, and silently directed him to leave.

"YOU CAN HAVE THIS BACK! ENGAGEMENT RING? IT'S CHEAP TRASH. GO AND SPEND YOUR MONEY ON BEER AND YOUR BIT ON THE SIDE! I NEVER WANT TO SEE YOU AGAIN. GET OUT!

Albert had not two timed her but upon reflection he could not commit to a woman with a fiery temper and rancour in her heart. The previous men had taken the remains of her self-respect, strip by strip. He saw her as a challenge initially and she love-bombed him with lavish attention and gratification of his marital rights before their engagement. Albert felt ashamed for giving into temptation, but it was offered on a plate, and she told him when they married, he would never be second best even when they had children; he would always be number one. Albert was lonely and she preyed on his weakness.

For Ena, another rejection was soon smothered with another man. But there was a significant difference this time because within nine months of the Register Office debacle, Albert married a popular, beautiful girl without a past, in All Saints Church in Sanderstead on Saturday 2nd May 1936, attended by her family and members of the community. The bride's elderly father suffered a stroke three years prior to the wedding but the purposeful stride of a proud parent accompanied his only child down the aisle, and gave her away with a hint of sadness, but reassured Albert would take care of her. Susan's grandmother paid for the elaborate elegant reception at Coulsdon Manor which presented the charm and character of a luxury country house hotel. Her close-knit family sat under the stewardship of a feisty matriarch: Grandma Nora. Although, some were more interested in the content of her bank account rather than a genuine interest in her health. Albert's family fractured after his father was killed in World War I. His mother disowned her children; did not want a connection nor reminders of her husband. She moved to Liverpool to live with her great aunt. Stanley's parents took in Albert and his siblings were adopted by a couple who subsequently relocated to Wales to work in a family business.

***

Every detail of the wedding was delivered to Ena in Alfonso's Hair Salon, in Croydon, by one of her regular customers who worked in Coulsdon Manor. Ena kept an overtly keen interest in Albert's marriage.

Jack was born in January 1937, a honeymoon baby, and his brother, Leonard was born 1939. Albert and Susan cherished their stable family life and their love for each other deepened.

Albert and Stanley willingly served King and Country as they set off for duty in 1939.

Susan and the children stayed with Grandma Nora in Castle Combe Village in the Cotswolds.

PTSD (post-traumatic stress disorder) knocked Albert off balance once he accepted Stanley would not be a part of his life again and the horrific circumstances of his death. The quintessentially English village, in an area of outstanding natural beauty in north west Wiltshire, sheltered him. A period of convalescence, in the idyllic setting, abated the nightmares which worried his wife and children. Grandma Nora extended an open invitation to stay but Albert knew it was important to get back to work and settle the children into a school near their home. His decision was supported by the unwavering loyalty of his wife.

***

Susan rendered her time in service to the church family of All Saints in Sanderstead in addition to the voluntary work at the community centre in Croydon. Ena invited herself to the autumn jumble sale and dragged her friend, Doris Docker, more of an acquaintance at the bingo hall.

Ena bought a silver-plated necklace inset with cubic zirconia stones releasing a long sleek shine.

Ena asked, "Is there a mirror? Nice to see how it looks."

"Yes," replied Susan, "I'm sure there is a hand-held mirror in the office." She recognised Ena, however, rooted in the

Christian Faith, forgiveness was forefront in her mind. She sought absolution for herself in prayer and empathised with Ena.

***

Ena explored options how to socialise with Susan. Bingo was not on the list. One of her customers mentioned the upcoming nativity play. An opportunity to volunteer at the church and with preparations inside the school. Ena was completely out of her comfort zone but motivated by bitterness.

Doris's daughter, Gillian, served a purpose which proved to be successful. Ena used as a ruse to inch her way into close connection with the Burtin family.

The other parents greeted the six-year-old with care and concern due to her fragile frame and tattered clothes.

Susan shared their concern and gave Gillian a woollen scarf and a cup of hot Ribena, and asked, "Would you like to sit with us? My sons are in the play and need lots of encouragement and applause."

Ena nudged her pseudo companion, "That'll be nice, won't it Gillian?"

The rising stars soaked up the applause and took a bow and they received a standing ovation. Susan looked at Gillian, "Did you enjoy the play?"

"Yes," Gillian replied, "don't know story but like songs."

"We have a book all about the first Christmas. Would you like it? Your mummy can read it as a bedtime story."

Ena stared at Susan in silent reproval and shook her head in response to the projected insensitivity. Gillian stared at the floor, there was no reply nor reaction.

The awkward glances between Albert and Ena were followed by equally stinging small talk.

"Sorry to hear about Stanley," said Ena.

"Cheers," Albert replied as he fought back the tears. "Terrible loss but he sacrificed his life for all of us."

Susan hopped in with an ice-breaker, "look, here they are, our superb actors!"

Albert ruffled their hair and the two boys felt embarrassed and nudged their dad.

Ena looked towards the Christmas tree and the modest multi-coloured glass baubles flickered in the candle light. Her reflection on the past was fragmented by Susan, "this is Jack and here's Leonard, or should I say Len, hiding behind his big brother as usual."

"Mum! Don't." A collective grumble prompted their mum to get ready to leave.

"No sister to keep you in order?" Ena's enquiry pierced the cautious conversation and Susan's heart. She called upon her spiritual strength, took a deep breath, and replied, "sadly no. We have our hand's full, with these two lively young men, they're 12 and 10. The years fly past. But we are blessed they are healthy, but a bit noisy, at times."

Albert ushered his sons towards the door as he knew the entente cordiale was fading fast.

"Goodbye, Gillian, hopefully see you again soon," said Susan. "We're making Christmas decorations at the community centre next week. Would you like to join us?" The attempts to make eye contact with Gillian were futile.

Ena returned the scarf and instructed Gillian, "say thank you!"

Susan looked at the child shivering, "you keep it, please, as a gift. Do you have to walk far? Quite chilly now."

"Be alright, her mum'll be here soon. Her friend's got a car, ain't gotta a clue how he can afford it."

Gillian's mother did not turn up, so Ena brought her home. A regular pattern during the next few months and years.

***

Albert worried about the increasing amount of time Ena spent with his sons. Gillian loved being with Ena because it was far better than being with her mother. Jack and Len liked Ena's sense of humour and robust character. The entanglement of friends extended to more events and encounters.

'Surely, Susan would spot any danger signals,' Albert thought, 'Ena will soon get bored and return to the pub.' Guilt muddied the waters of his instinctive disquiet. His work as a builder on the post war big project; constructing the new town of Harlow, resulted him staying away frequently. He stayed in bedsits with his workmates. Not much time for sleep nor travelling. Jack and Len were becoming increasingly boisterous and rebellious. Susan struggled to impose discipline on two strapping teenagers therefore she told her husband Ena's intervention eased the lid off the pressure cooker. Albert did not want to disbelieve his devoted wife and did not want to stop the development of the bond with Ena. but something was niggling at the back of his mind.

***

Ena tried to manoeuvre Jack to contact Gillian, but Daisy stole his heart at a St. Valentine's dance held in the Community Centre, in 1957. Jack, egged on by his friend in the band, asked Daisy for a dance and the rhythm sealed their fate.

Jack tolerated Gillian being the gooseberry and was flattered to have two women following him around. He compared Daisy's pretty features with the allure of Gillian, a temptation for most men.

Ena fervently hoped Daisy would wither however she blossomed.

***

Ena introduced the idea of going to the seaside for a week and promoted how much fun it is staying in caravans. She invited Jack and Daisy because it was clear the new parents were overburdened, and she championed the mantra 'a change is as good as a rest.'

Gillian and Daisy excitedly and endlessly talked about outfits and swimwear although Daisy focused on her distorted body image of a '*mummy tummy*' and dreaded the thought of a swimming costume. Gillian promised to bring a bag of make-up - broken rejects from the Woolworths stockroom, courtesy of her mother who worked as a shop assistant. Daisy's mum paid for an extra-large caravan to help the shattered married couple to relax. Ena managed to book the adjacent compact caravan: cosy but suitable for their needs.

Squeals of excitement emanated from Daisy and Gillian. A first holiday by the sea for Gillian and the first break since her honeymoon, in Margate, for Daisy. The sunshine, and a sky clear from the clouds and fumes in London, heightened their mood.

"Blimey, ain't goin' be like this all week?" Jack's grumpy tone matched the taut facial expression. "Doin' my head in!"

"Come on Jack," said Ena, "I'll treat you to fish'n'chips and a pint or two. Let them do 'girlie' things, they'll be yappin' all afternoon."

Daisy and Gillian, the early birds, sat outside each morning with coffee and toast, gossiping about the previous evening in the club house, and how the men were gawping at Gillian.

"Let's go to the beach today," Gillian suggested with anticipation, "have to show off my swimsuit."

"I'm not sure," Daisy replied hesitantly. "You've got a figure like a model, I'm all out of shape now, bit lumpy. Jack doesn't seem interested; you know!?"

They both sniggered. "Don't be silly, "said Gillian, "you and Jack looked cosy dancing whilst I was sittin' on my lonesome."

"Jack had a dance with you earlier," Daisy tried to cheer up her friend.

"Yeah, but he just took pity on me," Gillian pouted.

Daisy and Gillian paid for deckchairs on the beach and dipped their toes in the sea. Gillian tripped and Daisy grabbed her arm to pull her up out of the water and they giggled loudly. Their sun hats blew in different directions, lifted by the incoming breeze. Thin summer dresses pulled over the swimsuits, covered the self-consciousness on the way back to the Caravan Park.

Jack wolf whistled after Gillian walked past his sun lounger, "Saucy swimsuit, darlin'."

"Stop it!" Gillian protested and blushed. "Your wife is much prettier and dryer."

"Yeah, but ain't sexy!" Jack put his arm around Daisy's waist, "I'm only jokin' babe. Like a bit meat on the bone!"

Ena turned the pages of the magazine and observed the scene unfold in front of her and smirked.

***

"How are you two?" asked Ena, "looks as if you've been shopping?"

"We got a bus to Margate and went to Dreamland – a treat for the birthday girl. Do you remember Jack? When we went on the Big Wheel? Then you dragged me on the Octopus ride, I was so frightened - kept my eyes shut." Daisy excitedly recalled memories from her honeymoon in hope her husband would connect with the initial 'sugar rush' days of their marriage.

Jack grunted, stubbed out his cigarette on the ground, but did not look up from his newspaper as he sat outside the wooden structured cafe near the Caravan Park.

"Let me get you a birthday ice-cream," said Ena.

"Thanks, won't fit into my dress!" Gillian jokingly put her hands on her imaginary bloated stomach. "I'll burst soon! We've already had fish 'n' chips with bread and butter and tea; it was only 2'd. Finished our candy floss on bus back, driver didn't think it was funny."

"You'll be fine," said Jack and smiled, "thin as a stick!"

Ena tutted, "take it as a backhanded compliment. Jack needs to brush up on his English, don't you?" Her tone sounded like a parental telling off.

"I'll get you a tub with sprinkles and two spoons so you can share. All right girls?" asked Ena.

"Ah, don't I get to share? "Jack smiled and winked at Gillian.

***

Ena called out impatiently, "Come on ladies! Mr Bayley is waiting to take our photo. Can't keep him here all night. The band will have gone home by the time you're ready!"

"Okay, okay!" said Gillian as she emerged from Daisy's caravan after a beauty make over.

Jack stood with his mouth opened. "You scrub up well, girl."

Ena stared with annoyance at Jack, "He means you look nice."

"Both look alright," said Jack; conscious his compliments were increasingly one sided and he did not want to lose the chance to be in favour with his wife.

Mr Bayley arranged their positions; Jack, centre stage, with his hands clasped the two young ladies. Daisy and Gillian played supporting roles to the star. The director i.e., Ena stood on the perimeter next to Gillian.

Music and laughter filled the clubhouse as the smell of smoke and alcohol percolated through the ambience. Gillian and Daisy danced the night away to songs by Elvis Presley, Bill Hayley & His Comets, Chuck Berry and many more crowd pleasers played by the resident band. Ena filled their glasses regularly with Babycham. Gillian made eye contact with Rick, the drummer in the band, and her line of sight led to the bar. "Great beats! Do you have symbols?" Gillian burped and fell into the nearby chair.

"Best chat up line I've heard," said Rick, "what's a nice girl like you doin' in a dump like this?"

"It's my birthday! I'm 16 today! My friend is with me," Gillian surveyed the dance floor. "Where's she gone?"

"Is she as pretty as you, darlin'? Might be our lucky night!" It took a minute for the penny to drop, and Rick said, "too young, I'm afraid, you're too young sweetheart. Never mind I'll give you a quick cheeky kiss an' we'll dedicate a song to you later. What's your name darlin'?"

"Gillian, I'm 16 today," the slurred words became even more difficult to understand.

"Happy Birthday! You got champagne to celebrate?"

"Sort of, little glasses of Babycham, little champagne, ain't it?" Gillian smiled looking for approval. "Tell your boyfriend not to be such a cheapskate! We've gotta get back to work."

"He's not my boyfriend," Gillian mumbled, "it's my best friend's husband."

Gillian and Daisy took their shoes off and tried to jive although their sense of balance had long gone, and they slid on the polished parquet flooring.

Gillian held onto Daisy and called out as she waved to Rick. "He's a drummer."

"You don't say," Daisy laughed loudly. "What's his name?"

"Forgot to ask. But he knows my name," Gillian staggered to the centre of the dance floor but could not get his attention.

"Ladies and Gentlemen, we have a special birthday to celebrate tonight," announced the lead singer of the band. "It's Jill's 16th birthday! Where are you? Oh, there you are – give us a wave. Let's all sing together; 'Happy Birthday to you, Happy Birthday to you, Happy Birthday dear Jill, Happy Birthday to you!"

Instead of a courteous thank you, an unpleasant squeal followed. "My name's Gillian!"

"Sorry, my lovely. See what happens when you don't have champagne to celebrate. An unhappy birthday girl."

A few families collected money to buy a bottle of vintage champagne 'of sorts;' the best available in the club house i.e., it was Hobson's choice.

Lights dimmed and a slow dance accompanied the song, 'Tears On My Pillow' (written by Sylvester Bradford and Al Lewis). Daisy and Gillian held onto each other. Tears initially smudged the pink cream rouge on Gillian's face and flowed to elongate the thick black eyeliner. Ena guided the amateur ballroom dancers towards their table. "Can't be all that bad," said Jack, "you wait to you get as old as my Missus, then you'll have something to cry about!" The joke hit the wrong note.

"We can't all go out staggering together," said Ena, "goodness knows where we'll end up. Jack, can you help Gillian back to her caravan and come to collect or should I say carry your wife?"

Daisy's head rested against the tablecloth. Not the cosiest pillow but she was peaceful and reduced the volume for those on the adjacent table.

Ena winked at Jack, "No need to rush. I'll make sure Daisy is not disturbed."

Gillian asked Jack, "Did you know it's my birthday today? I'm 16."

"At this rate, we won't be celebrating your 17th birthday, if you don't stop falling over." Jack replied as he gripped Gillian's waist.

"You're so kind an' handsome. Oops! Shouldn't say that. It's so naughty!"

Jack winked and with a lecherous look said, "You can be as naughty as you like darlin'."

"Would you read me a good night story?" Gillian asked with an innocence of a child but the intent of a mistress.

"Ladies and gentlemen, hope you've all had a good evening. You've been a great audience and great dancers!'"

The holiday makers gave the band a rousing round of applause.

Daisy sat bolt upright, "Where am I? Where's Jack? Where's my husband? I love him so much."

Ena offered reassurance in conjunction with a false witness statement, "No need to worry, I'm with you. Jack will be back in a few minutes. Gillian looked a strange shade of green, said she wanted to be sick, so Jack waited with her an' then carried her to the caravan. You've got a good'un there, make sure he don't slip through your fingers. No rush, get your shoes an' bag."

Daisy rubbed her face, blue eye shadow spread across her nose. "Look!" Daisy shouted, "it's Gill's bracelet. Why's it on the floor? I bought it specially. Leo sign – zodiac thingy.

Lion too big!" Daisy got hiccups but rambled after each spasm. "Excuse me! I'm so rude. What was I sayin'? Oh yeah, bracelet, I must bring it to her for good luck."

"She'll be well in the land of nod by now, I'll leave it by her bed, she'll need lots of luck gettin' over the monster of all hangovers," said Ena.

***

"What day is it?" asked Gillian.

"Friday," Ena replied, "yesterday was Thursday 13th August – unlucky for some. Remember, your 16th birthday?"

"Yes, bits an' pieces?" Gillian's face reddened and she swerved into a different lane. "Music was good. Wish brass band in my head would stop playin' so loud!"

"Have some coffee," said Ena. "Daisy found your bracelet, I put it under your pillow."

"Cheers. Was she angry?"

Ena replied knowingly, "She's fine. We all mess-up now an' then"

Even a gentle cool sea breeze could not ease the burning fire in Gillian's heart. Sitting outside the caravans, in the shade, with toast and coffee summed up the day for Daisy and Gillian. After another mid-morning snooze, Daisy asked, "Did you get your bracelet?"

"Yes, thanks," Gillian replied, "sorry. Can't remember much."

Daisy rubbed her forehead, "Don't blame you! Ena said Jack had to carry you to the caravan after you were sick."

Gillian hoped her false grimace covered the truth adequately. "YUK! That's disgustin'! Ena can get 'im discount at launderette, one of her customers works there."

"He must've jumped out of the way. Only got a few extra creases in his trousers and your bright red lipstick on his shirt."

"Blimey, got more than he bargained for!" exclaimed Gillian. "Must've been fast asleep, dribbling, when he carried me. ICKY!" Horrible! How embarrassing!

As early evening approached Ena suggested Bingo for the last night entertainment in the club. She made fun of Gillian who was asleep in the caravan, "She's still green around the gills! What do you think Jack, good joke?"

"Don't give up your day job," Jack dismissed Ena; his private ethical tutor gaining more influence as each day passed.

Ena glared at Jack and replied, "Will have too soon. Alfonso is selling up. Business has gone right down-hill. Can't keep up with all those fancy new hair salons and styles. We ain't getting any younger. He's going home to Italy. Always called it home and didn't stop goin' on about better weather an' food. Don't blame him but leaves me high and dry. On a roll now, joke after joke!"

"Sorry," Jack's voice was childish and remorseful.

Daisy intervened, "You're so experienced. Could you start home hairdressing? You've got loyal customers and Jack's mum knows a lot of people at the church, sure she could put business your way."

A deafening silence fell between the two caravans, different in size and domesticity.

"Lads down pub could do with haircut an' soapy mouth wash. You'll make a fortune!" Jack babbled and could not believe his wife's tactless suggestion, by bringing his mother into the conversation.

"Cheers, but time for a change. Still life in this old bird," said Ena defiantly. "Anyhow who's up for bingo?"

Out of guilt, Daisy replied, "Yeah, be good fun. You'll have to teach me. How much money do I need?"

"My treat," replied Ena, "you'll soon get the hang of it. Come on Jack, it'll be a good laugh."

Jack used a brazen-faced lie as an excuse interwoven with hatred for anything that would lessen his ill-perceived macho image. "Wouldn't catch me at bingo! Prefer to watch paint dry. I'll go for a pint an' call it a day.

Gillian and Jack, intoxicated by lust and addicted to the adrenaline rush shared a few hours in his marital bed. Jack's inflated ego expanded but Gillian's crumbling self-respect deflated, already defiled throughout her teenage years by blunt dismissal after being used. Jack knew the fling was a bit of fun to reduce his frustration. *'I'll make it up to my missus*,' he thought. Gillian fantasised about being a long-term love interest, but reluctantly accepted Jack did not want this type of arrangement and did want to blight the life of her only friend.

***

Gossip travelled fast. Gillian tried to hide the indiscretion. Jack cared little for being called a rogue by his mother-in-law. It was not the first time and would not be the last. Daisy reverted to her defence mechanism i.e., denial. A survival strategy deployed throughout her marriage.

Len, moved to Wales after the summer in 1959. He accepted his brother's character to a certain extent but bragging about sleeping with Gillian breached the boundary wall. Len was angry no one tried to stop Ena manipulating Jack. She took little interest in him – Jack was the target. Len felt ashamed after abusing his mother. He blamed Jack throughout his teenage years but knew his involvement inflamed the torment. Len ran away from the moral culpability. The plan was to trace his uncle and aunt who moved to Wales with their adoptive parents in 1919.

Albert caught the threads of the circumstances and decided to put an end to the unhealthy influence Ena had on his eldest son. Although not cash rich, after paying the private residential home fees for his wife, following a nervous breakdown, he sold items of furniture to buy a one-way ticket to Dublin for Ena and the initial cost of renting a flat. He did not have the chance to see his grandsons as often as he would like but definitely did not want Ena to interfere with their lives. Susan gave a Christian welcome to Ena and naively thought she had forgiven Albert. Her sons liked being with Ena, and on the surface the situation, although awkward, appeared reasonable. Guilt plagued Susan which contributed towards her ill-health in conjunction with parental burnout. She was too embarrassed to arrange babysitters because Jack and Len had bouts of hostility, disobedience, and defiant behaviour. Jack started to be aggressive. Susan hid most of the bruises from her husband and blamed her clumsiness for the visible scars. She carried the intense pressure which resulted in a lack of sleep and loss of appetite. Ashamed to seek help from her elderly parents, she did not know what to do. Albert's absence due to the pressure of his work only increased the stress. Her relatives clashed furiously for a disproportionate share of Grandma Nora's estate which drained the last drops of energy. Finally, after every effort, her resilience shattered.

***

Martha showed Pam a colour photo of them standing by the door of the caravan, with Basil.

Pam teased Martha, "I remember. You brought your teddy on holiday, what a baby. I didn't bring a fluffy toy."

"Because you didn't have one!" Martha retorted.

Pam showed Maeve. "Look at your mummy with her teddy. What was its name? Oh yeah, Basil."

"Where is Basil now?" asked Maeve.

"He went to heaven with Granny Daisy when she passed away."

Pam mouthed "What?!" Martha held her finger to her lips. Pam raised her eyes in disbelief.

Martha did not want to remember or share how her dad had thrown Basil into the galvanised iron, household, rubbish bin when she was on her first date, with Micky, a volunteer at the community centre. Rage, jealously, and fear motivated him to show his only daughter a lesson. Rage roared because Micky had not asked his permission, jealousy jangled because of his freedom to date a younger woman, and fear frosted because he did want his daughter to be a sad single parent like Gillian; addicted to evermore quantities of alcohol and men. She suffered irreversible damage to her health, and it drove a wedge between her and Daisy; her only friend.

Martha did not replace Basil; determined her dad would not cause deep emotional pain again in her life.

***

Maeve's yawn triggered the end of their adventure and delve into a past mixed with fun, friendship, and vulnerability.

The space where the caravans were located represented the inevitable distance and dogmatism and divide amongst the principal characters. Echoes of laughter and tears and coercion could still be heard above the noise pollution of a chaotic world. Each memory generated a consequence and designed the blueprint for the foundation, construction, and content of the buildings labelled 'home.'

***

CHAPTER 17

The Y-shaped strap split, and scratched Pam's big toe and she cried out, "OW!"

"For goodness' sake," said Martha, "what have you done now?"

Pam limped by Martha's front door looking for sympathy. "Only bought 'em yesterday."

"Don't tell me, down the market," Martha snapped, "that'll teach ya for buyin' cheap thong sandals. Looks like a bit of cardboard on the sole."

"Better than your memory foam granny style with wide fitting for your elephant feet!?"

"CHILDREN!" Betty called out from the kitchen, "behave or you'll have to sit on the naughty step. Come on, make-up, and I'll make tea. If you're really good, you can have chocolate biscuits."

Laughter emanated from three friends who had experienced, endured, and enjoyed different platforms and climbed a selection of stepladders to reach this stage.

"Smells yummy!" said Pam.

"Yeah, Betty has cooked extra Yorkshire puds, roasties, and there's mint jelly and your real favourite – parsnips. Only joking. There's pair of old flip flops in my wardrobe, you can have them. Anything to keep you quiet."

Pam hobbled up the stairs and shouted, "NO PARSNIPS!"

The rustic ring box, made from natural walnut wood, fell on the floor as Pam rummaged through the wardrobe. She tentatively lifted the lid engraved with the letter M, in boho art style in modern calligraphy, and unwrapped the pink tissue protecting the claddagh ring. A tear drop fell but did not pierce the delicate wrapping. She tenderly returned an item of jewellery representative of a lost love and a lifetime commitment to care for her youngest daughter.

"Foods gettin' cold," Martha pronounced as she finished laying the table in the dining room.

"Not just for you," said Betty, "sharing is caring."

"Waste of time," Martha reaffirmed, "her ladyship can't lower herself to share unless it's with Bea."

"Did you leave food and water for Bea?" Betty asked.

"Left her favourite biscuits and bowl of water in garden. She loves me even more coz I bought the cat flap, she uses all the time."

Martha intervened, "Uh-hum!?"

"Alright, alright, M paid for it, but I'll pay you back. Honest!"

Martha acknowledged the promise with a sarcastic dressing, "Yeah, right! Far too early for fairy tale stories – save those for bedtime."

Betty asked Pam, "They look more comfy? We thought you got lost or fell asleep."

"No. Wiped my feet. With tissues, before you ask! Went into Maeve's room to look at her bookshelf. It's full up, no more space, even for a little one."

"WHAT!" Martha shrieked. "You didn't move anything?"

"No, I ain't silly. Do know what upsets Maeve, well, not everything. She told me about the Mary Poppins book when we were in Reculver an' I had a quick peep. Didn't touch it! You can check for finger prints."

"Calm down, and eat all your veg," Betty chortled.

"We don't need no education. We don't need no thought control." "La, la, la la. La, la, la; leave those kids alone!"

"Pam, stop making a racket," Martha pleaded, "you're scaring Tabitha; she's trying to have an afternoon nap."

"Only singing, coz Kids on summer holiday, remember song? Was number one for a long time."

"Yeah, long time after you left school," Martha quipped, "not that you went to school much."

Betty shuffled forward and carried Tabitha to the cosy chair and wiped the remaining cat fur from her skirt. "I know,

I know," Betty tried to appease Tabitha who displayed a most disgruntled expression. "Duty calls, better help Pam before she jams the dish washer door again."

Pam welcomed Betty's offer to help. "Cheers, could you make the coffee an' I'll keep fightin' with this stupid thing! What's wrong with Miss Grumpy Pants?"

"Mustn't forget sweeteners," Betty's muffled voice was partly caused by the intense concentration on following the instructions for the coffee machine and concern about Martha.

"I've wrapped left overs in foil and put 'em on oven tray," Pam unveiled her kitchen maid skills much to Betty's surprise. "Where's boring Brian? Suppose he'll be back soon?"

"No," Betty whispered, "he's staying with his sister."

"What, for good?" Pam sniggered.

"Ssshh! It's not a joke. Really don't know when he's coming back."

"Ah," Pam replied. She tuned into her comedy channel and adjusted the volume on a repeat of the coping broadcast."

"Shall I leave your coffee on the table madam?" asked Pam using her best impression of the butler in the TV programme 'Upstairs Downstairs.'

Martha had a sense of humour failure, "just shut up an' sit down! Where's the sweeteners?"

"Sorry, my fault," said Betty, "do you want anything else from kitchen? Tempt you with a piece of trifle?"

"Oh no!" Pam replied, "I'm stuffed. Think I'll have a snooze with Tabitha." Pam's expression straightened and her tone flattened. "Is Brian busy at work?"

"Don't know an' really don't care," Martha's sharp reply metaphorically hit Betty in the face as she returned to the living room.

"How old is Penelope tomorrow?" asked Betty.

Martha mocked her estranged sister-in-law, "Oooh! Never ask a woman her age!"

"Is Brian taking her out for her birthday?" asked Pam. "His takin' a day off work? How will they cope? The company will crumble!"

Betty conveyed a comment from her daughter which lightened the mood, "Sindy said on 22nd August 565 was the earliest sighting of Loch Ness Monster. They could have a joint birthday celebration."

"How is she?" asked Pam. "I mean Sindy not the Loch Ness Monster."

"She's travelling with a group of friends to the Isle of Coll. I think it's Inner Hebrides? Not good at geography; Ted will know. But scenery is wonderful and trip ideal for her - adventurous and watching the wildlife. She plans to study Physiotherapy in Aberdeen, her 1:1 Honours Degree in

Sports Science will definitely help. Is that right description of degree? Will ask Ted tomorrow. But do know she loved St Andrews University.

"Wow!" Martha exclaimed. "How's Ramsey?"

"He's really happy with Palma. She's super intelligent just like him, but I am biased. They enjoy studying at University in Malta. Both doing a Master of Science in Computers? Dreadful, can't remember correct name of their course. He achieved 1:1 Honours degree Computer Science at Plymouth University? I'll have to write them down especially before end of month when they're staying with us for a week. Sindy will come down so we can all have a good old catch up. Love them to pieces and we're so proud of them. Not sure where they've inherited their brains from but we're over the moon, they're making the most of all the opportunities. What's the film where Robin Williams says, "Seize the day?" Another question for Ted."

"Super clever!" said Pam. "They're just following our good examples," Pam nudged Martha, but she just rolled her eyes.

"How old is Ramsey?" Martha asked.

"He'll be 28 in October," Betty replied. "How could you forget? I waddled down the aisle in my over stretched matron of honour dress for your wedding. Your mum tried to let the dress out, but I was bursting out. Ted told me to breathe in. I had terrible indigestion never mind breathing in!"

Martha laughed as the scene flashed back into vision, "But was a nice colour dress an' extra big bows did hide some of the bursting."

Three companions continued chatting and reminiscing on the 'good old days.' The stability in Betty's life separated her from the chaos and tribulation and regret shared by Martha and Pam but there was an indelible link. Betty's children were stable and comfortable in their own skins. Their successful education results were a consequence of the investment of steadfast unconditional love from their parents.

Philomina and Maddy were adept academically, but their inner conflict and outward confrontational nature wrecked the chance to develop friendships with Ramsey and Sindy who could have fortified their development in education and emotion.

"I'll have to go get Maeve soon, poor Angela will be worn to a shred. Oi! Lazy bones, wanna come for a walk?" Martha looked at Pam who was snoring, dribbling, and leaning over the side of the couch. "Not a pretty sight!"

"Leave her," Betty said with an empathetic maternal consideration. "She doesn't usually eat much; Sunday roast must have been a shock to her system. Good to see her not so self-conscious at dinner table."

"You're right. I'll go and make sure Bea has food an' water, Maeve loves making a fuss of her – poor thing not used to attention. *Sleepy drawers* can stay here tonight, keep an eye on her."

"I'll make sandwiches for Maeve's tea," said Betty, "what's her favourite?"

"Boiled eggs will be great. Blue serviettes with small crowns are in drawer under knife and forks. She likes those. Helps keep her settled. Do you want anything from shops?

"No thanks," Betty replied. "Can you get chocolate buttons for Sleepy Beauty."

***

Ginger wagged her tail exuberantly in anticipation of the friendly visitor who sat on the bench in the front garden of Anchor Tale. The enthusiasm prompted Maeve to jump up and say, "it's mummy! Come on Ginger!"

"Are you well?" asked Angela.

"Yes, thank you. Sorry, didn't mean to disturb you. Have I woken Ginger from her afternoon sleep?"

Angela instinctively sensed the desolation in Martha's voice and the downcast body language.

"Would you like a cup of tea? Maeve cannot wait to show you the cupcakes she made, decorated with sprinkles, and beautiful butterfly wall stickers."

"Hope she has not worn you out?"

"No, not at all," replied Angela in a soft soothing tone. "Although Ginger will be going to bed earlier this evening, she does not sleep a wink when Maeve's here. Their friendship fits like a glove."

"Mummy, mummy," Maeve called out in great excitement. "Ginger and me have made these for you and daddy."

Martha surveyed the exquisite symmetrical design on the butterfly wings and said, "Thank you, darling, you two are clever."

"We thought you would like the shade of blue. Aunty Pam said you and daddy have been married twenty-eight years. Can we use the butterflies at your party?"

"What a nice idea and so thoughtful. Can we put them in a box for now?" Martha's request evoked a mixture of memories and tears. Angela interceded, "We can put them in the art and craft cupboard, out of harm's way, before Aunty Pam comes for tea on Wednesday."

"Oh yes," said Maeve, "Aunty Pam might sit on them. She is funny but a little clumsy at times."

Smiles spread throughout the dining room and Martha appreciated her daughters immaculate timing with regards lifting spirits.

"Maeve, could you help, please? Can you bring Ginger to her personal poodle parlour, she needs a facial and a thorough brush. She will be jubilant if you are the hairdresser?" Angela's request created space to have a conversation with Martha. "I hope you do not mind my observation; you appear to be carrying a heavy weight. Can I help?"

"Thank you. Sorry, there are a lot of ingredients in the mixing bowl, a sticky mess. Really appreciate the time you spend with Maeve, the change in her character is miraculous."

"Maeve is revealing her true self; the seal on the lid containing her potential has been opened. What are the plans for Maeve returning to school? Will the headmaster help you?" Angela held an innate scepticism of the modern school inspectorate programme and the neutrality and attitude of the governing authorities in relation to children with different abilities.

"I've had numerous meetings with headmaster. He said all the issues had been investigated thoroughly and the teachers told him it was a safe environment for Maeve. They are not listening. What else can I do?" Martha could not stop the tears and wiped her nose with the remnants of tissues stuffed into the waistband of her skirt.

Angela turned up the volume of the radio, tuned into Classic FM, to cover the outward sign of anguish, Martha had and carried for too many years. "Please allow me to help, firstly here is a fresh handkerchief. With your permission we can arrange a meeting with the governors of the school. They have a duty of care, and need to guarantee Maeve will be safe, both physically and psychologically. Also, we can explore the option of home schooling; my friend from church is a lawyer and she can study the Government's guidance documents. Maeve is blossoming and I fear she will regress to lacking confidence in verbal communication. Academically she is far more advance than her peers and this may make them insecure however Maeve is not to blame for their weakness. Unfortunately, her intelligence may unsettle the teacher and if he or she does not have the necessary skills it is far easier to ostracise Maeve than to find ways to affirm she is a valued member of the class."

Martha was taken aback by Angela's assertive statement although acknowledged it was rooted in values inherited from her father and her experience as a teacher. "You are kind, sounds a wonderful plan, but I do not have the money to pay for a lawyer and private tutors."

"I would like to be a sponsor for Maeve if you will allow me. Please do not think I am being intrusive. I cannot stand back and watch the system fail a girl as beautiful and gifted as Maeve. She deserves better and Victor intuitively left a trust fund for this eventuality. He said I should be a private tutor and, as always, he was right. I am unable to cover all the subjects on the national curriculum therefore we can arrange lessons with other teachers. Pam will be only too delighted to maintain the physical education and comedy classes."

"As long as she is not in charge of spelling, we'll be fine," Martha smiled. "Will Maeve be isolated? I am worried about no social contact with children of her own age."

"We will have to be creative however there are youth groups at church, the Royal British Legion organise events for all ages, the library arranges activities. We can make enquiries with the Girl Guides and the pièce de résistance would be to go to dance classes with Pam?"

Martha smiled and the weight on her shoulders felt lighter. "How am I going to explain my red puffy eyes to Maeve?"

"There must a plant in the front garden causing you to sneeze?" Angela hugged Martha in consolation and appreciation for bringing an energy and purpose back into her life.

"Wow! Ginger! You are a super model and the Oscar for best make up and costume – okay collar – goes to Maeve," Martha clapped and hugged her daughter.

"Mummy, can you take a photo, please?"

"Yes, of course darling. Ready, one, two, three. Say cheese!"

Maeve giggled much to the delight of her mother, "Ginger does not like cheese, but she loves biscuits." Ginger's reaction to the word, biscuit, was not a surprise and she jumped up to Maeve.

"If it is okay with Angela, we can give Ginger one more treat before we leave. We are going to visit Bea, make sure she is well and has food, and nice cosy bed for tonight."

Maeve's face lit up and she asked, "Is Aunty Pam going out with her friend again?"

"No, darling, Aunty Pam is having a sleepover with us tonight."

"Yaay!" Maeve squealed with delight.

***

Betty tucked Maeve into bed and made sure Owen, the plush barn owl was comfortable before reading the bedtime story *Grá* (Love) with a mastery in performing all the different voices.

Martha dropped the Clipper Card bag for life beside the sofa, "Wakey, wakey! Cosy dressing gown, pjs with slippers. Comfy clothes for sleep over."

Pam rubbed her eyes and asked, "What time is it? What day is it?"

"6 o'clock. In evening not mornin.' You ain't been out partying all night and it's Sunday 21st August 2016, all day!"

"Thanks. Urgh! My stinky breath's gettin' worse. Where're the mints?" asked Pam.

Martha grimaced, "In mixy up drawer, I'll get 'em an' clothes peg for my nose!"

"Love you too! Need to get a glass of water and swill my mouth out!"

"Not in my kitchen sink," Martha snapped.

"Don't be silly, in utility room. Gonna have ciggie first, don't start, tryin' my best!"

"Up to you! Stand at end of garden, use my trainers by back door. Don't want Maeve choking on your second-hand nicotine."

"Glass of wine or prosecco?" asked Martha.

"Whatever's open." Pam pulled her fingers through her hair and asked, "sleepover? Am I sleepin' with Betty?"

"No. She'd suffocate with all the gas from both ends." Martha laughed at her own joke.

"Not funny! My stomachs doing summersaults and you're takin' the mick!"

"Ah, didums!" Martha mocked before she turned to stare into the metaphorical headlights of the truck speeding into her life. She continued, "there's plenty of space although Philomina has locked her bedroom or studio as she likes to call it. She's with dearest Aunty Penelope and then goin' back to Edinburgh. She hates being here and is pining for Rune."

Pam looked bemused and asked, "Is he a student?"

"Keep up!" Martha tutted, "Rune is a girl, remember Maddy's sarcastic dig about Philomina's special friend?"

"Sort of. Dunno what we're allowed to say these days without gettin' into trouble," Pam protested, "they might as well throw the book at me, coz I've got a serious case of 'foot in mouth disease.' Well, I may be a piglet."

Martha interjected, 'bigot' not piglet. Not only ignorant but illiterate."

Pam hit back, "alright, alright! Keep your hair on. I maybe out of touch but what about prim' n' proper Penelope? How she's takin' the news?"

"She ain't got a clue coz Miss 'inclusive and diversity' don't want to be cut out of the Will!"

Pam gasped, "So, Philomina's special friend, Rune is not as special as money. She really is a piece of work! Does Rune know who she is involved with? Feel sorry for her."

Martha's anger burst the banks, "Philomina's told Rune all about her wicked, old fashioned, ignorant mother and how there is a ban on them staying or visiting our home. Of course, her father would welcome them with open arms and his values are set in 2016 and not with the dinosaurs. Best we keep away from each other for a while."

"Where's Maddy?" asked Pam. "Let me guess – hippy commune? Am I allowed to say hippy?"

Martha barked, "Oh, stop! Maddy is in Margate?

Pam, confused by the change in the landscape, asked, "in Dreamland or at another address?"

"She's stayin' with her boyfriend."

Pam dreaded the answer to her next question, "what's his name?"

"Phil Tern."

'Phew! Thank goodness it's not Mick.' Pam thought and breathed out slowly. She realised her reaction appeared to be exaggerated, even by her standards, and turned the awkward moment into another question. "What's Phil do?"

"He goes to art college," Martha replied, "and you've guessed it, Maddy, now, wants to go to the same college."

Pam did not grasp the implications of the next stage in Maddy's education and asked flippantly, "Long journey each day? She hates gettin' up early. Does her course start at midday?" "No!" Martha groaned, "gets better by the minute; she's movin' in with Romeo or Picasso – whatever she wants to call him."

"How long have they known each other?"

Martha spluttered out, "Couple of months! Yeah, I know – what can I do? Lock her in her bedroom?"

"Speakin' from experience," said Pam, "if you put your foot down, she'll only move further away with goodness knows who. Let her make mistakes. As long as there's a safety net - knows she always come back here. She's trying to get our attention because she feels left out. What did Brian say?"

"NOTHING! Leave it up to good old mum – she'll sort it out as usual, on her own!"

Pam looked at the anger etched across the face of a mother, a shadow of her former self and delivered an inappropriate intervention, "Hope he's going to treat you, big time, on your wedding anniversary?"

Martha remained silent and bit her nails.

Pam, startled by the lack of response and nervous body language, changed the subject, "do you want me to talk to Maddy?"

"Past caring. What a mess! Seaside is supposed to be fun; candy floss, penny arcade, fish'n' chips, ice-creams, and plenty of R&R. An escape from pressures in City of London and crazy Croydon. Running away don't solve everything?"

"Nope!" Pam replied bluntly, "bring all our baggage with us, and they're even heavier than my rucksack."

"Nothing's heavier than your rucksack!"

Pam laughed at the wisecrack and asked, "Is Bea okay?"

"Yeah, snug as a bug in a rug."

"Cheers! Wait a minute, where exactly is she snug?"

"In your bed." Martha replied. "Before you start moanin,' Maeve dug out a soft cosy blanket; don't know how she found anything in pile of clothes and tat in your wardrobe. Anyway, Bea is cosy and cute by your pillow, if you don't believe me – here's photo and this one is on Facebook. Wonder how many young men will be adding comments, "I recognise that bed!!"

"Ha! Ha! You're so hilarious," Pam sneered. "Have another glass of wine, might help you tell a joke that's actually funny!"

"Chill! Miss Touchy! Bought you these. See what is on front – Share Bag."

Pam muttered, "Dream on!"

"S'alright, nice big bowl of trifle in fridge with my name on it and with double brandy soaked in the sponge. Stop with dirty looks! Blame Betty, she made it."

"What are you blaming me for?" asked Betty.

Martha blushed, "didn't hear you come downstairs. Is Maeve okay? We're only joking about the trifle."

"How rude! And ungrateful! Takes a long time to create my tasty trifle using a secret recipe which I will not divulge for any amount of money!" Betty smirked and reassured Martha; explained how Owen the owl and Maeve were sound asleep.

Pam burped. "Excuse me, must be the roasties comin' back to say hello." "Stop! That's vile," Martha screwed up her face and held her nose. "Have you been drinkin' brandy? Where you hidin' the bottle?

"Ssshh up!" Pam slurred. "Lighten up, when's last time we had a girlie sleep over? I have other sleepovers, but they're like firework night!" Pam started to sing "I don't want you to work all day, but I want you, to be true, an' I just wanna make."

"ENOUGH!" Martha shouted. "If you wake Maeve up, I'll swing for you!"

"You'll fall over, you're so drunk," Pam hiccupped.

"If you're gonna be sick, go in the garden. I ain't clearing up after you!"

Betty called for order, "Girls! Girls! Do you want me to bang your heads together? I'll make black coffees and we can relax and watch 'Pretty Woman' for the fiftieth time. Okay?"

Pam returned to the living room; slouched on the sofa and whispered a quote from the film, "I want the fairy tale."

"Stop crying, you big baby," Martha chortled, "you know the ending. Your Prince Charming will only have to climb up one step to your bungalow. What you wanna watch now?"

"I'm goin' to bed," Pam yawned and staggered towards the hall.

Martha taunted Pam, "Lightweight! We used to stay up all night. Is there an urgent board meeting tomorrow with the CEO? Or are you meeting a new entry in your top ten?"

"Might be!" Pam replied defensively. "Bob's comin' around about 10ish."

"And, what does Bob do?" Martha was intrigued by the snippet of information however predicted the outcome.

"He's a builder but, uhm, does plumbing."

"What's wrong with your water works?" asked Martha, and Betty joined in with the banter. "Maybe he can fix Bea's water fountain."

"You're a good double act. Not! My washing machine's broken again."

Martha sniggered before asking, "so, you have Bob the builder fixing your washing machine which conveniently stops workin' each week? All you need is Dermot to fix your garden an' you'd be sorted."

Pam looked confused and over tired, "Dermot?"

"I'll explain later. Sweet dreams. Wonder if Bob has a white horse?"

Pam threw a cushion at Martha. It missed and hit the floor knocking over the cup of coffee.

Martha's face reddened and Betty came to the rescue, "I'll clean it up, you two go to bed!"

"What time's Ted coming tomorrow?" asked Martha as she pushed Pam up the stairs.

"Probably around 11, is that okay?"

Martha stifled a yawn and replied, "Yeah, stay as long as you want. Pam will be with her Knight in Shining T-shirt, first thing, so we can have a sensible, grown-up conversation, and I can have a look at your photos of bungalows. Sounds triffy? What's the word?"

"Terrific," Betty smiled. "We're viewing the one in Princess Avenue, Bermcliffe again. Most important, need good size rooms for Ramsey and Sindy. They'll always have a home with us. Anyway, tell you more tomorrow or should I say later today. I'll help with Maeve's breakfast; you are going to have a very sore head!"

***

CHAPTER 18

"Aunty Pam, aunty Pam! Can we go to say hello to Monty and Bud?"

Pam froze and flinched, "We really need to get back home, Ginger looks tired."

"Oh no, she is full of beans. Angela said I must not say biscuits," Maeve tried her best to whisper but Ginger's sharp hearing triggered a jump towards Pam who tumbled onto the ground.

"Aunty Pam, are you okay?" Maeve took Ginger's lead, but she was still over excited.

"Let me help you up," said Monty. "Are you hurt?"

"No. Pam looked at the crack in the sole of her new sandals and shouted, "DRAT!!" An apology followed, "Sorry Maeve – should not use that word."

"I know, Aunty Pam. Sometimes, daddy and mummy use those words. Maddy and Philomina use them all the time."

Pam picked up the two pieces of the broken footwear and said to Monty, "Thanks for coming to our rescue; wish I had half of Ginger's energy. Whatever you do, please do not say the 'b' word."

Monty looked at Maeve and mouthed, "What is 'b'?

"I will draw a picture. Ginger is very clever and can understand even if I spell the word. Aunty Pam is funny but does not spell every word correctly."

"Maeve, you are cheeky," said Pam and looked at Monty. "I'll explain another time."

"Maybe you could explain over lunch, tomorrow? The Vintage Sea Harbour restaurant is nice and has lovely cakes, but they do not match Maeve's expert baking skills."

"I'm not sure, my washing machine's not working, need to buy another pair of sandals, an' take Ginger for a walk, and help Martha an' Maeve, and telephone Betty." The list of excuses dried up, but one more came to mind. "We've had the yummiest afternoon tea with Angela, can't have another feast so soon."

"My, sounds as if you'll need a break. Have a think?"

"Oh, Aunty Pam," Maeve took on an authoritative attitude which surprised Pam and Monty and Ginger and Bud. "Mummy and me will finish the housework in the morning. Angela has invited mummy and me to lunch and promised to make egg salad. I cannot wait - it is delicious. We can take Ginger for a walk in the afternoon. Please go to the Vintage Sea Harbour restaurant. Angela told me they have portraits of King George VI and Queen Elizabeth; the Queen Mother, and you can buy souvenirs of old newspapers and postcards."

Pam dithered and tried to look eager, "Uhm! How can I say no? Sounds great."

***

A faded grey and white striped background set the scene for the pink cabbage roses with soft green leaves decorating the walls in the Vintage Sea Harbour restaurant. The famed fragrance of the homemade cakes complimented the delicate taps of the teapot lids.

Pam knocked into the table causing the antique teaspoon, dated 1937 to commemorate the Coronation of King George VI and Queen Elizabeth, to fall on the cream blue, heavy quality 100% wool, rug with a sculptured traditional Indian design. Monty caught the tea cup before it tipped over the edge of the saucer.

"Sorry for being late," said Pam. Her face reddened and she took a breath before delivering the monologue. "Thank goodness carpet's thick, need to be with me here. Sorry didn't arrive earlier. Said that already? Repeating myself again, put it down to a senior moment. Iris phoned me this morning an' told me, customer donated summer clothes, nearly new. She could only put aside sandals for a couple of hours, so picked them up on way here. Thought give 'em test drive. Not bad? Bit granny for me but they're a good fit in here. Pardon the pun! Better put bag under table otherwise everyone will be trippin' over, don't want any more accidents. Would've left earlier but Bea started playin' up. Normally she's good as gold but stupid water fountain broken again, so tried to fix it, gave up and left a saucer of milk an' Tupperware pot full of water. She'll be okay, left biscuits, her favourite's tuna but only had lamb flavour in Tesco. I'll share tin of tuna tonight; that'll make her happy. Then, would you believe it? Smoke alarm started beepin,' ain't got a clue what's happened. Had to pull batteries out, was drivin' Bea mad, poor thing. She's got cat flap, but poor thing was hidin' in wardrobe. It never rains but it pours! Cash machine's not workin' so had to queue up inside bank. Didn't expect it to be busy on a Thursday, where's everyone come from. Suppose silly tourists on summer holidays, don't understand why they come to Wishym Bay, must be better places to go. Mind you, it's warm today. Nice an' cool in here, good choice. I recognise that song. Wait a minute, oh, what is it? So annoying. Ah, I know, football, West Ham? They sing, 'I'm forever blowing bubbles.' Sure, they do? Used to watch football with, umm, mean on telly." Monty stared in astonishment at a lady in front of him resembling a wound-up toy, rapidly and incoherently moving from one topic to another.

'She'll run out of energy soon,' Monty thought as he looked towards the owner to rescue him.

"Have you had a chance to look at the menu?" asked Gladys.

"No, sorry, no, I'm talking too much, you go ahead." Pam looked directly at Monty as he waited patiently. "But can I have glass of water, please, my throat's dry?"

Gladys replied with a hint of reproval without crossing the line of a customer relationship, "Of course, probably the hot air, but nice to see the sunshine."

"What would you like?" asked Monty.

Pam looked at the menu and replied, "Can't make up my mind. Had a big breakfast so I'll have toast. Will have to ask Iris to find me a bigger dress if I carry on eating this much. Blame Martha for buyin' all those fish'n'chips, but be rude to say no."

"Would you mind if I interrupt you? But Gladys will be back soon and prefer not to keep her waiting, she's very busy." Monty ushered his new friend to decide and take a break.

"Did you enjoy your toast?" asked Monty.

"Yes, much better than out of my burnt out toaster," replied Pam. She hoped the fabrication about the big breakfast would stall his inquisitiveness. Her eating disorder was covered up, for the most part, however her acting skills were not fool proof to those who took the time to care.

Monty asked, "the cakes look and smell great. Can I tempt you?" He was buoyed up by the reciprocal brightness in Pam's response. "Fruit cake looks nice but can't eat slice on my own, we can share?"

"Good idea," Monty replied, "I'll get two forks."

Pam strained to listen, "like the songs. Can't remember who it is?"

"Vera Lynn." Monty floundered and took a deep breath. "Sally loved her songs, especially *'From the Time You Say Goodbye.'*

"Do you still miss her?" Pam gulped and thought *'what a stupid question.'* "Sorry, don't know what to say!?!"

Monty's eyes glistened, "No one does. Only been a year but feels much longer. I thought it may help to bring in the donation to the charity shop on the anniversary."

"Saturday 21st May?" Pam was overwhelmed with guilt about her reaction to Monty. "I'm sorry, felt so awkward. Your bag was slightly open, and did not what to do, especially as it was my first day. I think avoidance is best tactic but makes' things worse."

"I'm the same," Monty replied. "Even crossed the road to avoid one of my employees shortly after his wife passed away. I felt terrible but couldn't face him or our fleeting mortality. Our son, sorry, I mean my son, Lewis, emigrated to New Zealand with his wife and two children, shortly after Sally died. The grief was too much – he was and still is devastated. Sally doted on him and regrettably he was spoilt. But as an only child, it's not surprising but not wise."

"What does he do?" Pam stumbled over the words, "sorry, what's his job?"

"He learnt basic carpentry in my company; got on well with the lads but he didn't like working for his dad, so we paid for him to go to university. He came back to help with a few jobs but had his sights on bigger and brighter things. Sally and me were filled with pride when he became a Construction Project Manager in Manchester. And were staggered when one of the buildings won a prestigious award – achieved the highest ever BREEAM score of 95.16%. Sally was ecstatic when we travelled to Manchester to see The Queen and the Duke of Edinburgh officially open the office building to the public in November 2013. The name, One Angel Square, is poignant. I am so pleased she lived to see that day even though she embarrassed him, as mum's do."

Pam blinked rapidly to fight back the tears as she reflected on the indifference of her mum. "Incredible. Lots to lose, sorry, mean, your son lives a long way from Wishym Bay. Long distance flights not easy with children?"

Monty appeared despondent, "he has not returned, yet. But I travelled to his home for Christmas and New Year. Great to be with grandchildren but Lewis remained distant. He said I brought the grief with me; he became even more upset so cut short my trip."

Pam's voice lowered to a whisper, "really sad. Families act strange after funerals, sorry, mean loss."

"I will stop rambling," said Monty. "We can enjoy today especially with these delicious cakes. You have a lovely smile and nice fun character. Surprised no one has swept you off your feet?"

"Wot, in these sandals?" Pam pulled the comfort blanket of humour over her shoulders. "Only jokin.' I'm not nice. I'm a good actor." Pam hesitated before revealing more, but she proceeded. "Never been engaged, married or pregnant. Quick run through, not worth goin' round the houses." Pam grinned to hide the awkwardness and sadness. The noise of daily life blocked out the heartbreak most of the time but saying it aloud, exposed the nerve endings to the cold air and there were no prescriptive pain killers strong enough to treat the affliction.

Self-medication eased the sharpness temporarily, but it returned with vigour.

Glady's eased the tension with a question, "Would you like more drinks?"

"I'll have a hot chocolate," Pam replied, "no marshmallows an' no cream."

"Black coffee, please," Monty placed his order and said, "cake was scrumptious, no matter what they say, can't beat home baking."

Monty coughed lightly, "where are your family? Do you keep in contact with them? Excuse me if too personal."

"It's okay. None left! Well, none that I know about. Mum checked out, sorry, passed away in 1992. I looked after Gran for a while until she left us, passed away, in 1996. My step-uncle, not sure what to call him; mum's half-brother, Charlie, died in 2003. He was alright, left Croydon at first opportunity, no surprise, his dad was nasty, to put it mildly. Charlie joined Army Cadets and moved to Yorkshire, lived in a bedsit an' was a miner for a while. But work, booze an' cigarettes got better of him. Went to his funeral, tempted to stay there, friendly people an' stunning scenery but really cold. Martha talked me into comin' back."

"Glad she did," said Monty, embarrassed how he openly admitted his feelings. "I do not like cigarettes and what a dreadful smell. Remember when people smoked in pubs – how did we put up with it?"

Pam diverted attention from her fractured life and said, "Must buy postcards for Maeve. Which ones do you think are best?"

***

Over the next couple of months Monty and Pam met more regularly and felt more comfortable.

The Vintage Sea Harbour restaurant was a safe space, and the familiarity brought a contentment Pam could not understand. Gladys was pleased to see a reduction in the monologues and Pam started to listen and eventually they both learned to have a balanced conversation, with the occasional outburst from Pam.

Pam did not want to walk in the shadow of Monty's late wife therefore did not accept the invitation to his home. *'Maybe one day,'* she thought. However, her footsteps moved closer to the open door after each time they met.

***

CHAPTER 19

Loud gurgling noises and steam gushed from the coffee machine. The Barista worked hard to keep up with influx of orders on a rainy Saturday morning.

"Number 32, number 32!" The loud call soared above the hive of activity in Joanie's Caff Inn.

"Over here!" came the reply from a flustered rotund gentleman. "We had to move; Clive couldn't stand the smelly couple in the corner."

"Can't comment on that Sir, but long as you've got correct order, we'll all be happy. Yeah?"

"Cheers," said Clive, "sorry, don't want to make a fuss. Vince takes good care of me. Silly me, should say Vincent otherwise there'll be no ice-cream for dessert."

Joan, the owner of the cafe, winked and said, "No problem darlin' Enjoy your meal."

Pam pulled her threadbare black rucksack under the table but not before Joan caught her foot on the strap. "Oh no!" Pam exclaimed, "so sorry, you've got enough on your plate!"

"Not at moment darlin'! I'm clearing up empties," Joan chortled, "but I'm goin' sound like an air hostess, but don't look like one; keep your bag tucked under table. Otherwise, we'll be filling out accident book all day. Ain't got time to breathe never mind paperwork. On your own darlin'?"

"NO!" Pam replied abrasively. "Sorry, she'll be here soon."

"No problem, could take empty chair, give you more leg room. Give's a call when you're ready to order!" Joan scuttled off to the tumultuous kitchen.

Clive leaned over towards Pam, "So awkward when they're late. Come an' join us, better then looking like a singleton."

"Thank you," Pam replied. "Can't squeeze in there? I could try, but I'll cause even more of a rumpus. Anyway, don't want to butt in, enjoy your brunch. Maddy likes a lay in, she'll be here soon. She's my niece. Well, not really my niece, my best mate's. *'Just stop talking'* Pam thought *'just shut up.'*

Maddy's arrival halted Pam's entirely unnecessary elongated explanation.

"Here she is," said Clive, "worth waiting for. You make a cute couple!" Vincent pulled his shirt.

"Alright?" Maddy look baffled and turned to Pam. "You told me you'll be on your own!?"

Pam sensed the tension and apprehension in Maddy's stance and did not want her to leave and had to pull the coping clown out of the proverbial top hat, fast! "I'm on my own," Pam grinned. "Who'll put up with me? It's been all fun 'n' games in here. Clive an' Vincent are keepin' me company an' we managed to save your chair. You know, like on holiday, in olden days, people had to put towels on the sunbeds?"

"Yeah, whateva!" Maddy groaned. "S'alright, she rabbits on with everyone, no one listens."

"Miaow!" Clive jibed. "We'll leave you alone babe, have a good catch up with your friend or is it aunty?" Vincent kicked Clive's ankle under the table and mouthed, '*Stop!*'

Pam smirked. "Before midday, I'm impressed! Lookin' bit grey an' delicate. How was yesterday? Have a good birthday?"

"Yeah, went out for a drink with mates and then curry which weren't a good idea." Maddy belched.

"That's disgustin' but far better than last year when you re-decorated my bathroom!" Pam held her nose and grimaced.

"Ha! Ha! Taking jokes off mum? You make a right pair of comedians!" Maddy grunted.

"Just remembered, why I love you so much," Pam mocked Maddy's grumpy teenager act, "what do you want to eat – nice greasy fry up?"

"Don't think so, somehow! I'll have what you're having, nothing on toast?"

"Could stretch to strawberry jam," Pam replied, "why not, birthday treat, let's push the boat out. Get it!?"

"You're doin' my head in! Please stop for one minute!" Maddy whispered.

Joan burst into the conversation, "alright darlin'! See your friend's turned up. Nice cosy corner for two! What you gonna have?"

"Two toast and teas and a special treat of strawberry jam, for the birthday girl!" Pam taunted Maddy.

"HAPPY BIRTHDAY," Joan shouted, "how old? What am I sayin'? How young today?"

"Her actual birthday was yesterday," Pam replied with an escalation of excitement, "sweet 17!"

Maddy stared at Pam with the sharpness of a sword and mumbled, "keep this up and I'm leavin!"

Pam gave Maddy two gift vouchers and said, "here you go grumpy. Don't spend them all at once."

"Cheers, didn't think you had any money?"

"One's from your mum. Don't put it in the bin!" Pam pleaded. "And I've got piggy bank under my bed."

"Surprised it's not shattered into pieces with weight on top!" Maddy chortled.

"Very funny! Enough about my night-time, or sometimes, day-time activity! Are you okay? And your young man?"

"I was okay before hearin' about your antics. That's gross! Way too much detail!" Maddy screwed up her face in repulsion. "Phil's fine, finishing a painting when I left, bet he's gone back to bed. Tell mum, I'm alright, and thanks for voucher. Not ready to talk to her yet. But you'll keep an eye on her, won't you? Mum needs you; she won't admit but she does. We think you're the needy one but think about Mum for a minute."

Pam retaliated, "What, like you do?"

"Put your claws away," said Maddy, "she pretends to be strong, but she's broken hearted. I do know all about Ben."

Pam's voice flattened, "How did you find out?"

"Philomina told me I was a consolation prize – a poor replacement." Maddy shoved the solitary tear into her hair. "Bit of a delay, seven years? Miss Pampered thought she'd be only child, no wonder she hates me and everyone else in the family except darlin' daddy!"

Pam growled, "Good old Philomina, always rely on her for empathy and compassion. She's like a viper! Influenced too much by Aunty Pen."

"Don't make excuses for her," Maddy snapped, "she's just horrible, a spoilt brat! But won't be so spoilt when Aunty Prim and Proper finds out about her girlfriend. You know about Rune?"

"Yeah, your mum told me. None of my business, but she can't keep hiding Rune an' using us as a punch bag, coz she's frightened of being cut out of the will."

"You've heard Pen rattle on," said Maddy, "she idolises my ugly sister; expects her favourite niece to have a big white wedding to Prince Charming and they'll have a sweet girl and a brave boy! Can't wait until she finds out!"

Maddy changed tact and caught Pam off guard. "Did you ever want to get married?"

"Nah! Not me," said Pam. "Don't wanna be tied down!"

"The truth?" Maddy saw through Pam's bluff.

"Mr Right never called at my door. Should say, never stayed at my door! Had a bit of a mixed-up childhood. Mum not really interested but your Granny Daisy looked after me best she could. So, count yourself lucky, young lady. Don't take what you've got for granted and don't throw it away over a silly argument. Your mum'll come around. Aunty Pam will save the day!"

"Did you have kids?" Maddy asked.

"No!" Pam replied with sadness seeping through her bones. "Long story, but it's reason I keep banging on about health checks, for you and your better half! No chance for me now, ship sailed long ago. More time to keep an eye on you and your mum. While we're talkin' about children, go easy on Maeve, yeah? Give her a chance. Your mum loves you both the same, and, yes, know you were told you'd be the baby in the family. Really upsetting, I get it, but it ain't Maeve's fault. Your mum couldn't give her away in the jumble sale coz you an' flaky Phyllo didn't like her."

Maddy rolled her eyes, "But she's weird!"

"Not weird, just different. She's cleverer than you and me put together which ain't hard. Poor thing can't go back to school. Other kids are ripping her to shreds; started by callin' her names but it's gettin' worse. Angela's goin' to take care of her, like a minder but with a more mellow personality. Never know, when she's happier, you might like her, but won't hold my breath."

Pam tentatively asked, "all finished with Mick?"

"Yeah!" replied Maddy. "Yesterday's news."

"Good news," Pam remarked with an added sting in the tail, "best to have a fresh start - don't have dragnet behind you – never know what you'll catch."

"Cheers for not tellin' mum, but don't tell her any more lies!"

Pam laughed out loud, "talk about the pot calling the kettle black!"

"Everything alright, ladies? Can I get you anything else?"

Maddy pulled her shoulders back and said, "I'll have black coffee, please."

"Mornin' after night before, is it darlin? Those were the days! Can't remember last night out on the tiles. Can't even remember last time went out to the supermarket! Can you believe it's 1st October? Year's flown past. Christmas cards already in shops! Anything for you, aunty?"

"I'll have coffee as well," Pam replied, "caffeine keeps me goin.'"

"You're tellin' me, darlin. Back in a jiffy!"

Pam touched Maddy's hand cautiously. "If you need anything, give us a call. Don't matter if you're in trouble, we'll sort something out. Don't run away, we'll find you."

"Sounds like a threat?" said Maddy. "Give me some credit, I'm not a school kid. Nice to have a bit of privacy; won't have mum knocking on my bedroom door, asking if I want anything when she really wants to know who is with me. Dad don't care - Philomina is his life."

"Have to agree with you," Pam mimicked the look of shock by being on the same side of the road as her antagonist. "Unfair on all of you, but it's gone too far to change now. Cut him some slack though, his world fell round his ears, after losing his job in the City. But instead of talkin' or even helping your mum he finds distractions and focuses on Philomina with back up from his sister. Did you send your mum an anniversary card?

"What's the point?" Maddy hit back. "They ain't married, they just put up with each other when they can be bothered! Told mum: if dad's playing away from home why can't I?"

Pam put her head in her hands and replied, "Blimey, thought I was bad! That's goin' help ain't it? You ninny!"

"Bye ladies," Clive called out, "enjoy yourselves. We're off shopping. I'm buying a 'Kiss me Quick' hat!" Vincent waved listlessly but enthusiastically encouraged Clive out the door.

"Gotta go," said Maddy and proffered advice to her partner in crime albeit from a distance both geographically and demographically. "Don't give up. Mr Right doesn't have to be a sparkling toy boy. He might be disguised as Mr Stable. Don't judge a book by its cover!"

Pam reeled back in shock, "Phil's havin' a good influence - hope he's a stayer not a player."

***

Martha and Pam shared a bottle of white wine as they sat in deckchairs, on the beach. In unison they called out, "CHEERS!" and clinked their crystal glasses.

Pam boasted about Monty, "He cooks and brings food for Bea. He's fixed the washing machine, yes, and Bea's water fountain, refitted smoke alarm, bought me a new toaster, made, and fitted decking in garden. Can sit outside and have …"

Martha interrupted, "Stop trying to pretend, you ain't given up smoking."

"Not yet," Pam said apologetically. "Monty hates the smell of cigarettes."

"Might be incentive you need? Hee hee!"

"Shut Up! He's not tellin' me what to do!" Pam's prickly reply reaffirmed her fear that the brick wall she hid behind was slowly eroding away.

Martha raised her eyebrows and said, "Pushing you in right direction though. But you're as stubborn as a mule. He'll need the patience of a saint."

"What tune you humming?" Martha covered her ears. "Or you swallowed a fly?"

"What a cheek!" Pam sounded offended but a wry smile revealed her true emotion. "Heard it on TV this morning – advert for golden oldie hits – right up our street. '*A time to dance, a time to cry. A time to throw stones? ......There is a season turn, turn, turn...*' Tune is going around in my head but can't remember all the words."

"What a surprise!" Martha quipped. "That's a blast from the past! Mum liked the song. What's name of band? Come to me in a minute? Talk about something else an' I'll remember it."

Pam looked at Martha's glass, "Wanna a top up?"

"The Byrds! That's the name!" Martha squealed with delight.

"Plenty around here to join in with chorus!" Pam chuckled.

Pam was mesmerised by the shades of orange overtaking the hues of blue in the sky.

The cool breeze stirred her from the depth of the portrait, and she said, "tide is so far out. We'll have to walk miles for a quick paddle. Better than swishin' round our ankles– saltwater leaves a mark on our clothes. Remember when we tried to chase the waves?

Martha gasped, "how can I forget? You kept falling over. Strained my shoulder after number of times I picked you up. Martha took a sip of the chilled wine and paused before she asked, "Clocks go back on Sunday, do you wish we could go back?

Pam did not leave any room for doubt, "NO!" Can't go through it all again but wouldn't mind dancin' without creaking and aching. It'll be great when Betty moves here. Three Musketeers back in action."

"Three Stooges at our age," said Martha. "You jealous of Betty?"

Pam sighed and stalled and finally admitted, "Yep, she's got it all. Love her, despite her curly locks. She's a good friend but blood is thicker than water."

"Sure is." Martha's rapid response enveloped with emotion and surety prompted Pam to turn; with earnest expectancy etched in her expression, she asked, "How long have you known?"

Martha held Pam's hand. "All the time. And you?"

Pam echoed, "All the time."

The two sisters sat together soaking up the sun set.

***